She felt as though she were straddling two worlds. The boxes upstairs in her bedroom were her past, and yet as she touched the locket, there was another past calling her, and the possibility of a father.

Other Books by Kathryn Lasky

TANGLED IN TIME

BOOK ONE
The Portal

Kathryn Lasky

Book One

The Portal

HARPER

An Imprint of HarperCollinsPublishers

Tangled in Time: The Portal
Text copyright © 2019 by Kathryn Lasky
Interior art © 2018 by Fran Forman
All rights reserved. Printed in the United States of America.
No part of this book may be used or reproduced in any manner whatsoever without
written permission except in the case of brief quotations embodied in critical articles
and reviews. For information address HarperCollins Children's Books, a division of
HarperCollins Publishers, 195 Broadway, New York, NY 10007.
www.harpercollinschildrens.com

Library of Congress Control Number 2018948000
ISBN 978-0-06-269326-6

Typography by Carla Weise
19 20 21 22 23 PC/BRR 10 9 8 7 6 5 4 3 2 1
❖
First paperback edition, 2019

For Fran Forman, who through her art breathes light and air
into my word dreams in this story

TANGLED IN TIME

BOOK ONE

The Portal

Contents

The Greenhouse

The Locket

A Prince

Fashion and Style

Fashion World Takes Note of Tween Philly Blogger
by Uta Bradford

"*I'm tall for my age*," says middle school student Rose Ashley.

Indeed she is. At five feet, six and a half inches tall, the suburban sixth grader does appear somewhat older than her eleven years. But don't let that fool you. Through years of scouring thrift stores—or "thrifting," as she calls it—she has discovered fashion treasures that she adapts to her own style, which Rose describes as funk meets vintage. Thrifting, she is careful to note, is not yet an Olympic sport, but should be. "Much less expensive than all those gymnastic and ice-skating coaches." She pulls out a boxy jacket she picked up for five dollars. "Christian Dior—so it had a few moth holes. I thought, you know, I can work around that."

And she certainly can. A self-taught expert seamstress, she has yet to find anything she can't fix or sew from scratch. Her mom, real estate agent Rosemary Ashley, bought her an electronic sewing machine that Rose calls the *Millennium Falcon* of sewing machines.

On her blog, *Threads*, she shares snappy observations on fashion, pop culture, and sewing. The site is peppered with photos of herself and her friends wearing some of her more outlandish getups. Rose's following is building, with 20,000 readers each day.

The
Greenhouse

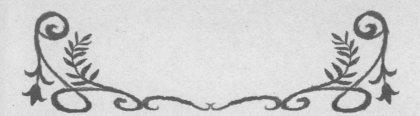

Chapter 1

Bow Ties
and Truth

*R*ose Ashley stood in the middle of the circle as the three girls spun around her. She clamped her eyes shut and tried to block out their jeering faces. The girls took turns picking apart Rose's carefully composed outfit.

"What's with the bow tie?"

"And the shirt! My little brother wears a shirt like that."

"Are you a man or something?"

"Maybe a Cub Scout. The shirt has those flap pockets with the snap buttons. Any badges?" hooted the one with the little brother.

Rose cringed. Did this have something to do with her

fashion blog? But she hadn't posted anything in over a month. How would they have found out about *Threads*? Of course the article had come out in the Philadelphia newspaper, but who read that paper in Indianapolis? Oh! And she'd forgotten the YouTube thing. "How to Raid Your Mom's Closet, or 75 Scarves She Never Wears and What to Do with Them." That had led into a mess of crafty projects, including the bow ties.

That scarf video had received more hits than anything she'd ever done. Following that, the bow tie of the month club on her blog really took off. Everyone was emailing wanting the instructions for how to make one. She even wrote an essay for school: "Not Just for Guys—Bow Ties." Within a month, the entire girl population of her middle school was wearing them. But that was in Haverford, near Philadelphia, on the East Coast. This was Indiana, smack-dab in the middle of the country. And these girls had somehow targeted her.

The girl with a bright neon-blue streak in her hair took a step closer. Her name was Carrie. She was short, squat really, and reminded Rose of a pug with a bad personality. Narrowing her eyes, Carrie took a deep breath.

"I know! Let's play the truth game with her. Find out who or what she really is!"

"Yeah, think of this as the Circle of Truth—we get the

facts!" Rose thought this one's name was Brianna.

Rose touched the bow tie nervously. She loved it. It was pale blue with little white daisies. She had made it herself from some scraps of material and tied it bat-wing style.

"Oh, bow ties not for guys—we get it!" Carrie said in the snarkiest voice imaginable. So they had seen the blog! "What else did you find in your mama's closet?"

But before she could answer, the third girl spoke up. "Never mind. Enough about the blog and the stupid You-Tube videos." This was Lisa. Very pretty. She had a sequin pasted onto her left eyebrow that pranced up to her hairline as spoke. She also had the deepest dimples Rose had ever seen. Flashing them constantly, she took a step closer. "You're not exactly Mia Ryles."

Mia Ryles! Rose nearly gagged. Mia was the thirteen-year-old YouTube sensation who was the complete creation of her fanatical mom, Monica Ryles. Talk about glitter! Mia was obviously Lisa's inspiration. Her mom had rocketed Mia into multiplatform deals with everything from social media to hair products to fashion. The fashion was ghastly in Rose's mind. She called it the baby-doll-cheerleader look.

"Okay, Rose, are you ready?" Carrie growled. Rose said nothing. It was as if her voice had taken a deep dive inside her. Her mouth was quivering. She felt a hot blister of tears behind her eyelids ready to boil over.

"For example," Carrie continued, "when I was little, I peed in the swimming pool and the water turned this color blue." She pointed to the streak in her hair. *Some inspiration*, Rose thought. Pee and chlorine! The other two girls were giggling madly.

"Guess what I did," Lisa of the glitter said.

"I don't know?" Rose croaked.

"I had a zit once. Once upon a time . . . a long time ago." She made it sound like a fairy tale. A fairy-tale zit that had escaped from a troll and accidentally landed on a princess's face.

"I did too!" Rose blurted out. "And yeah, I peed in a swimming pool once. It was at the Meadow Lark Community Swimming Pool and . . ."

"Don't talk!" Brianna roared. Rose knew that some might think that Brianna was beautiful in that skinny fashion-model way, but her eyes were too small and it gave her, in Rose's opinion, a kind of rodenty appearance. It looked as if she were always seeking out crumbs or the tiniest bits of food, or more likely gossip. What kind of rodent? Rose didn't ponder this too long. But definitely a rodent—rat, mouse, vole, whatever. A creature of the underground. Her hair was skinned back in a ponytail that made her tiny face look so sharp it might cut something. *Like blades!* Rose thought. She had heard that Brianna was a champion ice-skater.

She leaned in toward Rose. Something toxic seemed to

leak from her eyes. "Carrie does the talking. Asks the questions," she snapped.

"Right, Brianna. Thank you for recognizing that. I am the questioner."

Inquisitor is more like it, Rose thought.

"So what happened to your mom?" asked Carrie.

"She died."

"Your dad?"

"I don't know."

Carrie stuck her head forward as if she was trying to ferret out every tidbit of information. She was still shorter, much shorter than Rose. "Divorced? He abandoned you? Ran off with a prettier lady than your mom? Or dead too?"

Rose gasped. This was too awful. It was only her second day of school. They had obviously done their homework on her, finding *Threads* and then her YouTube stuff. She could never have imagined such a start to the school year. This was one for Guinness World Records. Rose was no stranger to first days in a new school. She and her mom had moved around so much she was practically a professional at first days! Her mom had been a real estate agent in Philadelphia. And for her mother, new houses were investments. After she moved into them, she would fix them up and sell them. She was a serial renovator. New houses in new neighborhoods had never really bothered Rose. Her mom always said, "I don't sell homes. I sell houses. Home isn't four walls and a roof. Home is you and me."

❊

For her second day at this new school, Rose had put together the perfect ensemble. The first day she hadn't done anything too wild. Just an old shirt of her mom's and leggings. A few months before, she had made a belt to wear with the shirt from all the lanyards she had woven in summer camp. One sixth grader had even admired it. The outfit was low-key. Her outfit today, however, was hardly outrageous. Bow ties and boys' collared shirts were so *in* right now. Or so she had thought. She had felt confident.

But today they had reshuffled the homeroom assignments, and she was put in with the three meanest girls in the entire school. Every school has its mean girls, but usually Rose managed to dodge them. These three seemed particularly vicious. Like mythical creatures, harpies perhaps, with human heads and bodies but the wings and talons of predatory birds. She was their prey. Fresh blood.

Yes, it all fits, Rose thought.

Once upon a time, there was a girl named Rose—Rose Ashley. And over three weeks ago, she became an instant orphan when her mom was killed in a car crash. Now she's surrounded by three of the most horrible girls—pardon, harpies—in a new school, in a new city, living with a grandmother she barely knows.

Their game was about to begin again. Rose hardly had time to pick up her backpack and flee when there was a screech from one of the girls. Rose looked up just as a boy in an electric wheelchair came crashing into the middle of the circle.

"Sorry, coming through. Didn't mean to crash into you, Brianna."

"Just buzz off, Creepo Palsy," Brianna sneered. Rose was shocked. It was a terrible thing to say. Her new homeroom teacher, Mr. Ross, had already told her that she would be sitting behind the boy in the wheelchair, Myles, who had cerebral palsy.

"Learn how to drive!" Carrie shouted. She gave Rose a sharp look and then the girls scattered, like flies shooed off food at a picnic.

"Uh . . . thanks," Rose said to the boy. "You're Myles, aren't you?" He wore very cool, squarish glasses. The lenses were thick and seemed to magnify his dark brown eyes. Shaggy black bangs fell across his forehead. He was cute— "a handsome lad," her mom might have said. Or if he had been a girl, "comely." Her mom had a penchant for old-fashioned phrases.

"Yes," Myles said. "The student in the wheelchair. My reputation precedes me." His head wobbled a bit as he shifted slightly. His left hand was bent inward and appeared immobile. His right hand hovered over the chair's controls, the fingers open and relaxed. "And you're Rose Ashley. The new student." His speech was thick, like cake batter, as if his tongue had to scrape and push the sentences out of his mouth.

"Uh . . . yeah, I'm Rose, and thanks for c-crashing into them." The very word was hard for her to say since her mom's accident. She hadn't been allowed to watch the news that night or in the days that followed the accident. Caroline, her mom's friend from work, stayed with her until they could figure out where Rose was to live. She had unplugged and hidden the cable box, so Rose wouldn't hear about the crash on television. But Rose still heard snippets of the phone calls whenever Caroline thought she was sleeping: "Engulfed in flames . . . died instantly . . . no remains."

I'm sort of a remain, Rose thought. In her mom's will, it said that Rose was to go to her grandmother's house if something ever happened to her and that proceeds from the sale of the house were to go to Rose.

"Yeah, Myles. You showed up at the right time."

"My pleasure," Myles said.

Rose looked off toward the girls, who had retreated to another corner of the schoolyard.

"The girl with the ponytail—she's Brianna, right?"

"Yeah, but the real ringleader is Carrie. The short one with the streak in her hair. Kind of the Cruella de Vil look, except the streak is blue and not white. She thinks it's cool and 'creative.' NOT. And that's Lisa. Uh . . . not much to say about her except she likes sequins, glitter. Sparkle on the outside. Dim on the inside." Myles tapped his head. "But she is a good horseback rider. Watch out for her spurs." He laughed. The chuckles sounded a bit like bubbles breaking through water.

Just then, the bell rang. He gave a jaunty salute with his right hand, then buzzed off in his wheelchair.

Rose was standing alone now. So alone. If her mom were alive, she would have gone home and told her about these obnoxious girls. And her mom would've said something like "Oh there's always kids like that. . . ." And maybe told her about some bully from her own school days. And Rose would've whined and said, "You don't get it, Mom." But now there was no mom to try to understand her. There was no mom for her to whine to. "Puleeze, Mom, gimme a break. Things have changed since your day."

There simply was no mom.

❊

The Philadelphia house had sold quickly, and the very next day Rose was bundled up like some sort of package and put on a flight to Indianapolis to live with her grandmother, Rosalinda. Caroline came with her to help "settle her in." But there was no settling in to speak of. Rose felt entirely adrift.

That first night she had been too tired, too shocked,

too sad, too everything to even eat. So Rosalinda's live-in cook sent dinner upstairs to her bedroom. But she just pushed the food around on her plate.

The next night she came downstairs when called and was surprised to find that she was to eat alone. Caroline had already left.

"Where's my grandmother?" she asked Betty, Rosalinda's caretaker.

"She likes her supper in the greenhouse," Betty answered. For the next twelve days before school started, this was how it went: Rose ate alone, her grandmother treated her with general indifference, and no one mentioned her mom. If Rosalinda was bothered by the death of her daughter, she didn't show it. The one time any mention of Rose's mother did come up was when Rose came out of the bathroom one evening and ran straight into Betty and Rosalinda.

"Betty," Rosalinda said, turning to the caretaker, "am I upstairs or downstairs, and who's this young girl? She looks so much like my daughter."

"She's Rosemary's daughter—your granddaughter, Rose," Betty answered, giving Rose an apologetic look. She pointed to a picture in a frame on a table. It was the one taken on a beach in Florida. Rose was just five or six at the most. In the photograph, Rose was wearing a bathing suit with mermaids on it and leaning up against her mother. Her mom wore a bathing suit that she called a mom-kini, as it was fairly modest. "She's almost all grown up now, Mrs. A, but just a little girl in that picture."

"Oh yes," Rosalinda answered. Rose looked up hopefully, but only for a moment. "I remember I had a daughter or a granddaughter once. I think I misplaced them." She giggled as if she were describing a missing remote from a television—oh dear, where did that remote go?

"Misplaced" was the perfect word, Rose thought. It seemed to Rose as if her father must have been misplaced as well. She had learned quickly as a child not to ask about him. Whenever she did, a strange mist that was not quite tears came to her mother's eyes, and a sadness seemed to cling to the air. Her mother appeared to nearly dissolve into some distant place beyond anything Rose knew.

❋

Rose felt very "misplaced" now as she returned to her grandmother's after her second day of school. Rosalinda lived in a stucco house that presided over the corner of two tree-lined streets. It was so different from the neighborhood where Rose had lived with her mom. They had lived on Sylvan Lane in a suburb of Philadelphia. Her mom joked that Sylvan as a name was wishful thinking, since it did not have a tree on it. All the houses had been built in the past ten years and were for the most part boxy, brick, one-story ranch-style houses with garages that took up a third of the lot. The lawns were severe squares of green grass with fiercely trimmed shrubs that stood at attention. But Rose liked it. It was home.

Her grandmother's house was on the corner of Meridian and Forty-Sixth Street. It was a neighborhood of stately houses, and though Rosalinda's was no more or less grand than the next, it had an otherworldly feel about it, as though it belonged to another time, another place. Ivy crawled up the walls, forming a patchwork of green against the pale yellow stucco. It reminded Rose of a map, where the ivy was the sea and the stucco made up the continents. Perhaps it was like one of those very old historical maps that showed monsters swimming through unknown seas with the inscription *Here There Be Dragons*. But instead: *Here There Be Grandmother*. Grandmother Rosalinda.

If anyone wanted Rose to settle in, it didn't help that she had to ring the bell to be let into the house. It sure didn't make it feel like home. Her mother had trusted her with a key to their house back on Sylvan Lane.

Everything was wrong here. She walked up the three steps and rang the bell. At the same moment, a cat leaped onto the broad top step. Its fur was tawny bronze, just the color of the changing leaves.

"Now where did you come from, cat?" Rose whispered. She noticed it had only three legs. The cat cocked its head to one side and looked her up and down as if to ask Rose the same question. Its limpid green eyes flashed with a slit of gold light. On this crisp day, the creature seemed to be the essence of fall. *September, that's what you should be called,* Rose thought. Then there was the loud click of the lock being turned in the door. The cat was gone! Betty stood in the doorway.

"Oh, hello, Rose." Betty blinked as if Rose were a stranger trying to collect money for some cause or asking that a petition be signed to protect the habitat of an endangered toad. Or maybe Betty had a fleeting moment of thinking that Rose was simply an unexpected guest, which was exactly what she had been just twelve days before.

"Betty, there was a pretty cat here just a second ago."

"Oh, that three-legged one. Yes, it hangs around. I don't believe in feeding cats. They can become a nuisance." She pursed her lips and shook her head in disapproval.

Rose believed in cats—in feeding them and cuddling them. She did not find cats a nuisance in the least. She found them soft, quiet, gentle, and for the most part accepting. She loved the feeling when a cat plopped in her lap. She often wondered how they could be so comforting without ever saying a word. How they could seem to listen, to understand. Her mom had bought a cat for her when she was quite little and Rose had named it a rather stupid name, Moon Glow. But hey, she was four. They had called her Moony. But Moony had died three years ago. It turned out she had feline epilepsy. Her seizures became worse and worse, and finally one day she staggered into the kitchen, started shaking violently, and keeled over, dead. Rose hadn't been there to see it, but she dragged every single word of how it had happened from her mom. Then they collapsed on the couch in the den, her mom folding Rose in her arms, and they cried and cried.

Her mom had made a big deal out of Moon Glow's funeral. She had invited Rose's friends over and served lemonade and cupcakes. There were pictures of Moony on a table with a bouquet of flowers. They had buried her in the backyard with a stone marker that her mom had found someone to engrave. It read "Here lies our friend Moon Glow. Indeed a bright light in our lives. RIP." Rose had actually made herself a mourning outfit. All black, of course, it was made from a slip of her mom's and part of a witch costume she had worn the previous Halloween. All very drapey and topped off with a black straw hat she had found in a thrift shop with her mom, to which she had attached a black veil. She wore it for three days and then got tired of it. Her mom had taken a picture of her standing by Moony's grave. She remembered her mom saying something about her looking like a teensy Jackie Kennedy at President Kennedy's funeral.

Then, just three years later, all the lights in Rose's life went out. And here she was at 4605 North Meridian Street in Indianapolis, Indiana.

There was no funeral for Rose's mom, because there

were no remains. There was a memorial service. She could not even remember what she wore to the service. Rose was barely conscious during it. She felt as if the minister was speaking about a stranger.

❁

"Your grandmother is in the greenhouse," Betty said. "Why don't you go out and visit her? Or do you want to go to your room first and freshen up?"

Freshen up? Who used words like that, except old people? Rose nodded, not an answer so much as a dismissal, and then stepped into the large, shadowy entrance hall. From the tall windows, the occasional shaft of amber light fell on the polished wood floors. A staircase rose majestically with a lovely curving banister that cried out for a kid to slide down it. But here was another hope dashed: there was a stair lift fitted to the banister that made it impossible to slide down. That was how her grandmother ascended to the upper realms of the house where her bedroom was, as well as various guest bedrooms, a study, and a small library devoted mostly to books about plants and horticulture.

"You know, dear, your grandmother is often at her best when she's in the greenhouse. Very alert when she's fiddling about with her plants," Betty said as she closed the front door behind Rose.

"Don't call it fiddling, Betty." Her grandmother appeared in the arched doorway beneath the stairs, leaning on her walker. "It's anything but fiddling." She was swathed in shawls. A pair of reading glasses dangled from a ribbon around her neck, and her thin, white hair looked as if it had been tossed with salad tongs, then pinned with what appeared to be chopsticks. A calligraphy of wrinkles creased her cheeks. Her eyes were a pale, almost colorless blue. She was neither thin nor fat but seemed rather shapeless. It was her feet, however, that fascinated Rose. She wore old-lady shoes that were black and laced up tight. Her feet were puffy, oozing over the edges of the shoes like rising bread dough in a small pan.

"Come along, dearie. Betty can have Cook send in a snack." Rose had noticed that the live-in cook was only ever called Cook—she wasn't sure if it was actually her name or not.

For the past twelve days, Rosalinda hardly seemed to acknowledge Rose, let alone the death of her mother, and now she wanted her to "come along"? Rose shook her head. "I have homework to do," she said, wondering: *Why is she asking me now?* She had spoken of Rose's mother as having been misplaced, not dead. Had she grieved at all? There was certainly no sign of grief. Did being eighty years old with dementia give one a pass on feelings?

Rosalinda was already pivoting with her walker to return to the greenhouse. "Oh, come along, we'll only be a minute."

But it wasn't a minute. For that was the first instance that time started to go a bit *catawampus*, as her grandmother would say. It was there in the greenhouse that time would begin to strangely warp.

Chapter 2

Dirt Memory

"It's a Tudor *greenhouse," Rosalinda said, emphasizing the* "Tudor" like it held some special meaning for Rose. She lifted her walker over the sill of the door, and then together Rose and Rosalinda entered the balmy glass space. The warm, humid air was laced with scents. It seemed as if she were untangling a skein of fragrances. There was definitely a rose fragrance, but as she followed her grandmother, she detected an exotic, spicy smell that began to nip at the sweetness of the roses.

As she stood beneath the soaring glass roof, she felt as if she had entered a crystal castle. Indeed, there were three intersecting roofs, as there were three different areas of the greenhouse. Large cupolas floated like bubbles at the junctures where the roofs met, their glass panes tinted different colors. There was a calendar propped on an easel indicating which plants, depending on the time of the year, were to be hoisted on a rope-pulley system into the cupolas for exposure to the light. But there were winding staircases to these lofty realms as well. "This is amazing," Rose said in a hushed voice, forgetting herself. "What are those?" she asked, pointing up to one of the cupolas where vines with white clusters of star-shaped flowers swayed in a spectral breeze.

"Jasmine, a tropical."

Rosalinda was now perched in her planting chair, which was adjustable so that she could raise or lower it a foot or so, depending on which table she was working at. The tables ran for thirty feet down the center of the space and held tray upon tray of small plants and seedlings. Rosalinda explained that when they grew big enough, these plants would "graduate" to another area. This explanation began their longest conversation to date.

"Uh . . ." Rose was not quite sure what to call her grandmother. Granny? Grandma? Her best friend back in Philadelphia had called her grandmother Nana. Cook and Betty called her Mrs. A. Surely she shouldn't call her that. She supposed Grandmother would be okay.

"Grandmother, why do you call it a Tudor greenhouse?"

"Because that's what it is. It was an architectural style back then. And it's not a kit, mind you. I designed it. After I built mine, they stole the design and made build-it-yourself kits. But none are like mine. Never could be. You can't stuff a century into a kit."

"A century?"

"Sixteenth," Rosalinda mumbled. Her reply was barely audible.

"What?"

"Never mind," she snapped. "I need you to thin out those ragged robin seedlings over there in that tray." She pointed. Her finger was gnarled and bent, the knuckles swollen into knobs. "But before you do that, get me one of those pie tins and put some water in it from that pitcher. I have to soak some seeds overnight. Gives them a good start. Then you can do the thinning out."

"Thinning out?"

"Yes, pluck out some of the little ones. The bigger ones need breathing space. Survival of the fittest, you know."

But if she was ripping out the weaklings, was it survival of the fittest or murder of the frailest? She looked at her grandmother again. She was over eighty and seemed pretty frail, but something had changed since her grandmother was in the greenhouse. She seemed more alert. Even her eyes had lost that vague look they always had. For the first time, Rose could see a resemblance to her mom.

"Ragged robin—funny name." She began pulling out the weaklings. It was an oddly restful activity. She felt as if she were allowing the other ones to breathe a bit.

"Nothing funny about the plant," Rosalinda replied. "The leaves make a fine tea, and their flowers are delicate and lovely. With any luck they'll be in bloom by Christmas. Let others have those hideous poinsettia plants."

"You don't like them?"

"I loathe them," Rosalinda snarled. "Their immodesty offends. Wanton showgirls!"

Rose almost giggled. She sneaked a look at her grandmother, who had a most determined expression in her eyes now. She continued thinning out the ragged robin. Within a few minutes she had finished. The notion of studying for the upcoming spelling games dissolved. They no longer had spelling tests but games where you did stuff like rearrange the letters in a word to get a new word, like "carouse" out of "discourage."

"Is there something else I can thin out, Grandmother?"

Rosalinda looked up. The trace of a smile played across her face and something halfway between a snort and a chuckle escaped. "Try that seedling tray next to it—the love-lies-bleeding."

And from there Rose went on to another table where there were more plants with names like heartsease, cupid's dart, scarlet snowcaps. Rose felt as if she were walking through a poem, or perhaps the shadows of very old legends. Stories swirled about her. Cook came and brought tea and small cakes. The afternoon faded into evening and Cook came again, this time with two trays of food, but neither Rose nor her grandmother was particularly hungry. Rose had learned how to take the seedlings that had become "plantlings," her grandmother's word, and move them into larger pots. It was a delicate operation. "Always let some of the old soil cling to their roots," Rosalinda instructed.

"Why is that, Grandmother?"

"Memory—dirt memory. Nothing comes clean into this world. It shouldn't. Spick-and-span, pristine, perfect— ridiculous notions." She had held up a young fern. "You see this fern here?"

"Yes, Grandmother."

"Ferns are among the oldest plants on Earth; older than time, they are. Now just think if I had cleaned off all these roots. It would be as if I had sliced them from their history. From their great-great-grandmamma's and grandpapa's spores."

"Spores?"

"One-celled little bitty things. They're found on the underneath part of the fern frond. They're in charge of reproduction. No romance. They can do it all by themselves. But still there's a history. So you always start them in a nice little mixture of vermiculite, peat, and some soil that their ancestors have grown in. People always say that when you die you can't take it with you. But with plants, especially very old plants, you can take it with you. So old dirt is good dirt. Let the soil cling—otherwise they'll wither and die." She paused and inhaled sharply. "It's almost as if they get lonely."

Rose shut her eyes. An ache swelled within her. Rosalinda reached out and touched Rose's hand. Above, a flash of moonlight filtered through the glass ceiling. And outside she thought she heard the meow of a cat.

"You know, my dear, I'm too old, but that staircase winds up to the central cupola. It's lovely on the night of a full moon. When shafts of moonlight fall through the tinted panes, it's as if there's a garden of light blooming up there. Go see for yourself. And say hello to the queen's petticoat. It'll have to be lowered tomorrow. We don't want the poor thing moon-blinked. You know too much moonlight can do that."

"What's moon-blinked?"

"Slight confusion and then . . ."

Rose was already starting up the spiraling staircase. She felt the pools of colored light falling down on her. An intensity of scents swirled through the air. There were cinnamon and rose fragrances, then the spicy scent again mingled with something like lilies.

"And then what, Grandmother?" she asked over her shoulder as she climbed the stairs.

"Won't bloom in its proper season—it will make a surprise appearance, too early or maybe too late," her grandmother was saying from below as Rose ascended the staircase. "It will go catawampus. Plants can do that when confused."

❈

The blossoms of the petticoat plant were lovely, tiny bells no bigger than a baby's fingernail. They hung on long green strands and swayed in a ghost of a breeze. The tinted glass showered them in an array of colors. Standing at the top of the winding staircase, Rose felt as if she were in the midst of a blooming rainbow. A calm stole through her. All the terrible words, the terrible images etched in her mind since that horrible day when her mom had died seemed to fade away. She felt free, and it was as if for the first time she could breathe again. She didn't care what those three horrid girls thought of how she dressed. She wasn't going to change because of them. She might even start writing her blog again. For some reason, her grandmother's words about spores came into her head: "Let the soil cling—otherwise they'll wither and die." She had lost so much, but she couldn't lose herself. She would wear her favorite skirt, one she had made out of a huge sweater her mom had bought for herself and then never worn. It had big deep pockets that Rose turned inside out, which made flounces on either side. She'd wear it with yet another bow tie—a big floppy one that she had made from a tablecloth she'd found in a vintage shop that specialized in lace. It made her feel good planning her outfit. She just wished the boxes with her sewing machine and other stuff would come. Caroline had promised to send them right away.

✳

Rosalinda was gone by the time Rose descended the staircase. Betty had come to take her upstairs to bed. Outside, however, she thought she saw a fleeting bright shadow. Could it be that cat, September? Her glass was still filled with milk from her snack. She could pour it into one of the little pie tins that were stacked for soaking seeds. She quickly filled the tin and then walked to a door at the back of the greenhouse and set it outside. She couldn't see the cat, but she sensed it watching her.

Rose left the greenhouse through the passage that connected it to the entry hall, where Betty was helping her grandmother into the stair-lift chair. Her grandmother leaned toward Betty and whispered, "Who's that girl?"

"It's Rose, your granddaughter."

"Oh, of course." But there was no hint of recognition. Rose sighed, saddened. It wasn't the first time since she'd arrived that her grandmother stared at her as if she were a stranger. An intruder. The vague look in her eyes had returned. There was a hum as the stair lift began to glide upward on its rail. Just before it reached the big curve, Rosalinda raised her hand and gave a faint wave, opening and closing her palm like a baby might wave bye-bye.

"Bye now," Rosalinda murmured.

Chapter 3

The Court of the Mean Queens

*A*s soon as Rose set foot in the lunchroom the next day, she saw Carrie, Lisa, and Brianna huddled at a table. Their eyes landed on Rose like vultures spotting carrion, and then Carrie said something that made all of them look to each other and giggle. Rose saw Lisa and Brianna slide their eyes toward her again. They all laughed even louder. Rose turned away and spotted Myles sitting at a table with two other boys. She decided immediately to join them after passing through the cafeteria line.

"Hi, Myles."

"Hi, Rose. Come on, sit here with us," Myles said as Rose put her lunch tray down. "Rose, these are my friends

Anand and Joe. They're in Mr. Beatty's homeroom. Joe's a champion ice-skater."

"Junior champion."

"Cool," Rose said.

"And I'm a junior tiddlywinks champion." Anand offered.

"Really?" Rose said.

"NOT!" the three boys said in unison.

"Anand's a mathlete, and so is Myles. They're just modest," Joe said.

"Mathlete? Like on a team?" Rose asked.

"School team," Anand replied.

"I . . . I'm not on any team," Rose said. Her voice felt a little quivery. She was actually tempted to say, "I'm an orphan." But that would be so lame.

"What do you like to do?" Myles asked.

"Uh . . . sew. Design stuff."

"I knew it!" Joe exclaimed, and high-fived Anand. "That shirt you wore the first day of school. I bet you got it in the boys' department at Schockman's, and the bow tie, perfecto!"

"Schockman's?"

"The department store downtown."

"Naw, got it in Philadelphia. Gilford's—boys' department. Cooler shirts in the boys' department." She had sewn three other versions of the shirt and special ordered the snap buttons.

"So you're not at Court, I see," Anand said.

"Court?"

Anand nodded toward Carrie, Brianna, and Lisa.

"Court of the Mean Queens," Myles said, laughing. His laugh sounded slightly more like a hiccup now than the previous bubble laugh had. "That's what we call them."

"Or sometimes the Trio of Doom," Anand added.

"That's when it goes beyond mere bullying and they cross over into their special-ops mode," Joe said.

"Special ops. You mean they go to extremes?"

"You got it. They can be very strategic. Myles's wheelchair batteries were stolen one time. We're pretty sure it was them."

"That is nasty," Rose said, trying not to look over at the girls.

Soul thieves, that's what they are, she thought.

"Nasty?" Anand said. "That's an understatement." He turned to Rose. "You mean you haven't got your passport yet?"

"What? A passport? What are you talking about?"

"See those two girls just sitting down with them now?"

"Yeah."

"They must have just gotten their passports."

"I don't understand."

"It's like this, Rose," Myles said. She was becoming accustomed to his way of speaking. "Once you've done enough of the Mean Queens' bidding—like nasty tricks and all—you get your 'passport.' It's a virtual passport that allows you into their small, foul world."

"Who would want to be in that world?"

"They always have some sixth graders in training," Joe said. "You know, some kids think it's cool to be accepted or just noticed by older kids—even the bullies."

"They long to belong!" Anand said. "See those two other girls trying to squeeze in at the table—those sixth graders?" Anand asked, nodding to two girls.

"Like remoras," Myles offered, and laughed again.

"What?" Rose had no idea what remoras were.

"Suckerfish," Myles replied. "They attach themselves to sharks. I did a science report on parasites in nature. Covered a lot—from strangler figs to remoras. Usually the relationships are mutually beneficial, but in the case of strangler figs, they kill their host tree. That one girl with the blond hair and the pink streak? She's a Carrie wannabe, obviously."

"What about the girl with the hair bow?"

"Sibby Huang," Joe replied. "She worships Brianna because of her skating. She belongs to the same skating club I do. She's good. Very good for her age."

"Should we—uh—get emotional about strangler figs killing hosts, or just chalk it up to one of the cruelties of nature?" Anand asked as they kept their eyes fastened on the sixth graders circling the Court of the Mean Queens.

"What do the remoras do for the Mean Queens?"

"Play fetch, mostly, like obedient dogs," Joe said. "And sometimes take the blame for their dirty tricks."

"What are their dirty tricks, or special ops, as you called them?"

"The Mean Queens do a lot through texting—gossip, spread rumors. Don't let them get hold of your cell phone. But they don't limit it to kids. They were really mean to Ms. Elfenbach last year too."

"The math teacher? She's so nice."

"Yeah, well, Carrie, who thinks she's God's gift to mathematics, was ticked off about her grade," Joe said. "She claimed Ms. Elfenbach was drunk or something when she graded a test last year. She started a rumor that she was an alcoholic. Carrie and the rest of the Mean Queens started calling her Ms. Alcobach."

Rose was aghast. "That's terrible."

"Yeah," Myles broke in. "That's what they consider really funny. So lame. Perfect example of their Trio of Doom behavior. Very destructive. Way beyond bullying."

"So, moral of the story," Anand said, "is: watch out."

❋

Rose did watch out. Until two days later, when she found herself alone in the hall. Her grandmother's driver, Calvin, was planning to pick her up that day to take her to an orthodontist appointment after school. He had told her he would be a few minutes late. It was a minute or two past three, and the halls were empty since school had let out at 2:45. She was just getting the books she needed that night from her locker when she heard footsteps, then giggles, and then felt one hand? Two? Maybe three, shoving hard against her back. Her head banged against the metal; then there was a slam. Complete darkness. She heard a click, a sickening click. *Trapped! I've been locked in my own locker.*

"Have a nice night in school!" a voice sang out. "Maybe you can write about it on *Threads*!" Another voice she didn't recognize squeaked. There were giggles from other girls. "You see—that's how it's done," Lisa said to someone. "That's how you'll get your passport."

"Let me out of here. Let me out!" Rose screamed. She beat on the door of the locker. The metallic sound reverberated down the corridor.

Panic surged through her. *Now just calm down,* she counseled herself. *Calm down, Rose. Someone will come—a janitor or someone. Do some deep breathing. Calvin said he'd be late. He'll wonder why I'm not outside and come into the building.* She suddenly realized she could call on her cell phone. Who would she call? Her grandmother? No—the school, of course. She'd google the phone number. She reached into her pocket for her phone.

Nothing! She turned the pocket inside out and heard

the clink of a penny and the dry rasp of some Skittles falling onto the metal floor. The phone had been there minutes ago. Joe's words came back to her: *Don't let them get hold of your cell phone*. They had it! Now what? There was an eerie stillness as the school grew silent. Then she could hear the school buses pulling away outside. And there was darkness, total darkness. The panic rose again.

Then, at last, a voice. "Rose. Rose, it's me. Myles." She heard something scratching on metal. Suddenly the locker door opened. There was Myles in his wheelchair.

"Nothing like a compass for picking locks."

"Myles, you're here?!" she said, stepping out of the locker as Myles backed away in his wheelchair.

"Yeah—why do you look so surprised? Well, maybe you should be. But I'm very good with my one working hand." He lifted his hand that was holding his compass for geometry. "Lucky we started that geometry chapter this week," he said, dropping the compass into a bag slung over the handles of his wheelchair.

"How long have I been in there?" she asked, glancing at the clock. It said 3:08. "Is that clock right, Myles?" He looked up at it, then at his watch.

"Yeah, 3:08."

"It was just five minutes. It seemed like forever."

"I heard the Mean Queens giggling and a sixth grader

was tagging along. They were saying something about shoving someone into a locker. I figured it was you."

"You did? How come?"

He looked at her and tipped his head. "You really don't know why?"

"I'm not sure . . . my blog, maybe?"

"Not maybe—definitely, Rose. They're just jealous."

"But I haven't written on my blog since . . . since my mom died."

"The internet, YouTube. Just google Rose Ashley and you show up." Myles stopped his wheelchair and met her eyes.

"Don't let them scare you, Rose. You should keep writing your blog. They'll get bored eventually. That skirt you made from scarves and ties, that was so cool. I showed my mom a picture of it on your blog. She thought it was great. And that bow tie of the month thing! Joe had this great idea."

"What's that?"

"Could you make us all bow ties? You should do some for girls too, of course."

"What girls would wear them?"

"Not all the girls at Lincoln are Mean Queens. Like Susan and Zora and Lydia. They've all checked out your website."

"Well, I have to wait until my sewing machine arrives. It's supposed to come any day."

He started up his wheelchair again, and they walked outside. Rose thought about what he was saying. His electric wheelchair suddenly shot ahead.

"Hey, slow down. Doesn't that thing have a low gear?"

"Oh, sorry. I thought you were a fast walker."

"Not today."

"Are you all right, Rose?"

"Yeah . . . yeah . . . as right as one *can* be after being shoved in a locker. Just thinking about what you said."

"Someone's waving at you over there."

"Oh, that's Calvin, my grandmother's driver. I have an orthodontist appointment."

"Okay, see you tomorrow. I hope those girls get what's coming to them for that. It was a mean trick."

Rose turned on her heel. "Don't tell on them, Myles. It will make it all the worse—for me. I . . . I can handle it."

"I'm sure you can, Rose. Never doubted you. But I am going to tell Joe and Anand. We'll be on the lookout for you."

❋

"I'm not really hungry," Rose said when Betty opened the front door. "My teeth hurt. The orthodontist tightened my braces. Have my boxes come yet? Caroline said she sent them two days after I left."

"No, but they will get here. UPS is very reliable."

Rose said nothing, but she was truly upset. The remnants of what had been her life were in those boxes—the sewing machine, yards of wonderful fabric, books, her sketch pad and three whole folders full of designs, her own designs for outfits past and those that she had hoped to make. But admittedly it was hard to even think of a future without her mom. And getting back to her blog? She might not be ready yet.

"No snack? No dinner?" Betty asked softly.

"Nothing."

"I'm sure Cook could fix you some soup. And there's angel food cake that Cook baked. That's very soft, you know. Your grandmother will be so disappointed. She enjoyed her time with you in the greenhouse."

But Rose was already off, tearing up the stairs to her bedroom. She flung her books on the desk and flopped onto the bed. Beating her fists into the pillow, she sobbed, "Why . . . why did you have to die, Mom? How could you?"

There was soon a sodden patch against her cheek. It was as if she had cried an ocean into that pillow. The last thing she remembered hearing was the scraping of her grandmother's walker outside her bedroom door and then Rosalinda's voice. "Leave her be, Betty . . . leave her be."

It was the plinking of raindrops against the window-pane that woke her up. Outside there was only pitch black. The glass of the windowpane was a sheet of sliding water. Except for the sound of the rain, the entire house was quiet. She felt a gnawing hunger and decided to go to the kitchen and find something to eat. Passing her grandmother's room, Rose could hear Rosalinda snoring softly. She made her way down the stairs toward the kitchen. She dared not turn on a light, but her eyes had grown accustomed to the darkness.

Under a glass-domed platter, a cake perched. It had already been cut into and seemed to invite her to take a slice. There was a knife set beside the platter. Quietly she removed the dome cover and cut herself a piece. She was just about to take a bite when she looked through the kitchen window that had a fine view of the greenhouse. She noticed that the glass roofs seemed to glow. *How could this be on such a pitch-black and moonless, rainy night?* she wondered. It was as if the greenhouse possessed a moon of its own. She set the piece of cake on the counter and went out through the kitchen pantry and across a hall that led into the glasshouse from the rear, the door Cook always used when delivering dinner to Rosalinda.

As she stepped into the greenhouse, the air swirled with the scent of the jasmine vines that now tumbled from the cupolas, almost reaching the floor. The tray of love-lies-bleeding that she had thinned out had burst into bloom, with dangling blossoms like pendulous ruby necklaces. Foliage that had barely unfurled was now thick and stirring softly in a phantom wind. It was as if magically a fragrant jungle had sprung up around her. There were no longer trays neatly arranged in rigid rows awaiting her grandmother's tender attentions.

She looked up once more at the cupolas, but there were no cupolas. A flawless blue sky stretched overhead, and beneath her feet was a woodland path. Ahead she heard a meow. September? Rose stopped abruptly and listened. All was silent, and then suddenly she heard a giggle.

"Grandmother?" she called out softly. Hesitantly she continued down the path and soon heard footsteps. She realized that she must be far beyond the confines of the greenhouse. There were no walls of glass. The roofs had dissolved into this bright new morning, and straight ahead there was a girl. She wore a sapphire-blue dress that reached the ground. It was trimmed with ornate braid. The bodice was tight-fitting and heavily embroidered. From beneath the hem of the skirt peeped pointy-toed scarlet shoes. *Those shoes!* Rose thought. What she wouldn't give for those shoes! The girl's bright red hair was arranged in a circlet of elaborate braids atop her head, although a few strands streamed out from the braids like escaping flames. They looked at each other, startled.

"Guards! Guards!"

What in the world? Rose wondered as a man came around the bend in a fitted jacket emblazoned with brass buttons, gold epaulets, and ballet tights! Had she stumbled into a Shakespeare play? She didn't wait to ask but turned and bolted.

She ran breathlessly through the thickets of shrubbery laden with large exploding blossoms, burrowed through openings in the tall hedges and tangles of brush. Soon she smelled the familiar muggy odor of the greenhouse and the path gave way to the neat aisles with the tray tables of seedlings. The long, dangling vines of the jasmine had retreated in an orderly fashion to the airy realms of the cupolas. She heard the welcoming patter of the rain against the glass. It was once more pitch black. She raced up the stairs and back into her bedroom, where she shut the door firmly, then slid a chair beneath the handle to jam it, to lock out whatever it was she had encountered.

This was a dream, just a dream, she told herself. It couldn't have happened. None of it. It was as if she had just emerged from a fever dream. She was afraid to go to sleep. Sketching always calmed her. So, sitting at her desk, she picked up a pencil and began to sketch what she could remember of the shoes and the dress. The shoes were incredible. There was a circular jeweled buckle on them, and from that a brighter red piece flared like a single batwing. Bat shoes! How cool was that?

Then, going to her computer, she decided to type her first entry in her blog in nearly two months.

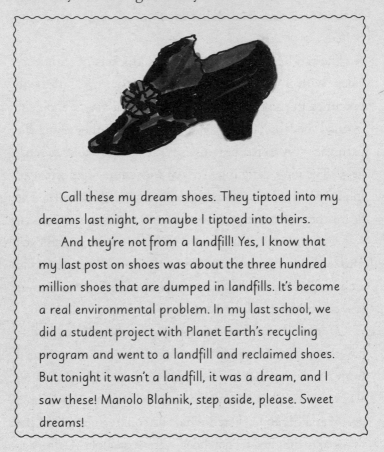

Call these my dream shoes. They tiptoed into my dreams last night, or maybe I tiptoed into theirs.

And they're not from a landfill! Yes, I know that my last post on shoes was about the three hundred million shoes that are dumped in landfills. It's become a real environmental problem. In my last school, we did a student project with Planet Earth's recycling program and went to a landfill and reclaimed shoes. But tonight it wasn't a landfill, it was a dream, and I saw these! Manolo Blahnik, step aside, please. Sweet dreams!

The next morning when she went downstairs, Cook greeted her warmly with a twinkle in her eyes.

"Didn't like my cake, did you? One bite and left it on the counter."

"Oh, sorry." She looked down and saw scratches on her arms, as if they had been torn by thorns or the brambles of a thicket. *Then it wasn't a dream?*

Chapter 4

"I Don't Exactly Hate You . . ."

Rose's phone was turned in on Monday. It was "found on the school grounds," a likely story. She expected the Mean Queens had done something awful with it, but so far it seemed all right. Rose was relieved. She even began to think that perhaps it had fallen out somehow when she, Myles, Joe, and Anand had gone outside to collect leaves for microscope slides in science class that day. So life went on uneventfully. But as hard as she tried to banish the thoughts of her strange experience in the greenhouse, the memories lingered. The girl in the sapphire-blue dress, the wonderful pointy-toed red shoes, the guard in tights, the cupolas that had dissolved into the sky of another day, a new morning. The more she thought about it, the more dreamlike it became. Except for that meow. She had heard the meow just before she glimpsed the girl. The cat's cry lasted longer in her mind than the scratches on her arms from the brambles.

She began once again to help her grandmother in the greenhouse. She wanted to prove to herself that in fact the jasmine had not miraculously grown long enough overnight to reach the ground. And she was right. The flowers were still suspended a good twenty feet above the floor of the greenhouse. And the seedling heads of the loves-lies-bleeding were sealed shut, with perhaps just a thread of the deep red color showing through.

"Oh, it will be another month or more until they open," her grandmother said when she noticed Rose looking at them so closely.

Rose looked around. Her grandmother seemed quite alert, especially compared to nights when she would stare at her blankly. So often Rose felt as if she were a stranger in this household, or at best treated as some kind of gentle intruder. She didn't really blame her grandmother. She knew she was teetering on the edge of some sort of dementia. Yet here in the greenhouse her grandmother was always alert. She seemed "grounded" in this soil, this old dirt that Rosa-linda had called good dirt.

Rose continued to help. And each night after her

grandmother went up to bed, Rose would set out some milk in a tin pan with some crumbled biscuits for the cat. She rarely saw the cat, but she had the sense of being observed by those tilting green eyes. She had decided September was a "her." And occasionally she did hear her meowing. When she did, she always thought of the girl with the pointy red shoes. She loved those shoes!

And she loved September too. She wished the cat wasn't so shy. September, she decided, was not an ungrateful cat. Just an eat-and-run cat. Cats were odd creatures. One had to give them time. *Never rush a cat*, Rose thought. Perhaps someday she might write a book about cats. *Tips for Cat Owners*. But that was the catch, of course. No one ever really owned a cat.

❋

There were always new things to do in the greenhouse. New seeds to plant—some of which had to be soaked overnight to give them a good start—and trays to be fertilized. Plants that had grown too big needed to be transplanted into larger pots. It was Rose's task to prepare the new pots with a mixture of peat and the granular stuff called vermiculite. She used Rosalinda's formulas, all neatly written in a book.

Rosalinda's attitude about homework was rather casual. She told Rose that she would learn much more from working beside her in the greenhouse. And one evening when

Rose brought her laptop down to look up some plant information on the internet, Rosalinda was captivated. "Such treasures!" she exclaimed. For indeed Rose found a solution for controlling the bugs that wreaked havoc on her grandmother's tiny ruby-red carrots, and then five minutes later discovered a special kind of bonemeal as a nutrient for stunted toad lilies. From that point on, Rosalinda insisted that Rose bring her laptop with her every evening. Dinner continued to be served in the greenhouse. As the days began to grow shorter, the night fell earlier, turning the glass house into a starry empyrean, a timeless place of simultaneous seasons and the endless blossoming of flowers. Yet never during their evenings had the cupolas dissolved or the aisles transformed themselves into woodland pathways as they had before. It had been a dream, surely just a dream. Rose had almost convinced herself.

❀

On this particular evening, her grandmother had just gone up to bed and so Rose, as had become her habit, stayed a bit longer and ascended the spiraling staircase to one of the cupolas. Rosalinda had started some winter violets from cuttings, and Rose herself had sown a flat of violets that afternoon that needed to be elevated into the cupola. As she carried the tray, for it was too large for the pulley lift, she heard the ping of a text message—most likely it was Joe, who'd gotten into the habit of texting her with questions about homework. But she didn't reach into her pocket now—not until she had put the plant tray down safely.

She was in the largest of the cupolas, where they kept the orchids. Orchids were brought down only for brief periods—mostly on holidays to decorate the house. There was also a myriad of lilies, bromeliads, and hibiscus up here, all of which thrived in the warm, moist air in the upper levels of the greenhouse. Rose felt as if she had been transported to a rain forest. She set the rootling violets down and took out her cell. The green text bubble floated up on the screen: *I don't exactly hate you, but if you were on fire and I had water, I'd drink it.* She didn't recognize the number it came from, but it wasn't hard to guess that it was one of the Mean Queens. Well, she supposed this was bound to happen. Had she really expected them not to bother her once they had her number? She should have changed it.

There was another ping and another bubble. This time, Rose gasped. Nausea swept through her. There was a screenshot of the front page of a newspaper and a photograph of a car on fire—the inferno her mother had died in. She felt herself growing dizzy. A strange sensation of powerlessness flooded through her. She grabbed the railing tightly and watched her knuckles turn white. She shut her eyes. *Don't fall, don't! You'll die if you fall!* But then the strong fragrance of the jasmine swirled through the air and filled her senses. She opened her eyes as the vines grew before her, stretching all the way to the floor. Shakily she began walking down the staircase. It was happening again! She no longer felt nauseous. Not even frightened. By the time she was on the bottom step, the concrete floor of the greenhouse had become a grassy path, and she felt something soft brush across her leg. "September!" she gasped. It was the cat. She did not sprint off but turned around and peered at Rose as if to say "Come along."

She began pressing through thick foliage, the streak of gold just before her like a light in the green leaves, or a maverick autumn leaf. The foliage soon gave way to an expansive lawn, and she was now on a wide drive that curved around the edge. Then September disappeared into some brush.

A voice behind her suddenly spoke.

"Come along, girl. I can't do this on my own. Two pails we have to get up to the palace. I could certainly use some help." Rose turned around slowly, hardly daring to breathe. A small scrap of a girl stood before her, leaning on a crutch and carrying a pail. She had white-blond hair and a scattering of freckles that stretched across her nose and cheeks. Her eyes were an astonishing blue—blue as any sky, blue as any sea, blue as the bluest flower that ever bloomed. Rose was unsure why she used a crutch. Her skirt was long, but it seemed as if her left foot turned inward. This was a girl just about her own age.

What had happened to her?

"Who are you?"

The girl did not answer immediately but squinted at her as if she was trying to place her face.

"Franny," she replied slowly. "I work in the dairy. And if you'd go back over there"—she pointed to a low, thatched building—"I left another pail of milk right by the door. You could save me a trip if you'd bring it." She nodded at her crutch. "The crutch robs me, you see, leaving me with only one working hand to carry."

"Yes, of course." But Rose did not move. She continued to stare at the girl. Franny.

"God's kneecaps, what are you waiting for, girl?"

"Uh . . . don't you want to know my name?" Rose asked.

"Oh, yes," Franny replied somewhat indifferently.

"I'm Rose—Rose Ashley."

"Oh, one of the Ashleys."

"You know my grandmother, Rosalinda?"

"I don't know any of them. They've been serving Her Highness—and the family—for a long time here at Hatfield. Since before she was born. Makes sense you coming. They're fiercely shorthanded up there. They'll hire you soon as they set eyes on you. Very thin on staff to serve her."

"Who's 'her'? Who's 'she' exactly?"

"Blimey! Are you daft? She is the royal princess."

"Royal princess?"

"Elizabeth, daughter of Henry! Henry the Eighth and the late and cursed Anne Boleyn." Rose noticed that she almost couldn't say the name Boleyn. "Now, Rose Ashley, have you had the skittles knocked out yer head?" She laughed warmly.

Skittles! Somehow Rose sensed she was not talking about the candy that was in her pocket. She reached for her pocket, but there was no pocket. There was no jacket. Gone too were her jeans. She was wearing a long voluminous skirt of a coarse brown fabric. Instead of a T-shirt, she wore a loose blouse tucked in, with generous sleeves. There were little tucks around the wrists of the sleeves. *Nicely made!* Rose thought. Hand stitched. A machine could never do such work, not even the *Millennium Falcon.*

"Go on, Rose, fetch the milk pail. I'll try to show you as much as I can. Course, I'm a tad lower than scullery, and I think I heard they were looking for someone to serve upstairs in the princess's chambers. You should do."

"Me? Why me?"

"They say that the princess thought she saw someone t'other day who she felt might suit."

Then it hadn't been a dream, Rose realized. The girl she had seen with the blue dress and the pointy red shoes had been the Royal Princess Elizabeth and they had each seen the other. But that princess, all those people, had lived almost five hundred years ago! How could this be? How had she jumped backward in time nearly five centuries?

"Now run along and get that milk." Franny said this merrily, as if she were inviting her to join a game.

Rose walked off in a daze. The pail of milk was right where Franny had said it would be. She picked it up and walked back to where Franny was waiting.

"Thank you. It'll make it so much easier for me. You know, my leg. Well, I guess you can only see my foot." She smiled, and a dimple flashed in her cheek.

"What happened to your leg?"

"Got the fever when I was a baby. I don't always need my crutch, but the weather's been bothering it lately. Then I took a tumble yesterday and that didn't help any."

"What kind of fever did you have?"

"The midwife called it infant apoplexy. Your muscles seize up. Lots of children die from it. But it just twisted up my leg and weakened it. So I can't complain."

Franny struck Rose as having an unusually sunny disposition. She liked her a lot, but she could still not begin to understand what had happened and how she had arrived in this place, walking with this girl, Franny. One moment she had been looking at that horrible newspaper picture of her mother's fatal car crash, and the next she was here in this new place. Hatfield, Franny had called it. And where was September?

"You know, Franny, I can carry both pails. It's not a problem for me."

"Oh, that would be very good, because then we could stop at the henhouse and I could collect some eggs for Cook. Saves me another walk."

"I'm happy to help you."

Rose paused a moment. "Have you seen a cat around here?"

"I thought I saw one the other day. And you know, it's funny, but I think Princess Elizabeth saw the cat too. She sent out a guard looking for it."

"Really? Was it by any chance orange?"

"Yes. Rather like a maple leaf. And thank you for helping with the pails."

"Oh, it's nothing."

Franny stopped and looked at her. "But it is something, Rose. You'll probably be a house servant. That's way above me. I can't think of one house servant, and there are almost fifty, who would pick up a milk pail, let alone go to the henhouse. You will go to the henhouse with me, won't you?"

"Of course. Why wouldn't I?"

"I don't know. You're a bit odd, Rose."

Rose was tempted to say, "So are you," but refrained. They continued on the path.

Rose scanned the countryside. If she just looked at the gently sloping hills, the grand old trees that swept green expanses, it might have been any fancy country estate in the America of her time, or like the country club where her mom often played golf with a friend of hers who belonged. But this was no country club. No golf courses visible. Rose knew she was not in her time. She was not going to come across a putting green or a reenactment of some episode in history where twenty-first-century people were dressed up in old-fashioned clothes to give a lesson on how life was in those olden times. This was the real deal!

She glanced discreetly at Franny. Her stockings were torn. The clogs she wore were wooden, good for mud. In fact, they looked as if they had animal poop stuck to them. Not dog poop either. Cowpats, undoubtedly, as there were some pieces of straw mixed in. Her skirt hadn't been washed in a long time. There were stains on it. And then of course there was Franny's odd way of speaking, not simply her accent but these outlandish expressions—God's kneecaps! The most fun swear ever, Rose thought. She pictured God sitting on a throne of cumulous clouds. His flowing celestial garments hiked up a bit, exposing knobby old knees crowning skinny, slightly hairy legs. Maybe God would be groaning a bit—"Oh, lamentations! My arthritis is kicking up again." To the left of the wide drive they were walking on was a vast lawn. A wonderful scent of freshly mowed grass swirled through the air, and beneath an oak tree was the hunched figure of a girl. Rose couldn't see her clearly, as her face was buried in her hands, and her shoulders shook.

"That girl over there. She's crying. Who is she?"

"That's her, poor thing." Franny sighed.

"Her? You mean the . . ."

"Yes, Her Royal Highness. Princess Elizabeth."

"Of course," Rose whispered, because it made sense to her now that everything she thought to be true could change in an instant. Her mom's life had ended in an instant. Her own life had changed in that same instant. So why should anything surprise Rose now? And though nothing seemed quite real to her, she kept looking to test reality, scouring this scene for certain touchstones of reality like the stains on Franny's skirts or the poop on the clogs. But nevertheless, she was surprised. And now she had been told that the weeping girl beneath the tree was royal. She could hardly ask to see her blue blood. Wasn't that the color that flowed through royal veins? And what proof could she offer them, offer to Franny or possibly this princess, of her own identity? Would they believe that she, Rose Ashley, had slipped from her grandmother Rosalinda's greenhouse in Indianapolis in the twenty-first century, and now she was here in England in what must be the sixteenth century?

"If they take you on, Rose, it's a fine job. I think she'll like you."

Rose was only half listening, as she had spotted September peeking around the immense trunk of the oak tree. Her tilting green eyes were fastened on the princess.

"I . . . I . . . hope so . . . but why is the princess crying?"

"Banished."

"Banished?"

"Banished from court by her father."

"Her own father banished her?"

"Well, he's king, you know. He can do that."

"But she's his daughter!"

"He's not just any king. He's King Henry the Eighth. He can do whatever he wants. He chopped off her mother's head."

Rose gasped. She knew this, of course, from history books, from televisions shows, from movies. But now she knew this because she was *actually here*. Had she slipped through some crack in time? She wavered a bit and set down the pail.

"Are you all right, Rose?"

"Yes . . . just takes a little getting used to."

Franny nodded. "I understand. First day on the job and all. I was a bit skittish my first day at the dairy."

"But tell me," Rose asked, "why was the princess banished? Did she do something bad?"

"Oh no, not at all! You see, every time the king remarries, he has a tendency to banish Elizabeth and often her half sister, Princess Mary. I suppose in a sense he wants to wipe the slate clean . . . you know, for his new bride."

"How many times has he married now?"

Franny paused and tapped her chin. "Let's see, first there was the Spanish queen. Catherine of Aragon, Princess Mary's mum. Then there was Anne Boleyn, Elizabeth's mum. Then Jane Seymour, Prince Edward's mum, before Anne of Cleves. Oh, nearly forgot Catherine Howard. He chopped her head off too. So, what are we up to?"

"Five."

"And now this queen, also named Catherine, the third Catherine, Catherine Parr."

Rose blinked. "A lot of Catherines."

"Indeed."

"Funny that they all spell it the same way, too, isn't it?"

Franny blushed. "I . . . I'm not sure. I haven't really learned my letters and scriving all that well. No time, you know."

"Oh, I'm sorry. I didn't mean to . . ."

Franny cut her off. "Oh, don't apologize. But do you know scriving?"

"You mean how to write?"

"Yes." Franny nodded. A wonderful smile began to steal across her face. Another dimple appeared. Her eyes twinkled like blue stars in a white night. "Of course you do! I should have known. You must be related to John Ashley. He's courting Princess Elizabeth's tutor, Kat Champernowne, or so it is rumored. The Ashleys are very bright."

In that instance, Rose realized she had a part to play and not simply a job attending a princess. "Yes, yes, Franny. A very distant cousin, I believe. Never met him." She of course had no idea who these Ashleys were. It was a pretty common name. There were two in the suburb of Philadelphia where she had lived and they were always getting each other's mail. But they were not related in any way. Could she be related to these more distant Ashleys?

"Course not, as you're probably from East Ditch near Letty Green."

"Exactly, and they're from West Ditch," Rose replied.

"Yes, West Ditch over by Tyttenhanger," Franny filled in. This was going well, Rose thought.

"I say, Rose," Franny said suddenly, "might you teach me some scriving?"

"Well, I suppose so. I mean, if there is time with my new job."

"Oh, that is so nice of you." Franny grabbed her hand. "I think you'll do well serving the princess. She's sad. But you'll make her feel better. Just as you have me. You'll be my friend, won't you?" A smile crinkled her face. "I mean, you can hardly be my servant." She giggled. "I don't need a servant; nor do you, I suppose. Just a friend." She stepped closer to Rose now. "So funny. I feel as if I have met you before. You remind me of someone."

"I don't know who that could be, but yes. I'll be your friend." She paused. "I only know your first name, Franny. What's your last name?" The color drained from Franny's face. She mumbled something.

"What?"

"Corey." She paused. "Franny Corey," she said in a stronger voice.

"Franny, this is such a nice summer day, isn't it?" She looked around to drink in the joys of the weather and the clear sky.

"Yes, summer. July is always the best month here, I think."

"What date is it exactly?"

"Not sure. But at least two more months until Michaelmas."

Michaelmas? When was that? And dare she ask the year?

Chapter 5

"You Are Mine"

They had arrived at the palace. Rose followed Franny around to
the kitchen yard, where they delivered the milk and
the eggs.

"Follow me. We'll go to the entrance for the inside palace servants. Normally I'm not allowed. But they're all in a
dither, being short staffed these days."

Franny went to a door, lifted the clapper, and knocked
loudly. They heard a bustling, then the sound of a bolt sliding. A plump, red-faced woman with her hair tucked under
a flouncy cap opened the door.

"Don't tell me no eggs this morning."

"No, plenty of eggs, Mrs. Belson."

"And who be this?" The woman ran her eyes up and
down Rose.

"Rose Ashley," Franny replied almost smugly.

"She be an Ashley?" The look in the woman's eyes brightened.

"'Tis true," Franny said. "And right in the nick of time, eh, Mrs. Belson?"

"I'll say. We've never been shorter staffed. Especially in the princess's apartments. Begging your pardon, Franny, but you know we can't have scullery and girls who muck about with chickens serving up there."

"Course not, Mrs. Belson."

"Wouldn't be fitting and proper-like." Mrs. Belson nodded at Rose. Rose nodded back.

"Now it might be temporary, dear. But we're in a pinch and beggars can't be choosers. You know the king banishes the princess and keeps most of her staff for his new queen. Doesn't seem quite right to me. Now wait here. I'll fetch Mrs. Dobkins. Franny, you run along, as you know how fussy Mrs. Dobkins is about egg and dairy girls at this entrance."

"Yes, ma'am."

The door closed and they were left alone.

"Franny, I'm . . . I'm not sure what has just happened," Rose said.

"What happened is you came in the nick of time and Mrs. Belson thinks you're fit to serve for the upstairs. You got yourself a fine job in the princess's apartments, even if it's temporary."

"Okay. . . ." Franny looked at her blankly, as she had a couple of times earlier. Rose suddenly realized that her speech must sound very American. The word "okay" was completely foreign to Franny. "I mean, yes, I suppose I did arrive in the nick of time, Franny. Thanks so much. Wish me luck."

"Oh, you'll do fine. You don't need any luck. I know it. Now I need to hurry along before Mrs. Dobkins comes round. So you wait here."

"All right. Thank you again."

Rose didn't turn around as Franny walked away, but she felt Franny's eyes on her, looking back. *She's trying to figure me out. And so am I!*

❊

"Who is she?" Franny whispered to herself. There was some-thing about Rose Ashley that stirred a memory. She had a headful of copper curls. Her complexion was tawny, and her eyes were very dark brown but had glints of bright amber. She was odd. That was for sure. It was almost as if she had never heard of Princess Elizabeth, or King Henry for that matter. She looked rather blank at their mention. But she was plenty clever. Knew her letters and scriving, and best of all she said she could teach Franny! Those words that Rose had said still rang in her ears: *I'll be your friend.* And Franny thought how she really did *need* a friend.

Her younger sister, Ellen, had died two years before

when the pox came through. Franny had somehow been spared. She heard her mum mutter to her father the night that Ellen died, "Surely, Alfred, we can't be struck twice. I pray not Franny."

"Thrice that would be," her father had added. "If you count Franny's leg."

"But she didn't die, Alfred."

Then it suddenly came to Franny why Rose's face seemed to have an echo of familiarity. The locket! She had found it perhaps two or three years before. She hadn't known it was a locket then—had thought it was just a pendant on a chain. She had glimpsed it on the verge of the main drive up to the palace. It was quite early in the morning, that time just before dawn, when the land seems to sleep. Every dewdrop on every blade of grass and flower suddenly becomes a prism, splitting the light into half a dozen colors. She spied a radiance turning the gray fuzz of a dandelion gone by into bright gold. When she walked over for a closer look, she saw that a small link chain was snagged in the bracken behind the dandelion head. On the chain she found a lovely pendant in the shape of a rose. It was a fine piece of jewelry, and certainly she could not be accused of stealing since she had found it by the roadside. Nevertheless, she felt she must tuck it away. A girl like her, from a family like hers—her mum worked in the laundry of Hatfield, her father was a simple yeoman farmer with a small plot of land, with one-tenth of his crop taken by the palace—there was not a spare farthing for such extravagances as pendants.

So for two years she had kept it hidden away. However, it was only a few months ago that she discovered that the rose was not simply a pendant but a locket too. The petals at the center of the rose were a paler gold than those around the edge. Beneath one of those petals was a tiny pin that if pushed in just the right way could open the rose. In each half there was a picture—a picture like none she had ever seen. Not painted, nor etched in pen and ink, but so real it seemed like a kind of magic. The surface was glossy, and the face that stared out at her was of a girl of perhaps six years. She was wearing the oddest clothing, and so was her mother. She supposed it was her mother, as they looked so much alike. But the two of them were half-naked. More than half-naked!

And that nearly half-naked girl looked very much like Rose! Not exactly. It was hard to tell, as the little girl's face had that chubby roundness to it of a six-year-old and her hair seemed much lighter. But there were resemblances. A Rose in a rose! The other picture was that of a handsome man with a close-clipped beard and a flat velvet cap, the kind artisans often wore. There was something about their eyes and the way they all smiled. It was almost as if they each had a secret. But how could this be?

Franny needed to run back home as fast as she could. She simply could not live another minute without checking the picture in the rose locket. If this was the case, if it really was Rose in that rose, then it must belong to her—and Franny would indeed be a thief if she kept it.

✤

Rose heard the door open again.

"Ah, what luck! Another Ashley, Mrs. Belson told me. Ashleys are always good! Couldn't have come at a better time!" the woman exclaimed. She was as thin as a scarecrow with her hair slicked back into a tiny bun the size of a Ping-Pong ball.

"Follow me, dear."

She moved in a sprightly manner as they wound their way up the twisting stone staircase. "Now it must be understood that you are not a companion to the princess. Your sole responsibility is to keep her quarters tidy. Check her gowns for stains and small rips that can be easily mended by you, not the head seamstress. We don't bother her with those tasks like buttons or darning. That's for you or Sara, the wardrobe maid, to tend to. You are also to wash the princess's undergarments—petticoats, drawers, and so on. But that is only required once every few months when she changes them."

"Eeeewww!" Rose exclaimed.

"What is that noise you just made?" Mrs. Dobkins

turned around quickly as they made their way up the stairs.

"Oh, nothing . . . I thought I felt a sneeze coming on. That's all."

Mrs. Dobkins nodded and continued to explain her duties as a chambermaid to Princess Elizabeth. "Well, we're here now." Mrs. Dobkins knocked on a massive oak door.

"Enter!" a young voice called out.

The door creaked. "Milady, this is the new chambermaid, Rose."

The princess was still wearing the blue dress. Her red hair was no longer in braids but flowed freely over her shoulders. Rose managed a curtsy. She had seen this done enough in movies. When she straightened up from the curtsy, her eyes and the princess's met. There was more than a glimmer of recognition in the princess's eyes. But she did not call her guards this time.

The room they were in was opulent, with tapestries on the walls and rich fabrics covering the furniture. But the fabric of the princess's dress was absolutely sumptuous. There was a triangular piece of material, narrow at the top and wide at the bottom, that extended from the waistline of the dress and made the skirt flare. The edges of the triangle were outlined with minuscule ruby-red beads. *So cool!* Rose thought, as she made a mental note. She would sketch it when she got back—if she got back! That thought was a bit startling, yet she could not help but marvel at the dress. And to think that a seamstress did all this with no sewing machine! She wished her own sewing machine would arrive. The boxes Caroline had sent from Philadelphia were taking forever to get to Indianapolis. When she got back to her own time, she was definitely going to google Elizabethan clothing.

Through an arched doorway, Rose glimpsed another room. She couldn't tell if it was smaller or larger.

"So you're the new maid, are you?" Princess Elizabeth said, then turned abruptly to Mrs. Dobkins. "You may leave, Mrs. Dobkins."

"Certainly, milady," Mrs. Dobkins said as she curtsied and backed out of the door.

The girl sighed and suddenly broke into sobs, burying her face in her hands.

"Oh, miss, what can I do?"

"Are you a ghost?" the princess asked, drawing her hands from her face.

"A ghost? Of course not."

"There was a girl who once was a servant here. She fell into a well and drowned." She paused. "I thought I saw a girl about your age a few days past on a pathway. I called my guards, as I thought it was the ghost of the drowned girl at first. But now I see you look nothing like Becky the servant girl."

"Not in the least. I haven't come to haunt you but to serve you. I am no ghost."

But in that minute Rose realized that it was she who had fallen into a ghost world. She was real, but everyone else was a ghost of a time long past, centuries gone.

"To serve me—yes! Of course." The girl pulled herself up and squared her shoulders. Despite her pink nose and tearstained face, she suddenly looked quite severe. "Well, to begin, you can address me properly—Your Royal Highness. For though I am banished, I am still, so far as I know, a princess! And the first time upon meeting a princess, one says 'Your Royal Highness.' Subsequently you may use an abbreviated form."

"And what is that, if you please, Your Royal Highness?"

"Milady."

"Yes, milady." Rose dipped into a small curtsy that somehow she knew was required, even though she was curtsying to a girl at least a few years younger. Dare she say a little more? "I . . . I . . . am so sorry for your situation." Elizabeth looked up at her now.

"Is that what you call it? A situation?" The princess's face seemed to soften.

"I'm sorry, I meant no offense."

"No need to apologize. You are the only person in this whole palace who has actually expressed sorrow for my plight. My father has a temper. He banishes me and my half sister, Princess Mary, on occasion. Mary doesn't mind it as much as I do. As you probably know, I do not have a mother. . . ."

Oh no, is she going to tell me about the beheading? Please no! Please!

"And what is your name?"

"Rose Ashley, milady."

"Oh. Kat, my governess, might have mentioned you. She's away now. Quite ill actually. She broke her leg and then contracted pneumonia. She is engaged to be married to John Ashley. Must be another branch of your family. Yours of course a lower branch, not the John Ashley branch."

"Yes, milady, another branch." *The twenty-first-century branch?*

"You seem agitated. You're wringing your hands."

"Me?"

"Yes, you, Rose. Who else would be wringing your hands?"

"True, milady. I just feel so bad for your troubles."

"Well, it could always be worse," she said ruefully, and plucked at a stray thread on her dress. *Does she mean she could be beheaded by her own father?* Rose wondered.

The princess sniffled again. "There's always hope."

"Yes, milady, there's always hope."

"You're just saying that to agree with me."

"No, milady, I would never do that. I . . . I take words seriously." The princess cocked her head slightly and regarded Rose.

"Do you now? How interesting."

Rose thought carefully before she spoke. "I know little of your plight, but I see before me an intelligent young princess and . . ." Before she could finish her sentence, Elizabeth's face broke into a smile. She rushed toward Rose and clasped her hands.

"You are right, so right, and guess what! I think the queen—Catherine Parr, my new stepmother—sees the same. I wrote her a month ago, and she wrote me back directly. So quickly, within one month, perhaps it was two." Rose blinked—two months. She thought that was fast? Well, she thought, it had been almost six weeks so far to deliver her boxes from Philadelphia.

Elizabeth chattered on. "She said I was too bright a princess to languish in the dim shadows of banishment. She urged me to be patient. That she will speak to the king and plead my cause, but my patience is wearing thin. Do you understand, Rose?"

"Yes. I believe I do."

"You really think Catherine likes me?"

"I'm sure she does."

"My father just has his moods. Does your father have moods?"

"I . . . I have never known my father."

"Oh, I'm sorry. That's very sad. And your mother—does she have moods?"

"My mother is dead."

"Oh dear!" Elizabeth exclaimed. "Then you are truly an orphan. I'm only a half orphan. I think you're the first whole orphan I've ever met. Fascinating!"

At that moment there was a knock on the door.

"Come in."

Mrs. Dobkins entered again and curtsied to the princess.

Shafts of sunlight were pouring through the windows and striped the floor. It had been close to dawn when Rose had arrived. There had been a quietness found only in those earliest hours. Now birdsong strung the air. She could hear it through the glass.

Mrs. Dobkins nodded at the princess. "Milady, I have just received news that the Princess Mary shall be arriving by luncheon. So, with Your Highness's permission, I might send Rose in to inspect that chamber and dust it up a bit."

Princess Elizabeth's face tightened. Her delicate features turned sharp. Her dark eyes became darker and as hard as agates.

"She can inspect her quarters, but she is in no way whatsoever to serve Princess Mary. Is that understood?" She glared at Mrs. Dobkins, then turned toward Rose. "Understood, Rose? As a matter of fact, I do not want you anywhere near me when Princess Mary is around. She has a tendency to take things that are mine." The princess paused. "And you are mine!"

The words stung in Rose's ears as she curtsied and left the room. *"You are mine"? What does that mean?*

❁

How many times had Rose's mom insisted that she clean her room before watching television or going out with a friend? "Your room, Rose. It's a complete disaster. You must clean it up. It will be condemned! I found a half-eaten Snickers bar on your desk from who knows when. You want to attract mice?"

Cleaning up her room was boring, but cleaning this one was not, and there were definitely no Snickers bars, although she found traces of mice. There were fabrics she had never seen. Gilded furniture and ornaments. There was a dressing table with a pearl-studded mirror. But not much clutter at all.

So it took Rose no time at all to clean the chamber that Princess Mary would be using. She plumped pillows, swept the hearth. Then, standing on a footstool with a broom, she brushed down the heavy curtains. She'd once helped her mom do this in a house she was about to put on the market, for her real estate business. No one had thought of brushing these curtains at Hatfield. She had to re-sweep the floor after she had finished with them. Rose knew she was not the tidiest person on Earth, but the hygiene habits of these people—royal people—left something to be desired. Imagine only washing your underwear every few months!

She began wiping the leaded windowpane. "Hello!" a familiar voice hissed.

"Franny!"

There was the sound of her crutch against the stone floor of the chamber. "I brought these." She was holding a bunch of twigs.

"A bouquet of twigs."

"Not a bouquet for decoration, silly." Her bright blue eyes sparkled. It was as if two little pieces of blue sky had come into the shadowy chamber. "Just a bunch of bayberry and juniper twigs for Princess Mary's teeth."

"Her teeth? Whatever is she going to do with twigs?"

"Clean her teeth, of course."

Another hygienic quirk. Rose imagined that the entire concept of toothpaste squeezed from a tube onto a real toothbrush would seem completely bizarre. And weren't twigs as real as a plastic toothbrush with its nylon bristles? Twig toothbrushes at least made a lot more sense than only washing your underwear once every several months.

"You know, Rose, we're in great luck."

"And why is that?"

"Princess Mary is coming. They hate each other."

"Then why is she coming?"

"They like to spy on each other. Not to mention the fact that Princess Mary delights in Elizabeth's banishment. But Elizabeth never wants any of her personal servants around when Mary is here. She even locks up all her jewelry."

"Yes, Princess Elizabeth mentioned that her half sister likes to take her things."

"Last time she took one of Elizabeth's favorite footmen. But you see, this gives us plenty of time together. My work is done."

"What shall we do?"

"Well, we could go for a swim?"

"A swim?"

"In the River Lea. We can fish there too. See, this is the first really hot day and I haven't had a bath since . . . I don't know, maybe Christmas."

Gross! Rose thought.

"So, you know how to swim despite your leg."

"Despite my leg! Oh my goodness, I swim better than I can walk. Not many people do swim. But I am one. I feel free in the water."

"But what about a bathing suit?"

"Bathing suit? Whatever are you talking about?"

"What do you wear?"

"I wear my nether things and sometimes my chemise. Why waste time to wash your clothes separately when you can swim in them and make them clean? And there's a place where the eddies get quite boisterous. It's wonderful for scrubbing out dirt."

Yes, Rose thought, *like a spin cycle on a washing machine.*

And she realized that *nether things* must mean stockings and underpants.

"Then we can just lie out on the grassy banks and be dry in no time. Oh, it will feel so good after all these months with nary a drop of water on my skin. Very cold winter. Ice on the well. Then only so much wood to heat up enough water for the teakettle and cooking. Couldn't waste it on bathing."

A blast from a horn seared the air.

"It's the princess!" Franny said, grabbing Rose's hand. "Princess Mary is arriving. Follow me. I know a place where we can see her best."

Rose marveled at how nimble Franny could be with her crutch on the twisting staircase that led up to a central brick tower. A window in the tower looked down on the portico where Princess Mary's carriage was just pulling up.

"They're taking wagers in the servants' quarters." Franny whispered.

"Wagers; you mean bets?"

"Yes."

"About what?"

"How soon Elizabeth will bow to her sister."

"Why does she have to bow to Mary and not Mary to Elizabeth?"

"Mary's older."

Elizabeth was standing stiffly on the steps. Her face

was rigid. A woman descended from the carriage.

"Older? She's ancient, Franny!" Rose gasped.

"Oh yes, almost seventeen years older. She's nearly thirty."

"She looks fifty. So how old is Princess Elizabeth?"

"Ten or eleven, I think?"

Suddenly Princess Mary looked straight up.

"Oh my God, does she see us?"

"No, terrible eyesight. See how she squints. . . . Look, Elizabeth hasn't even begun to curtsy yet." At that moment, Franny began to murmur. Was she counting? It didn't sound like it. Finally, after what seemed like hours, Elizabeth curtsied. "All right, that was one full Paternoster and a half."

"Paternoster?"

"The Our Father. You don't know it?"

"You mean the prayer?"

"Yes, I recited the entire prayer once and then had another go-round and got to the words 'our trespasses' before Elizabeth curtsied. You know: Our Father, which art in heaven, hallowed be thy name. Thy kingdom come, thy will be done, on Earth as it is in heaven. Give us this day our daily bread, and forgive us our trespasses . . ." Franny was tipping her head from one side to the other rhythmically as she recited the prayer. Rose realized it was her way of counting. How peculiar! But of course, the girl didn't wear a wristwatch or a stopwatch. She supposed it made a certain kind of sense.

"And you see, Elizabeth is not ducking her head as one is supposed to, but glaring right at Mary. Very exciting. Wonder if my pa won a farthing or two. Though Mum would be angry if he bet." *So*, thought Rose, *this is what passes for entertainment at Hatfield?*

"Let's go swimming!"

Chapter 6

The Man in
the Ruff

They were both *floating on their backs now in the calm waters* beyond the eddies. There was the scent of summer on the soft breeze. The air was tinged with the smell of freshly mowed grass. But never the sound of a lawn mower. They must use scythes for cutting the grass, Rose thought, or perhaps sheep munched it. But in this moment Rose felt only peace. She looked over at Franny, whose pert face tipped upward to the sun. Franny was a good swimmer, just as she'd said.

"I have a question, Franny."

"What might that be?"

"If, as you say, the two princesses hate each other, what

do they do all day?" Rose asked as she gazed at the flawless blue sky.

"Pray. Princess Mary is very religious. She spends a lot of time in the chapel."

"Does Elizabeth pray with her?"

"Only if forced to. Mostly the two princesses try to wheedle information out of each other. It's a great game—sort of a cat-and-mouse game."

"But Mary is not next in line for the throne."

"Oh no, that would be their half brother, Prince Edward, but he's sickly and frail."

In other words, Rose thought, *he could die. Wait, what do I mean? He does die, and Mary becomes queen*. It was then that the utter weirdness of Rose's situation struck her full force. She *knew* what would happen. She had read someplace about the young prince dying after he had been king for only a short time, allowing England's most horrific monarch, Bloody Mary, to rule. Her passion for God and burning Protestants had earned her the name. And yet Franny did not know this. She knew nothing of this. *But I do!* Rose thought.

At that moment Franny rolled over onto her stomach and began treading water, for they'd reached a deep part of the river.

"Rose!" There was a desperate note in her voice.

"Are you all right?"

"Yes, yes, but I . . . I must ask you something . . . uh, no, not ask you. I must show you something. Something very disturbing."

"What is it?" Did Franny know her secret? Did she know she was from the future? Another century, nearly five hundred years ahead in time?

They swam to the riverbank. September was frolicking on the grass, nipping at flies. "Oh, there's the cat that was with you when I first saw you. Your cat?"

"Uh, sort of." Rose was surprised; she hadn't realized that September had tumbled through time with her. A feline time traveler!

"Sort of?"

"She's a stray. She follows me about."

"Pretty, she is. Bright as an autumn leaf."

"Yes, I call her September."

Franny leaned forward until her nose was almost touching Rose's. "I have to ask you something, Rose Ashley. Something important." Franny's forehead crinkled into lines and she suddenly seemed older than her years. She began scrabbling on all fours to where she had dumped her skirt and blouse higher up on the bank. Rose felt as if there was something almost desperate in the way she was crawling. She finally reached her skirt, and her hand disappeared into a deep pocket.

"This!" she said, and held up a chain with a pendant on it.

"A necklace? Wh . . . what does this have to do with me?"

"You're sure you don't recognize it?"

"No, it's not mine."

"Let me show you something." Franny held the pendant. She pushed a small, nearly invisible pin, and the rose popped open. On each side, there was a picture. A photograph.

Rose gasped. "That's me! Me at the beach with my mom. Me when I was six years old."

"Why are you dressed that way?"

"Oh, Franny, it's so hard to explain."

Franny looked into her eyes sympathetically. "I understand," she replied in barely a whisper. "And who's that man?" Franny asked.

"I have no idea." The man had a ruff—a type of large, round, and frilly collar—and a neatly trimmed beard. He wore a funny little hat.

"He ain't noble 'cause he'd have ermine on his cloak if he was. Only royals are allowed to wear ermine. Sumptuary laws, you know."

"Sump-cha what?"

"Clothing rules, how you dress. Certain people are allowed to wear certain things depending on their rank and birth."

"That's terrible. It . . . it must be unconstitutional."

"Un-concha-what?" Franny asked.

"Never mind, it's just not fair." Rose wanted to wear a dress, make a dress like Princess Elizabeth's.

"Well, forget if it's fair or not, Rose. This gentleman, he looks quite a bit like you. Could he be related to you?"

"I have no family left," she whispered, and remembered the mist in her mother's eyes.

Rose sank her fingers into the grassy bank of the river. And just as she did, she felt something pulling her back, back to a newer century, back to where she'd come from. Every fiber in her body resisted. *No!*

The
Locket

Chapter 7

Ambush!

Rose wasn't sure how she'd gotten back from that grassy bank. She had dug in her fingers, trying to hang on for all she was worth, but it hadn't worked. She had to find out how the picture of her and her mom had shown up in sixteenth-century England! When she returned and looked at the time on her cell phone, only five minutes had passed since that dreadful text about her mother's accident had come in at 9:55 p.m. It was now ten o'clock. But it felt as if she had been gone for an entire day in that other world of Hatfield, in that other time out of time.

It seemed impossible. It had been early morning when she had arrived in Hatfield, met Franny, been taken up to the palace, met Princess Elizabeth, cleaned Princess Mary's chamber, then gone swimming. The sun was slipping down by the time they had swum ashore and Franny had shown her the locket.

Now she was back in her own century, in her own bedroom, and was trying to make sense of it all. Had this really happened? Had she dreamed it? But her bed was still made. Unslept in. And this man—he didn't look anything like her. She was sure. She popped open the locket. *Not me. Not me at all. No resemblance whatsoever!*

She had no desire for sleep. How could she? She and her mother did look a lot alike. The same curly copper-colored hair. And the same nose with the same band of freckles scattered across it come summer. It had been summer when that picture was taken, her mom in the mom-kini and Rose in her Little Mermaid bathing suit, her Aguaphile swim goggles with cartoon frog eyes on top slung around her neck, and clutching the Mickey Mouse pocketbook that she carried everywhere, and of course her Disney water bottle too. How much Disney merchandise could one kid wear? How did one explain Disney to Franny? Or, for that matter, to Her Royal Highness Elizabeth? She was a real princess and not a Disney one. How could any of this be explained? Possibly the man in the picture was dressed up for a costume party? Halloween, perhaps? Otherwise how could there be an actual photograph of a sixteenth-century man? There were only paintings then. The more she thought about it, the weirder it got. And she sensed it would keep getting weirder.

She climbed into bed and tried to fall asleep but couldn't. Around midnight she got up, went to her computer, and googled "portraits of Elizabeth I." There were many, but she was already queen by this time and usually wore a crown. One portrait intrigued Rose. She was older, in her fifties but still quite beautiful. In her hand it appeared as if she were holding a clear plastic tube. Impossible! Plastic hadn't been invented. There was a Latin inscription: *Non Sine Sole Iris.* Rose then went to Google Translate for the meaning. "No rainbow without sun." So the "tube" was really supposed to be a rainbow. The queen herself was draped in a dazzling array of jewels, but what fascinated Rose was the collar. "Epic!" Rose whispered to the image on the screen. "That collar is absolutely epic!"

It was ruffled, of course, for that was the style back then, but this one was made of gossamer-thin lace. It was as if the most fashion-conscious, elegant craft spiders, if such creatures existed, had woven that collar. Like a web, the collar spanned from her neck to her shoulders. In the fifth grade her class had done a unit on spiders. There was one spider that the teacher called the bling spider because of its jeweled appearance. Should the bling spider be her new name for Lisa of the Trio of Doom? She rarely appeared in public without a spritz of glitz, glitter in her hair, or a sequin on her eyebrow. And the bling spider was known not simply for its dazzling appearance but also for its intricate web weaving. Rose enlarged the view of the spectacularly ruffled lace collar. "This would definitely qualify for a bling spider creation," she whispered.

The Google entry mentioned all sorts of things about the symbolism in the painting—the rainbow for hope, the crescent-shaped jewel in her crown for the goddess of the moon from ancient times, the pearls for purity. An elaborate snake on one sleeve was said to symbolize wisdom. She couldn't get the collar out of her mind. She downloaded it and posted it on her blog under the topic "Fashions That Inspire."

Talk about majestic—this is total awesomeness!!!

Rose kept googling into the night. She was searching for portraits of men to see if any resembled the man in the locket. She had taken a photo of the picture in the locket, emailed it to herself, downloaded it to her computer, then enlarged it. *He doesn't look like me—no, not at all.* And she began listing all the differences in her head.

Coloring much ruddier. Ears awfully big. Eyes? Well, similar color, but they slope down a bit—they look kind of sad, she thought. Suddenly she had an idea. She would text her mom's friend Caroline back in Philadelphia and ask if she and her mom had ever gone to a costume party.

She looked at the clock. It was just one minute after midnight, but Caroline stayed up late.

She began to text:

Hey, Caroline, I know this is a weird question but did you ever go to a costume party with Mom? Or know if she went to one on her own?

Less than a minute later there was the ping of a text coming in.

You're up late, girl! No, as far as I know, your mom never went to a costume party. Not her kind of thing. Did the boxes come through yet?

Rose attached the picture of the man, replying:

No boxes!!! Lame. You're sure about the costume party? Take a look at this picture. Is this anyone you know?

Another ding.

Cool-looking dude. Wish I did know him. Costume looks very authentic. He does look vaguely familiar, but I can't quite place him. I'll check on the boxes again.

Vaguely familiar, thought Rose—but who did he vaguely look like? She went into the bathroom and peered at her own face in the mirror. *Not me!* She tipped her head ever so slightly. There was a window by the mirror that looked out on a big oak tree. Moonlight drizzled through the leaves of the tree, making the shadows dance in the night. One errant shadow fell through the window and briefly sliced across her face. Her chin darkened the way the beard darkened the lower part of the man's face. She stiffened. She suddenly felt as if she looked different, like a different person but indeed vaguely familiar. One who she could have been had she been born a boy. The moonlight shifted. The shadow vanished. She felt relief. *No, just me. Just me*, Rose whispered into the mirror. *And possibly a zit on my chin!*

She reached into the cupboard. There was a small plastic bottle of Clean and Pure, but it had nearly been used up. She took off the top and shook out a couple of drops. *That should do it*, she thought, and dabbed some on the suspect. She looked at her reflection in the mirror with the dab of pink lotion on her face. Then, raising her hand slowly, she waved to herself. "Bye-bye, O zit, you little demon pustule, wrecker of beauty and dreams."

Finally, she went to bed, but it seemed as if her head had hardly hit the pillow before her alarm went off. Darn! She cursed, looking at the clock. Going to school was the last thing she wanted to do. But she had to.

Then three hours after arriving at school she walked into the girls' restroom. The Mean Queens were there. It was as if they had been lying in wait for her. A total ambush.

I don't exactly hate you, but if you were on fire and I had water, I'd drink it. The words from the text message slammed in Rose's head. She froze. The three of them were primping in front of the mirror, dabbing on lip gloss. Which one of them had sent the text and the horrible picture?

"What shade do you think I should wear for the Snow Show?" Brianna asked, leaning toward the mirror.

"Snow Show? It's not even Halloween yet," Lisa said.

"Yes, but skating rehearsals start in a couple of weeks. If I make the cut, that is."

"Of course you will," Carrie answered. "But oh . . . look who's here!"

Rose touched the locket lightly. Like a vulture spying carrion, Carrie's eyes tracked her gesture as Rose reached for it. She desperately wished someone else would come into the restroom.

"What is that around your neck?" Carrie asked.

"Uh . . . nothing, really . . . just a . . . a pendant." Thank heavens she said pendant, and not locket. If she had said locket, they might become curious. Too late! Carrie was already moving toward her.

"Let's see it," she demanded.

"I'd rather not. It's . . . it's fragile."

"She'd rather not?" Carrie sneered. "Belonged to your late mother, I presume." *The Queen of Snark*, Rose thought. Carrie's eyes narrowed. She took a step closer. "An heirloom, perhaps?" One of Carrie's tinted blue eyebrows took a hike toward the blue streak in her hair.

"An heirloom for a nobody?" Brianna giggled. Her pointy little rodent snout wiggled just a bit, giving her a comic touch in Rose's mind. *You might be a champion ice-skater but you don't have the snark down, Brianna. Gotta work on it, Rat Girl*, Rose thought.

Ugh, I might be Wonder Woman in my head, but I'm pure Jell-O inside. Rose felt as if every vital organ were quivering and on the brink of collapse. The numbers on her internal

Richter scale were climbing. She was heading toward a seven quake—body quake, that is.

"I don't know what you're talking about," Rose replied, trying to steady her tremulous voice. Lisa now slid toward the bathroom door and rested herself firmly against it to block anybody coming in.

"Tell her what you found out, Brianna."

"My mother heard that your grandmother never had a husband, and her daughter never had one either. Your mom. But of course she's dead. And your dad seems MIA."

"MIA?" Rose's voice cracked.

"Missing in action." Carrie spat out the words. Rose's hand moved to her throat where the locket rested, a secret inside it. Might he look like her? Then she would no longer be a nobody. Perhaps somebody's daughter instead? Somebody who just might be alive and not dead.

"So where in the world would you get an heirloom? An heirloom is a valuable object that has belonged to generations of a family. What family?"

"It's none of your business." Her heart was clamoring in her chest. She folded her hand around the locket. Around the secret that she might not believe. A secret father? But how could that be?

"Now there's where you're wrong, Rosy!"

Carrie lunged toward her and had her hands on her neck. "Let me go. Let me go!" Rose screeched, and at the same moment a voice thundered from the other side of the door.

"This door needs to be opened immediately. I have a sick student here who needs to get in."

"Oh God, the Elf." Lisa quickly slid away from the door and Ms. Elfenbach entered with a greenish-looking sixth grader who promptly vomited on Carrie's shoes. "Ick! That little creep."

"Stop that, Carrie." Ms. Elfenbach quickly guided the girl to the sink, where she vomited again.

Rose fled from the bathroom.

"Gosh," Anand said, coming around the corner. "You look like you've seen a ghost."

"If only," Rose muttered.

"What happened?"

"Them!" She glanced over her shoulder. Carrie, Lisa, and Brianna were walking behind Ms. Elfenbach as she led the girl to the nurse's office.

"Mean Queens?" Anand asked. His dark eyes grew darker. "What did they do to you?"

She nervously fingered the locket. "They were trying to trap me in the bathroom. Then Ms. Elfenbach came in with that poor girl who threw up on Carrie's shoes. Carrie called her a creep."

"She called a sick kid a creep?"

Rose nodded. "Listen, we've got to go or we'll be late for math."

Ms. Elfenbach was also late for math, and Carrie, Lisa and Brianna weren't there at all. She was relieved when she saw Myles and Joe instead. *Lucky,* Rose thought, as this stuff that Ms. Elfenbach had started teaching about linear equations and graphing a slope intercept was not coming through at all. She would definitely have to go over it with Anand. But she was completely distracted. She could feel the locket against her chest. She needed to escape to someplace where she could open it and look at the face of that man, who in fact looked so much like her. Why hadn't she seen it before? She saw Anand whispering to Joe. Then she saw Joe scribbling a note. He passed it to Anand, who passed it to Susan next to her. Rose opened it.

There was a scrawled message. *Don't worry. We've got your back.* She mouthed back to them: *Thanks.* But in all honesty, she was worried. What could they do? Their very efforts to protect her could make matters worse. Susan looked at her sympathetically. Anand must have told Susan something about the Mean Queens targeting her too. Susan was a shy girl with glasses that had very thin, round black frames that really set off her pale complexion. There was something almost unearthly about her paleness. It was as if she had been created out of vaporous matter—clouds, mist, fog.

But her hair was fantastic. Jet black and densely frizzy. She spoke in a sandy whisper. It was as if she was afraid to speak up. She sometimes hung out with Joe, Anand, and Myles, since she was into sci-fi and they all were super *Doctor Who* fans. Rose sensed that Susan had a crush on Joe. Every time she talked to him, her voice almost vanished, and a storm of rapid blinks seemed to seize her eyelids.

"Rose!" Ms. Elfenbach said as she gathered her math book and papers to leave. "Might you stay a moment, dear? I'd like to speak with you."

Oh no, was she going to get blamed for that scene in the bathroom? She walked up to the desk.

"Can you tell me what was going on the girls' restroom?" Rose looked down. Her mouth was dry. "I know you weren't to blame. I know, Rose," she said more emphatically. "Those girls, Carrie, Lisa, Brianna . . . they . . . they're . . ." She seemed to be searching for a word. Was she going to say "difficult"? A nice word to use for ugly stuff. "Dangerous." A darkness seemed to invade her gray eyes. It was as if she didn't want to say that word but had to. Rose saw from the hard look in Ms. Elfenbach's eyes that she had no regret. "They always have to have someone to pick on. I know. I was one of their victims last year." Rose said nothing. "You heard, I suppose." Rose nodded. "Look, Rose, I know it's hard for you coming here to a new school, a new city, to live with your grandmother. Do you feel that you would like to speak to someone about this? It might help. Ms. Fuentes, the principal, is concerned. It must be so difficult to lose your only parent."

Oh great, I'm becoming a cause. Lincoln Middle School's favorite orphan. She bit her bottom lip lightly and shook her head. "No thank you."

❋

Somehow she got through the rest of the day. When she walked toward her bus, she saw Calvin waving to her.

"Calvin? What are you doing here? I don't have an orthodontist appointment."

"No, Rose. Not orthodontist. Horseback riding."

As if this day could get any worse. "But I said that I didn't want to learn how to ride horses."

"Your grandmother must have forgotten. But there's really no saying no to her anyhow."

"C-could . . . c-could . . . couldn't we just drive around and pretend I went horseback riding?"

Calvin's shoulders slumped, and he suddenly looked much older. He had told her he'd just turned sixty, and Rose said that she read that sixty was the new forty. They had joked about it. But now he looked almost seventy.

"Rose, you're not really asking me to lie to your grandmother, are you?"

"Well, just sort of a fib."

"It's not the truth, Rose. Call it what you may."

❋

They drove through the gates of the Hunter Valley Riding Academy.

"It's hardly a valley," Rose muttered.

"Not many valleys in this part of Indiana, but if you go down to the southern part of the state—Brown County—it gets a bit hillier."

"Look, every car here is an SUV and lots have trailers attached."

"Folks trail their own horses."

"But I don't have a horse to trail. So shouldn't that disqualify me?"

"Don't worry, your grandmother has leased one."

"Leased one already! She doesn't even know if I can ride."

"She has great faith, your grandmother. Don't you know that?"

"No, how would I? Sometimes she doesn't even know who I am."

"Not when you're in the greenhouse with her. She's as alert as any of us have ever seen her."

"But what if I hate it?"

Calvin pulled up in the parking area, turned off the engine, coughed slightly, then turned to face Rose.

"Rose," he said. His warm brown eyes looked at her kindly but very gravely. "If you do hate it, don't say anything."

"You mean don't tell the truth. Lie."

"I wouldn't call it lying."

"What would you call it?"

"I would call it not complaining. It will make your grandmother feel a little bit better. You know she's been better since you arrived. She seems not to be so forgetful, so . . . lost."

"What do you mean lost?"

"Hard to explain . . . just lost, lost in time."

"Lost in time?" Rose said vaguely. A shiver ran through her.

"Yes, sometimes she just comes out with the oddest things. And she has spells when we have to call the doctor or an ambulance."

"Ambulance?"

"Sometimes she has these little episodes—her blood pressure drops suddenly. She becomes faint. They have to take her in and readjust her medications. But she hasn't had one of those since you've been here."

At this moment a man in riding jodhpurs and boots came up to the car. Calvin lowered the window.

"Holy smokes, is this a 1958 Bentley?"

"Yes, sir, it is."

"Series One?"

"Indeed."

"Well, I'll be."

"My boss is particularly fond of British automobiles," Calvin replied. "British things in general. She also has a very sporty Aston Martin, 1934. But she feels she's too old to be racing about in such a car."

The man slapped the car and poked his head in farther.

"I'm Peter Elkins, and I bet this is Rose Ashley. In a few years when you get your license, maybe she'll let you race about in this baby." He patted the hood of the car.

"Maybe," Rose replied. She was tempted to say she would much prefer to take driving lessons than horseback riding ones.

"Well, we're ready for you. Your grandmother sent along your riding clothes, I believe."

"Yes," Calvin said. "In the trunk. I'll get the valise for you." Rose reluctantly got out.

"You can change in the girls' dressing room, Rose. It's right next to the tack room in the east barn," Peter said, pointing to a gray clapboard building with white trim.

"Okay," Rose said. She picked up the "valise" and wondered why Calvin didn't just call it an overnight bag.

As she headed into the barn past the tack room, she saw the door to the dressing room swing open.

"Oh, we meet again," Lisa said brightly as she came out. Now really, could this day get any worse? Maybe the horse would rear up, fall on her, and crush her to death. How had she not remembered that Lisa was a champion horseback rider?

"You two know each other!" Peter exclaimed. "Of course, you both go to Lincoln, right?"

"Right!" Lisa said. She had deglittered herself but now she turned on a full-wattage smile.

"Well then, you can show her around a bit after her lesson."

"More than happy to. You know, I can tell she's going to be good." Rose was alert. She recognized this kind of behavior. Lisa had lapsed into sleeper bully mode. Make nice in front of the adults. "She's got just the right . . ."

"Posture?" Peter said, walking away.

"That's it. You always say if you have good posture off a horse, you'll sit well in the saddle."

"You run along, Lisa. Harry is waiting for you on the jump course with Miss Dimples. Rose, meet me right outside this barn. I'll have Ivy waiting for you."

"Miss Dimples. That's your horse's name?"

"Yes, sort of named after me. My mom's idea because I have such deep dimples."

She flashed another smile. *I might barf*, Rose thought.

What a stupid name for a horse—Miss Dimples. Rose was infinitely relieved that her horse had a simple name.

"Bye, girlfriend!" Lisa actually came up to Rose and

high-fived her. Now the glint in her eye gleamed suspiciously. "Watch it!" she hissed. Rose flashed back her best stink eye. *Keep this up*, Rose thought, *and I'll be ready for the Olympic Stink Eye competition.*

❋

There was one good thing about her lessons. Her grandmother had bought her brand-new clothes for riding, and they were beautiful. Pale tan jodhpurs with leather patches on the inner leg to protect from rubbing against the saddle. A fitted darker tan jacket. She looked in a mirror. Pretty good, she thought. If only she didn't have to ride! *Always a fly in the ointment*, as her mom used to say. "Oh, Mom," she sighed as she went to find Peter, waiting for her with a dappled gray horse on a lead.

"This is Ivy, Rose—hey, how about that? Rose and Ivy. Sounds like a pub, you know, a bar in England. Doesn't it?"

"I don't drink, but maybe," Rose replied. Peter laughed.

"Ivy here is technically a pony, because she is just fourteen hands tall. The first thing I'm going to show you is how to bridle Ivy. And here, give her a lump of sugar first, and she'll be your friend forever. Hold your hand flat now and let her just lick it off your palm. That way Ivy won't accidentally crunch your fingers."

She held out her palm with the sugar. Ivy lapped it up. Rose liked the rough feel of her tongue, warm and just slightly scratchy.

"Now this is the bridle that I'm holding." He began to give a few quick pointers in the basics of bridling a horse. Rose took the bridle from him and gave it a try.

"Excellent!" he proclaimed. "You're a natural."

How can I be a natural? Rose wondered. *I'm not even on the horse yet!*

But she liked the process. There was a quiet orderliness to it. She found it almost soothing. And Ivy herself was patient—she seemed, in her wordless way, to understand her.

Rose's legs were long and she didn't need a mounting block. She easily slipped her foot into the stirrup and swung into the saddle. Peter led her from the barn into a ring. After her new teacher went over the basic positions of how to sit in the saddle, she flexed her heels down in the stirrups and began to walk Ivy around the circle. Toward the end of the hour, she trotted a bit.

"Amazing!" Peter called out. "I'm not even going to have to teach you to post. You're already doing it. Posting."

"Posting?" Rose asked as she pushed up in the stirrups. "What's that?"

"What you're doing right now." Rose felt the locket thumping softly against her breastbone each time she rose from the saddle.

"You've got the rhythm and everything. A natural, isn't she, Lisa?"

Lisa! Lisa was watching her! Rose felt herself suddenly bobble and bounce wildly in the saddle, losing her balance. *I'm going to fall ... I'm going to fall!* She gripped with her knees and tried to tuck her butt more firmly into the saddle.

"Great recovery!" Peter shouted. "Slow to a walk and bring Ivy to the center of the ring."

Peter walked over to her and slapped the calf of her boot. "Great first lesson. Wonderful instincts, Rose. Most new riders yank on the reins if they begin to lose their balance. Always a bad mistake. You handled it like a pro. Gripped with your knees and settled deeper into the saddle. Don't know what happened back there, myself. Because you seemed to have hit the sweet spot of Ivy's rhythm. Hard thing to do on the first lesson. So did Ivy spook a bit? I didn't catch it."

No, don't blame Ivy. I spooked, Rose wanted to answer. *Spooked by Lisa.* But she said nothing. Her heart was still racing and yet she wasn't frightened. An odd sort of joy pulsed through her.

"There must have been some great riders in your past. You've got the genes."

"Really?" She turned to Peter and smiled. It felt almost strange to smile. A foreign sensation. It had been so long.

Peter led her back to the barn. There was a boy carrying a saddle.

"Hey, Jamie, this is Rose. Could you help her dismount and show her how to brush Ivy down?"

"Sure, Pete."

Jamie was perhaps a year older than Rose. He had curly hair that tumbled over his tanned forehead and intense blue eyes. His cheeks were ruddy. He wore a faded plaid shirt tucked into his jeans. And his jeans were tucked into cowboy boots, not the fancy English-style leather boots. He had a distinctive way of walking—very long rhythmic strides, as if he carried a secret music inside.

"Hi," he said as he took the reins. "You know how to dismount?"

"I suppose the first step is taking the reins in one hand, then taking one foot out of a stirrup and then swinging that leg over the backside of the horse."

"You've got it. Then just slip on down."

Rose felt a shadow slide between them.

"She's fast, Jamie," Lisa said. Then giggled. "Fast learner." Rose's stomach clenched. She felt the blood rising to her face. Her foot seemed to catch in the stirrup and she began to fall.

"Whoops!" Jamie said. "I got you." She felt his arms grab her around the waist.

"Oh . . . oh . . . I'm sorry. I'm such a klutz."

"Hey, no. Don't feel bad. Look, Ivy didn't even shy."

She looked at Lisa. A bitter light was pouring from her eyes.

To think that minutes before Rose had felt herself smiling. What a day this had been. Well, she decided, no way was she going to let this idiot girl wreck her riding lessons. She had loved it. Peter was nice. Jamie was cute. And the clothes were so cool. She was coming back, definitely.

Chapter 8

The Diary

Rose smiled again. As soon as she walked in the door, Betty greeted her.

"Look what finally arrived."

"My boxes!" Three large cartons stood in the hallway.

"I told you they would come. Just took a little side trip to Carmel, Indiana, apparently. The zip code was two digits off."

Rose dropped to her knees and hugged one of the boxes. It was as if part of her life had come back to her.

"Want me to help you upstairs with these?" Calvin asked.

"Oh sure. Thanks."

As Rose followed Calvin up the stairs, once again she felt the locket thumping softly against her chest. She liked the sensation. The day had started out so horribly with the Mean Queens' ambush in the restroom. Then it seemed as if things had only gotten worse and worse. But in fact, the day began to improve in the most unexpected ways. The riding lessons had been fun despite her near fall, and Peter had declared her a natural. *You've got the genes!* But what genes? Her mom had never mentioned riding, and it was hard to think of her grandmother riding. Could it be him? The man in the ruff?

As soon as Calvin set the boxes down in the bedroom and left, she found the tiny pin just beneath the one petal of the rose and pushed it. She peered at the man. *I have no father.* The words seemed to cut her.

"I might," Rose whispered now. "I just might." And perhaps, she thought, he was a rider. *The source of my genes as a rider!* The thought thrilled her. She looked again at the picture. Between the ruff and the sleeveless jacket, he wore another close-fitting but longer jacket. There seemed to be a sprig of something in that jacket's buttonhole. She couldn't quite see what it was. She strained to look but soon gave up, as she was eager to open a carton and touch those relics of her own life that seemed unbearably precious.

She took the box cutter that Calvin had brought up, sliced the mailing tape, and tore open the flaps of the carton. She plunged her hands into the annoying Styrofoam peanuts packing materials. There were books. But the first "book" she touched was the diary that her mom had given to her as a birthday present just before her fatal crash. The key was still taped to the back of the diary. Rose had never written in it. Never even unlocked it. Her life had ended on that day in August, and she had no desire to relive any days close to that. She was tempted to throw the diary out. Put it in the trash can in the alley behind her grandmother's house. She would! She seized it now and quickly ran downstairs. Trash collection was still two days away, but she wanted the diary out of the house.

She knew it was a feeble gesture as she dropped the diary into the can. A kind of tattered symbolic act suggesting one could banish the day her mom's life had ended. But she also knew that she couldn't live with that last gift from her mom. She imagined it sitting on her bookshelf staring at her every day, taunting her with the days it held, the blank pages scowling at her. August 15, a monstrous date demanding her acknowledgment. No, she simply would not do it.

Returning to her bedroom, she took a deep breath and began to carefully unpack the rest of her life from the three boxes. There were clothes and fabric for clothes she had yet to make. But best of all, her beloved sewing machine was here at last. The *Millennium Falcon*. "Millie!" she whispered, and embraced it.

She was only eight when her mom gave it to her for

Christmas. The people at the sewing-machine store felt that it was perhaps too complicated for a girl her age, but her mom said no. That Rose had been using a rickety old one and was ready for something more complicated that could do the kind of meandering or S-curve stitching that she liked for decorative and appliqué work. It had a touch screen for selecting new stitches. Patterns could be scanned in, and there was a program with which Rose could create her own designs. When Rose first unwrapped it that Christmas morning, she gasped. She never thought her mom would spend so much money on a sewing machine. "Mom! This . . . this is the *Millennium Falcon* of sewing machines!" she screamed. And thus her first project had been a Princess Leia gown. Both she and her mom were huge Star Wars fans.

In anticipation of her sewing machine's arrival, Rose had cleared a place on a table in front of the window that looked out on the northeast cupola of the greenhouse. She had also cleared a bookshelf for her stacks of fabric. Her button box she put in a desk drawer.

With each object she touched she felt a rush of joy and yearning. These things were the last tendrils that connected her to what now seemed like a charmed life with her mom, an enchanted time. She spied a piece of the daisy-patterned blue silk that she had used to make the bow tie she had worn that first day of school. There were a couple yards or more of chambray fabric. So perfect for soft, swingy skirts. She had made one in a lovely peach color for her mom. Perfect for a garden party her mom had been invited to. Tears sprang to her eyes as she remembered her mom going off to that party. "Wish me luck. Lots of potential real estate clients there, and I'll be sure to tell them that my skirt is designed and made by you." Her mom had even ordered labels that read *Designed by Rose*.

There was a soft tap on her door.

"Yes?"

"It's me, Rose." The voice creaked.

"Gran?" Rose got up quickly. Tucking the locket inside her shirt, she went to open the door. Her grandmother had never come into her room the entire time she had been living here.

"Hi," Rose said, opening the door. Her grandmother was fragilely propped up on her walker. Betty stood behind her.

"Gran? That's what you've decided to call me?"

"Oh, sorry. I meant to say grandmother."

"Don't be sorry, child. Gran is fine. Very efficient. Why waste syllables? I'm Rosalinda. Your mother's Rosemary, and you're just plain Rose. Seems simpler. Doesn't it?"

"Yes, I guess so."

"And how was the riding lesson?"

"Fine." She paused. "Good, actually. He said I was a natural."

"Did he now?"

"Yes, Gran." Rose looked at her grandmother directly. "Said I had the genes."

"Peter? Peter Elkins. What is he, a geneticist?" She harrumphed. "Horse breeding, I suppose. But you're hardly a horse." She cackled. "Come downstairs. I want to thin out some of the herb seedlings. Dinner in the greenhouse, as per usual."

"Yes, Gran."

She watched as Betty led the old lady to the banister stair lift.

"All aboard!" Betty exhorted as she guided Rosalinda into the chair.

"My specs, Betty! My specs!"

"Right around your neck on the ribbon, Mrs. A. Here, I'll help you on with them." The huge oval frames dwarfed Rosalinda's face. Her pale, nearly colorless blue eyes were magnified and appeared to quiver slightly as she peered at Rose.

"My horse!" she exclaimed. This time she didn't cackle, but snorted. Indeed, just like a horse. Betty rolled her eyes.

"All right! All right! Off we go. Tallyho!" Rosalinda waved merrily as the soft whir of the stair-lift motor hummed and she glided down the curving banister.

"Be right down, Gran!" Rose called.

Then she heard her grandmother mutter something unintelligible to Betty.

"That's your granddaughter, Mrs. A. Rose, that's who she is."

"Oh yes. Just plain Rose."

❃

A few minutes later Rose came down.

"We'll have dinner over on the table with the winter herb trays. Second table to the left after the winter lettuces. I planted those lettuces two weeks ago, I think. Take a look and see if they've started sprouting."

How could her grandmother remember where she planted what and when, yet not remember at times that she had a granddaughter living with her in her own house?

"Oh, and look at this, dear."

"What, Gran?"

"The bud on this rose. A damask rose. A true old damask rose. Very different from these newfangled hybrids. It should bloom by Christmas. Out of season here in the greenhouse, but why confine it to summer? And you know it is the rose of a royal house."

"Really?"

"Yes. I think your mother might have had it in mind when she named you Rose—just plain Rose."

"Really?"

"Why do you keep saying 'really,' dear? It's as if you disbelieve everything. Not to mention you should be trying to expand your vocabulary. For example, you might say 'how incredible' or 'unimaginable.' Now please go check on those winter lettuces."

Rose peered over the lettuce tray. The dark, rich soil showed no sign of any "sproutlings," as her grandmother called the stage just before they graduated to become true seedlings. Behind the sproutlings' tray, there were some bright nasturtiums beginning to climb up a dozen or so thin stakes.

"See anything, Rose?"

"Nothing. . . . Oh, wait." She hunched over the tray. Did she spy a little bit of green? "Yes, actually. I think so."

"Like little green snouts, like . . . like pixie snouts?"

"Yes, exactly." Rose giggled. Suddenly she had an idea. "Hey, Gran, can you come over here on your walker?"

"Why?"

"I want to take some pictures of us together with the seedlings and those flowers; the nasturtiums on the stakes make such a nice background."

"Us together? But how? I'll have to ring for Betty to take it."

"No, Gran, a selfie."

"Selfie? What in heaven's name is a selfie?"

"I'll show you. Let me run and get my selfie stick. I'll be back by the time you get to the pixie snouts."

Rose was back, and Gran was posed rather rigidly by the lettuce trays. She slid her eyes toward Rose as she opened the selfie stick and put her camera in it.

"Good Lord, what a contraption!" Rosalinda said. Rose stood next to her.

"Now look up and say cheese."

"Nasturtiums!" Gran blurted.

A few minutes later Betty arrived with their dinner trays.

"Betty, Rose saw some sproutlings in the trays. We'll have herbs and lettuce by the spring equinox. Tuesday, March twentieth, six thirty a.m."

They ate their dinner mostly in silence, but when her grandmother did speak, Rose marveled at how she knew the location of every single seed she had planted and when it might sprout, and she even knew the precise date of the equinox.

"Gran! How in the world do you know the date, the day, and the very hour of the spring equinox?" Her grandmother looked up and cocked her head.

"Not really sure. I'm a gardener. Certain things just stick in one's head, you know. While others . . ." She paused. "Just . . ." Her voice grew faint. "Just fade."

The cry of a cat scratched the evening air.

"September!" Rose gasped.

"Oh no, dear, March. It's always in March. The September equinox just passed."

"Uh . . . not that September. Another one."

"Another? How many Septembers can there be in one year?" She emitted a tiny giggle.

"I'll be right back, Gran. Just want to check something outside."

She went out the rear door of the greenhouse and into the back alley.

"September?" she whispered into the thickening dusk of the evening. "September, where are you? Did you stay behind? September?" She stood still and listened. This day that had started so horribly had by some miracle turned into a good day, but did this mean she could never go back to that other world—the world of Hatfield and Franny and a lonely princess? She felt as though she were straddling two worlds. The boxes upstairs in her bedroom were her past, and yet as she touched the locket, there was another past calling her, and the possibility of a father.

She heard Betty's voice through the greenhouse door. "Rose, your grandmother wants you to check on the other herb trays before I take her upstairs."

"Yes, I'll be right in."

"Looking for that cat, were you?" Betty smiled and winked at her when Rose came back inside.

"Yes, I thought I heard her."

"She hasn't been around for the longest time," Betty said, and turned to Rosalinda. "She was looking for that cat, Mrs. A. The one that hangs around on our block."

"Moved on to a classier neighborhood, most likely." Her grandmother sniffed. "One of those places north of here. Ostentatious, palatial, ugly things. Unsightly."

"Oh . . . oh, I hope not," Rose said, thinking of Hatfield, the turreted brick palace where the princess lived. Had September stayed back there? Had the cat wanted to live in a real palace?

"Rose, dear," her grandmother said, "give me a report on those winter herbs. I sowed them a month before those lettuces."

"Oh yes, sorry, Gran." She walked over to the table. "Well, the parsley does need thinning. And . . ." She bent over the tray next to it, where very vigorous seedlings were crowding each other out. She blinked. The robust herbs looked exactly like the sprig she had seen tucked into the buttonhole in the man's jacket in the locket picture. "What are these, Gran? Their label seems to be missing."

"What are what?"

"They have needles like miniature evergreens."

"Oh, rosemary. I named your mother Rosemary. Rosemary for remembrance. How is your mother now, Rose? Just plain Rose." A frail giggle escaped.

"My mother?" She felt a lump swelling in her throat. "My mother is dead, Gran." She blurted this out. She had not meant to say it that way. It sounded so harsh. She wasn't angry, but she wished her grandmother could just remember that her mother was no more.

"Oh dear . . . I forgot. And here rosemary is for remembrance and I forgot. If that's not irony for you, I don't know what is." Then in a sad voice, her grandmother began to trill.

> *"There's rosemary and rue. These keep*
> *Seeming and savor all the winter long.*
> *Grace and remembrance be to you."*

She turned toward Rose as Betty led her away.

"That's from Shakespeare's *The Winter's Tale*, Act Four, Scene Four," Rosalinda called back over her shoulder.

"Your grandmother knows her Shakespeare, Rose," Betty said.

As well as the equinox, Rose thought. What an odd person Rosalinda was! Or perhaps it was her brain that was so odd—like a Rubik's Cube of some sort, full of twisty puzzles of time and fragments of memory.

"And!" Rosalinda's voice boomed. The moon just rising showered light through the greenhouse cupolas. Momentarily Rose felt caught in a dazzling crossfire of splintering moonlight.

"And what?" Rose called back.

"Where rosemary flourished, the woman ruled."

"Who said that, Gran?"

"Oh, for heaven's sakes, how should I know?" She laughed gaily now.

Rose watched as the shadow of her grandmother stretched across the countless trays of seedlings and fully grown plants that were flourishing out of season. Plants that did not appear to know their proper time. But then again, Rose was beginning to doubt what proper time was.

She thought once again of the seemingly scattered contents of her grandmother's mind. The point of a Rubik's Cube was to get all the surfaces to show only one color. In short, for everything to line up. But how boring that would be—a world or a time where everything lined up. Who knew if proper time would be as interesting as time out of time?

She heard the ding of her cell phone. A text message. Ever since the dreadful text about her mother, it was all Rose could do to look at her phone. But this was from Susan. Susan had never texted her before. Maybe the Mean Queens had gotten ahold of her phone, or even worse, maybe they had converted her! It was awful to live in such dread. To flinch at the very sound of a text ding.

Hey, want to go to those vintage, secondhand shops I was telling you about?

Rose decided to be safe and called Susan back.

The phone rang twice. It was definitely Susan's voice that answered.

"You just sent a text, right?"

"Yeah."

"Uh, sure, I'd love to go. When?"

"They open at eleven. I checked."

"But school . . ."

"Did you forget? No school tomorrow. It's Indiana State Teachers' Conference."

"Oh wow, yes. Let's go."

"I can walk over to your house, say around ten thirty. We can get to almost all of them just walking. We might have to take the bus to one downtown. But most are pretty close by, in Broad Ripple."

"Great, see you tomorrow."

After they hung up, Rose looked at the pictures she had taken of her grandmother and herself. They were good. Maybe she would start a little project where she'd photograph the trays for her gran, documenting the progress from sproutlings to seedlings to full bloom. She bet Rosalinda would like that. She decided to post the pictures on her blog, along with a close-up of the tray of pixie snouts and a caption:

My Gran is a little bit camera shy, but she let me take a picture of her shoes. She wears the coolest little-old-lady shoes! Oh, and here is a picture of a seedling tray of herbs. Gotta admit those shoes get me in the mood for some thrifting. Plan to scope out Goodwill and some vintage shops. This is all new territory, after all. The Midwest—prairie chic? OMG, how I loved *Little House on the Prairie*. Laura Ingalls Wilder, here I come. I'm envisioning a kind of sass-meets-power look. No briefcases puleeze! Mom never carried one and she was named top Realtor in the Philadelphia area twice. She had an adorable flowered backpack she found in Back to the Future, our favorite thrift shop.

Chapter 9

Thrifting

"**O**ld Souls," *Rose said. "What a great name for a vintage shop!"*

"Yeah, I thought you'd like it," Susan said. "I've been in here a lot, but I don't have the knack, really."

"What do you mean, the knack?"

"Style. You've got style, Rose. I don't exactly know how to put things together. I wind up looking . . . schlubby."

"Schlubby?"

"You know, kind of a mess, unattractive, clumsy. That was Carrie's nickname for me last year. Susan the Schlub."

Rose was shocked. There was nothing new about bullies calling kids cruel names, but it was as if Susan was accepting

Carrie's word on this. She was letting herself be defined. Thinking of herself as a schlub. That was really sad.

"Look, you're not schlubby in the least. I'll find something for you."

"But you put things together so well, like lace and plaid and that sweater skirt you wear a lot."

"The sweater was my mom's. I just—how shall I put it—reconfigured it and sewed it up."

"I need a lot of reconfiguring, Rose." Susan's shoulders drooped, and it seemed as if she were sinking into the sidewalk. Low self-esteem, Rose's mother would have said. Poor Susan was drowning in it.

"Don't be ridiculous. You don't need to change. We just need something that fits you. Not your size, necessarily; your personality."

"I . . . I don't really have a personality."

"Yes you do. You're just shy, quiet. Stand right there. Let me study you."

Susan froze. She looked as if she were in a lineup at a police station. Rose sensed it was useless telling her to relax.

"Okay, you have very pale skin."

"Almost translucent, my mom says."

"And you have very black hair. The glasses are a terrific fashion choice for you with those frames. Now does all this suggest anything to you?"

"I'm kind of black-and-white?"

"Yes, and with your pale skin, silky, chiffonlike fabrics in pastels might work. But ice blue would be great too, and LACE. You are made for lace with your hair."

"Oh, I hate my hair, it's so frizzy. And I can't straighten it because I'm allergic to the stuff."

"It would be a crime to straighten that hair. I'd give anything for your hair. It's like . . . like three-dimensional black lace." She grabbed Susan's hand and gave her a yank. "We're going in!"

As they stepped through the door, Rose knew immediately that they were in vintage heaven. It was stuffed with Old Souls clothing and furniture.

There were several racks of lace things ranging from curtains to dresses. She speedily pushed through the racks, murmuring as she slid the hangers. "No . . . no . . . no . . . no . . . no . . . no . . . YES!" She pulled out a faintly yellowed long lace gown with a high collar.

"It's beautiful!" Rose exclaimed. "You don't find this kind of lace anymore."

"But look, it has a huge stain on the skirt."

"Who cares about the skirt? It's the top part. Those are leg-of-mutton sleeves."

"What?"

"It's a kind of sleeve that's puffy at the top. I guess it's supposed to look like a woolly sheep's leg, and the bodice is beautiful."

"But what about the rest of it? The skirt?"

"We cut that off and use it for something else. But this top will make a beautiful blouse. You're getting bat mitzvah'd, aren't you?"

"Yes, in March."

"I see this matched with a gorgeous velvet skirt, and chunky shoes with maybe satin ribbons that tie over the top."

"Velvet?" a voice shouted out. An adorable little lady came bustling around the end of the rack. "I'm Elsie, the Old Soul, in other words the proprietor." Elsie hardly reached Rose's shoulder. "We have it over there on the far wall. Twenty-five linear feet of 1930s velvet evening gowns—very old-style Hollywood."

"Let's go!" Susan said. *Aaah!* thought Rose. *She's getting into the spirit of things!*

By the time they left the store, they had the lace dress, which Elsie originally asked twelve dollars for, but Rose talked her down to seven. Their most expensive purchase was the ice-blue velvet evening gown for twenty dollars, which they would literally split, both the cost and the dress. The bottom half for Susan, the top for Rose. Rose would make her a soft skirt to go with the lace blouse and then she would do something cool with the top for herself. There was also a beautiful black lace dress that Rose spotted—a perfect match for Susan's hair—but Rose couldn't persuade her to buy it.

Elsie came over. "It is a lovely gown. Got it at an estate sale. You know, common folk in Merry Old couldn't wear lace like this."

"Merry Old?" Rose felt her heart race.

"England, my dear. Clothing laws. I mean, it's one thing when restaurants say no service for people in bare feet or whatever. But you could be put in prison for wearing furs like ermine, or certain colors—like purple! Very bad to wear purple unless you were royal, of course. So undemocratic. God bless America!"

"Really?" Susan said.

"Yes, really," Rose whispered. Franny's words rang in her head. *He ain't noble 'cause he'd have ermine on his cloak if he was. Only royals are allowed to wear ermine.*

"Well." Susan's face scrunched up as if she were trying to solve a very difficult math problem. "What was the cut-off line for wearing fur or velvet?"

"Oh, not sure, dear. You know, noble birth—princesses, dukes, duchesses. Below that lairds or landowners, artisans, craftsmen, and merchants. The laws eased up for them, but no ermine, no purple, no cloth of gold. Though they couldn't wear pure silk, there were blends of linen that could be woven into very lovely brocade patterns. The coarse fabrics were left for the yeoman farmers and such."

It was all Rose could do not to pop open the locket right here and try to figure out the fabric of the man's waistcoat. Not a prince, but what was he? Laird, farmer, blacksmith, artisan?

※

As soon as she was back at her grandmother's, she went to her room and opened the locket. She squinted hard at it. Then she remembered she had downloaded the picture to her laptop. It was impossible to tell the fabric. But maybe he wasn't a farmer. A farmer wouldn't wear a ruff like this man. A merchant? Artisan? An artisan would be nice. Or maybe a merchant, if he owned a clothing store. She laughed to herself as she imagined a little sign in Old English script above the shop—*Vintage Before It Was Vintage*, or maybe *Vintage Is Now!* Rose hoped the cool dude in the ruff didn't own something like a butcher shop.

After Old Souls, she and Susan visited three other stores and found a few more items, but Rose's favorite of all was a red velvet pocketbook. She posted a picture on her blog of the pocketbook and the lace dress she planned to reconfigure for Susan.

IT CALLED TO ME: A red bag on a red chair in a red room. How could I resist?

It was almost midnight by the time Rose completed arranging a batch of new trays in the greenhouse. She began to wander the aisles of plants. It was as if the seasons had tangled. Some things were in full bloom and would be moved into the conservatory when they were reaching their peak. There would be peace and prayer lilies for the Christmas season and tumbling cascades of creeping wintergreen, then surprise clematis, which normally only bloomed in summer. But as her gran would say, *Why restrict these starry blossoms to just July? July has fireworks, January has nothing.*

And now she found herself in front of the damask rose, a rose for December, and yet, she thought, it was only October. She looked at the tight buds of the rose and touched her locket. She crouched down to observe it more closely. Was there a tiny seam of red, bloodred? She heard the soft meow of a cat. The rose seemed to unfurl as she felt a brush of fur against her calf. "But it's not December yet," she whispered to the cat. What was happening?

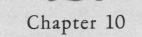

Chapter 10

"She Stole It!"

Suddenly she could feel the cold stone under her feet. And Rose knew she was back. She had been told to always remove her shoes when stealing into the princess's chambers to open the curtains in the morning. Mrs. Dobkins had trained her well. "Gently, gently. You must wake up Her Royal Highness quietly. You slip into her chambers like a ghost. Tiptoes and stocking feet."

Maybe I really am a ghost, Rose thought, reversing her earlier idea that they were the ghosts and she the real living person. For she had a sense that not only had she been here before in Princess Elizabeth's chambers, but she felt as if she had done this before as well. There was nothing unfamiliar about it. She knew the routine but wasn't sure how she knew it. Perhaps she had dreamed it while asleep in her own bed in her own century. But it was not unknown to her. She had *lived* it in some way.

She heard the princess yawn, then sit up in bed under the brocade canopy fringed with gold tassels. Elizabeth tipped her head to one side and felt a place on her chin. She groaned. "Oh no!"

"What is it, milady?"

"A spot!" She brushed her fingers across her chin. "I can feel them coming before they get here. Rose, when you put the lavender in the face-washing bowl this morning, put a half cup more in. I think I might vanquish the spot before it arrives."

Vanquish a zit? She makes it sound like a military operation! Rose mused. "Certainly, milady." She slid her eyes toward the princess. When she had last been here, first been here, actually, the princess was just about eleven years old. But she was clearly a bit older now, and unfortunately entering the acne zone.

"God forbid. I don't want to look like Princess Mary. I'd perish if I had a complexion like hers."

Lavender? Rose thought. *What she needs is Clean and Pure acne cream. Or better still, Zitbegone.*

"You don't think half a cup would be too strong, do you?"

"No, probably not."

"Do you ever get spots, Rose?"

"Oh yes, sometimes, milady. No escaping it, I guess."

"What do you do?"

"Uh . . . well . . ."

"Well what?" the princess snapped as she swung her legs over the side of her bed. "Slippers, please."

"They're right there, milady."

"What do you mean right there? They are at least half a foot to the right. I like my slippers directly under my feet when I prepare to climb out of bed," the princess snapped. *Imperious!*

"Imperious" had been on Rose's spelling list in school. They had to write sentences using five of the ten words that they were tested on. She had skipped "imperious" because she couldn't think of a sentence. Well, she could now!

"Yes, milady. Sorry, milady."

"Now tell me, what do you do about spots?"

What in the world was she going to say? She had to think fast.

"Well, milady, I make a paste."

"With what?"

"Lavender's part of it, and a little salt, and . . . and . . ."

"And what?"

Rose glanced at the huge fireplace. "Ashes." *Genius*, she thought. She had learned that in fourth grade when they were studying the Pilgrims. The Pilgrims made soap out of lye and animal fat and ashes. That must have been . . . oh darn . . . when did the Pilgrims come to America? Sixteen something? It was 1620, that was the date! And what was it now? She had looked up Elizabeth's birth date online. It was September 7, 1533. And Franny had told her that Elizabeth was ten or eleven. So it must be around 1544. So yes, 1544 was seventy-six years before 1620. Still, soap with ashes could have been invented. But Rose thought they should use it a little more on other parts of their body and not simply their faces. Royal or not, hygiene totally sucked here.

"Kindly make some up for me tout de suite!"

"Tout de suite?"

"Yes, immediately. That's French."

"You speak French?"

"And Italian."

"Really?"

"Yes, really. You know, you say 'really' quite a bit. I think you could expand your vocabulary."

Rose gasped. Things were too weird. Hadn't her grandmother just said that to her?

"Why are you looking at me like that, girl?"

"It's nothing. Nothing at all."

"Well, tout de suite with the lavender paste."

"It takes a few days, ma'am, as it must boil a long time and then I must strain it, let it sit, and then add the salt gradually." Rose was making this up as she went along. No chance of a CVS near here where she could dash out and get some Clean and Pure, stuff it into what might pass for a sixteenth-century bottle or jar, and give it to Her Royal Highness.

After breakfast had been brought into the princess's chambers, it was time for her to dress. Another maid, Sara, came in to help with the clothing. She ranked higher than Rose. Rose's job was merely to fetch the garments after the princess had decided on a dress. But going into the princess's closet—actually an entire room—was a fabulous adventure for Rose. Talk about the layered look! Rose had made a list in her head of the layers. It went roughly in this order:

A slip, sometimes called a chemise

Silk knee stockings

A petticoat

A kirtle, a one-piece garment worn over the slip

A gown

False undersleeves (foresleeves) attached with buttons or ties

*A stomacher, a kind of pre-spandex tummy-flattening
    contraption (Rose began to wonder when spandex had been
    invented)*

*A headdress or coif called a French hood (in Rose's mind it
    looked like something a nun might wear)*

Then there were the optional items: a farthingale, which was a hoop skirt in linen or in silks, with rope, reeds, or a cane hoop, and a partlet—a kind of fancy scarf tucked in and made of silk or fur for winter.

Rose not only was making a mental list of these garments but was determined to try to remember their design and construction. If she only had a pencil to sketch some of the details. But pencils most likely had not been invented yet. She loved the idea of false sleeves and studied carefully how they were attached to the main part of the dress.

Sara's task was to actually dress Elizabeth. It took at least a half an hour. First there was the chemise. Next came the silk knee stockings. Then came the stomacher that flattened everything out that was beneath the dress. But the princess was very skinny and did not need much flattening out. Yet it did give a smooth look to whatever dress she wore. However, on some days when less formal attire was appropriate, she merely wore a kirtle. Today she would wear the stomacher. Princess Mary was again in residence and there was an undeniable rivalry between the two, from morning through evening, of which clothing was only one part.

"So, Sara, what is Princess Mary wearing to chapel this morning?" Elizabeth asked.

It was Sara's job to sneak into Princess Mary's chambers and see what had been set out.

"The magenta brocade with the jewel-encrusted sleeves."

"She is so plain," Elizabeth muttered. "She feels she has to gild herself already in the splendors of a queen."

"Exactly," Rose said, surprised by her own boldness.

"Exactly what?"

"She is so very plain. Dumpy."

"Dumpy!" Elizabeth laughed gleefully. "I love that word, Rose. Say it again."

"Dumpy." The princess and Sara giggled.

"Be careful!" Elizabeth had a mischievous glint in her eye. "This could be treasonous—calling a royal dumpy."

"All I meant, Your Highness, is that she has no natural beauty." *Unlike you*, Rose thought. And there was no doubt that Elizabeth was beautiful, with her milky skin and red hair that she usually wore free, spilling like a soft sunset over her shoulders.

"And what might I then wear to compare, Rose?"

"I wouldn't try to compare with her."

The royal princess tipped her head to one side and studied Rose. She began to speak slowly. "Then what, pray tell, might I try to do? Speak honestly."

"The Princess Mary is harsh and all angles. Her skin is sallow. There is something lifeless about her. She needs the jewels to sparkle. But I think they only make her plainer."

"Are you suggesting that I not wear such adornments?" No doubt about it, Rose realized, Elizabeth was a quick study.

"Yes, I guess I am. You do not need such fripperies."
Fripperies, Rose thought; where had she ever come up with such a word? It sounded centuries old. Rose began in that moment to realize that although she might be straddling two worlds, she too was a quick study, a fast learner. She seemed to have unconsciously absorbed so much about palace life at Hatfield and her mistress, Princess Elizabeth.

"Then what might you suggest that I wear?" She opened wide her dark eyes that were a soft brown in the morning light. They were almost the color of cinnamon and seemed to complement her hair.

"Something quite simple. Not brocade. Nothing bejeweled. No gold cloth or silver embroidery. Simplicity."

"Go to my wardrobe and pick something out."

Rose walked through an arched door and entered a large closet the size of her bedroom at her grandmother's house. Sara followed her. A strong scent assaulted her as she entered, and she sneezed. "What's that smell?"

"Camphor, miss. Prevents mold, you know."

"Oh."

It was almost like walking through a forest of dresses, hanging on parallel rods. She began wandering through the aisles.

"The full ones, ball gowns, and those for masques are in another closet."

"Masques?"

"Oh, you know. The courtly entertainment that the king often holds—but seeing as we have been banished, we haven't been to such entertainments lately."

"That's all right." Rose had walked to the end of one aisle. Her eyes fastened on a soft moss-green dress with simple folds. "This is perfect. The color will look so good with the princess's hair."

"Yes, I agree," Sara replied. "And she usually wears these sleeves." The sleeves were a darker green and embroidered with a meandering stitch just like the ones her sewing machine could make, except of course these had been laboriously hand stitched.

"Not encrusted, Rose. No jewels on these sleeves."

"Yes, but . . ."

"But what, Rose?"

"I'm thinking a soft, draping wing-style sleeve like, uh . . . Princess Leia."

"Who?"

"Oh . . . oh, just an obscure princess from some fairy story my mother once made up."

"She made up her dresses too, along with the story?"

"Yes, yes, my mother was very imaginative."

"Well, there's this?" Sara said, pulling a set of white sleeves from a hook.

"Oh, that will work perfectly. See how they drape? That's just the look." Oh, what she wouldn't do to give

Elizabeth the Princess Leia hairstyle, what her mom had described as oversized twin bagels. But in truth, Elizabeth's hair streaming over her shoulders like pale fire would be best.

"And a ruff?" Sara asked.

"A ruff?"

"A ruff like these." She picked up one from a pile in a basket. "These are to be thrown out, actually. They're quite dingy. We have some new ones that the seamstress just made."

Rose immediately thought of the ruff the man in the locket wore. It was a signature Elizabethan piece of clothing. She hadn't seen Elizabeth in one, but Princess Mary had worn one on her arrival at Hatfield.

"I don't think I've ever seen the princess wearing one," Rose said. Then she quickly realized this could constitute a slip. Shouldn't she have witnessed this as the royal princess's chambermaid?

"Well, Rose, you haven't been here that long, and she wears them mostly for court appearances, not every day."

That settled it. In keeping with this new strategy of simplicity, Elizabeth would not wear one.

"No tiaras in this closet?" Rose asked out of curiosity.

"Oh goodness no. All royal jewels are kept, for the most part, by the cofferer."

"Cofferer?"

"Yes, Master Parry, the treasurer of the royal household. But you said simplicity, Rose. So no jewels. Right?"

"Of course. So no ruff either. Simplicity is key, I think."

"You're right, Rose. Princess Mary is going to look cheap, a positive hoyden."

"Hoyden?"

"Yes, crude. Like ill-bred folks putting on airs."

Well, thought Rose, *let us release Princess Mary's inner hoyden and Elizabeth's inner queen.*

Twenty minutes later, Princess Elizabeth stood in front of the large oval dressing mirror.

"Yes, yes." She nodded. "Quite lovely. Princess Mary will look positively tawdry. But . . ." Rose peeked around the princess's shoulders as she gazed at herself. "I think it needs just a touch of . . . of glimmer. Rose, what's that around your neck?"

Rose's heart lurched. She clapped her hand over the locket.

"It's just a pendant, milady."

The princess whirled around. "Take your hand away this instant."

"What?"

"Are you deaf, girl? I command you to take your hand away." Rose slid her hand slowly to one side. The princess's eyes narrowed. "You dare wear the Tudor Rose!"

"The Tudor Rose, milady?" Rose asked weakly. "My

mother gave it to me," she lied.

"I don't care who gave it to you. It's a Tudor Rose. Only a Tudor can wear it. I command you to give it to me this instant."

Rose's heart was beating wildly. She began to take it off but fumbled with the latch.

"Sara, help this servant take off that necklace."

But it's mine . . . mine . . . mine. The words screeched in Rose's brain. And at that moment she knew the image in the locket was not simply that of the man in the ruff but was actually her father. She was certain of it now. So much had been taken from her. Why now this too? She shut her eyes tight. Within the locket, not only had two centuries collided but history and destiny as well—and they were hers, hers alone. Not the Tudors', not this princess's, but hers! Rose Ashley of Indianapolis and Philadelphia.

Rose's hands dropped to her sides. She felt helpless. What would she do if the princess discovered the pin for the locket? If she opened the rose and saw the picture of her mom and herself in her Disney bathing suit and pocketbook and . . . and her father?

Rose was quaking inside as she watched Sara fasten the pendant around the princess's neck. Had this imperious little snot of a princess just ripped her father from her life? Should she have fought harder? She had just stolen what might be the only picture of her father, and Rose had willingly submitted to this . . . this . . . hijacking!

"Perfect!" Elizabeth exclaimed. "The utter simplicity is lovely. Rather timeless, I think. Don't you?"

Timeless. The word seemed to vibrate in Rose's head. *Does she know what she's talking about? Are we in a galaxy far, far away?* Rose squeezed her eyes shut as if to extinguish the sight of the princess's reflection in the mirror with the burnished locket hanging around her neck. And yet the image inside the locket burned brighter in her mind's eye. She saw it all now. The things that she was unwilling to see that night when she had peered in the mirror as the shadows played through the tree outside the window. This man had her high forehead. The bridge of his nose was very narrow like hers. *And,* thought Rose, *he's not a butcher—but perhaps a merchant or an artisan? Or crafter of fine things? Just like me.*

Chapter 11

"Princesses Aren't Supposed to Steal"

"What? She took it?" *Franny said. They were in the dairy, as* Franny was churning butter.

"She stole it!"

"But why?"

"She says it's a Tudor Rose and that only Tudors can wear it. Is that true, Franny? Is that one of those whadidya call it? Sump . . ."

"Sumptuary laws?"

"Yeah, the kind that says who can wear what, like ermine and stuff."

"I don't really know all the laws. I mean, what would folk like us do if we were going about in heavy stuff like brocade and such? Could hardly churn butter, I tell you. Better to just wear homespun. But wearing a rose pendant? I suppose it was the fact that it was gold."

"But she stole it, Franny. Princesses aren't supposed to steal."

"No, they aren't, and they don't."

"What do you mean they don't?"

"They command."

"Well, you call it commanding. I call it stealing."

"It's their right, Rose."

"No, I disagree. It's their wrong."

"A king or a queen can't be wrong. Nor can a princess who might someday become queen. It's their divine right."

"Are you telling me they are God?"

"They are given the right by God."

Rose slapped her forehead in disbelief. "You have got to be kidding."

"Kidding?" Franny looked perplexed.

"You know, joking. Not real."

"No, not joking at all, unfortunately." Franny sighed. "Here, take a turn at this. You're so angry it'll be butter quick as a wink."

"I'll get the locket back, Franny. If it's the last thing I do, I'll get it back."

"I don't want you to wind up in the Tower, Rose. You're the best friend I've got here." Franny was very quiet for several minutes as Rose churned.

"I have a better idea for you, Rose," she said.

"What's that?" Rose replied sullenly.

"Instead of bedeviling yourself about the locket . . ."

"Hush . . . she doesn't know it's a locket. And I pray to God she won't discover the pin."

"Why not try to find him—your father? The real man, not just the picture in the locket. Everyone has a father. You've just never met yours, Rose."

Rose stopped churning and stared at Franny. "Do you really think that it's possible, Franny?"

"Anything's possible, Rose." She paused. "Anything. Now you'd better run along. The princesses will be back from chapel and ready for their morning ride. I saw Andrew delivering their boots from being polished in the saddlery."

❉

Franny watched as Rose went up the road. Andrew soon joined her with the princesses' boots. She took one pair and they walked together. Franny watched as Rose disappeared around the bend, chatting amiably with Andrew, but couldn't help wondering where she had come from. How long might she stay? Would she disappear the way some of the others had? Or at least Franny suspected those others were *that kind*, as she thought of them. If Rose was that kind, was she in danger in that other world? And why had she come here? All these were thoughts she should not be having, but she could not help it. Her mum and da would be furious. She just prayed Rose would not do anything foolish.

❋

"So you say you just arrived, Rose?" Andrew asked.

"Yes, just a bit ago?" She tried not to stare, but he did bear a resemblance to Jamie from the Hunter Valley Riding Academy. His hair was black and tousled, and he had that ruddy look of someone who spent a lot of time outdoors. But he looked somewhat older than Jamie, closer to seventeen. Or, if you took in the elapsed centuries, almost five hundred and seventeen years old. And he had a similar way of walking. Long rhythmic stride. Even with her own long legs she had to press to keep up with him.

"And what do you do?" Rose asked. "You're in the stables."

"My father is the horse master of Hatfield, but we are short staffed here. So I work in the saddlery, and I tend the kennels as well."

"The dogs! That must be fun."

"Fun?" He cocked his head and looked at her. "Yes, I suppose so. Not as demanding as tending princesses, perhaps." He gave a nod to the palace. "We don't have a full kennel here. Just fifteen dogs."

"That's not full?"

"Oh no. The king's estates have the full complement of

hunting dogs. At least one hundred. Three divisions: fox-hounds, buckhounds, and otterhounds."

"My" was all Rose could say. She had no idea what he was talking about, but Andrew seemed nice enough. She looked at him more closely. He was one of those boys on the brink of being handsome. But his nose took a wiggle at the halfway mark that gave him a somewhat quirky look.

"Oh, sorry," he said suddenly.

"Sorry for what?"

"I tend to walk too fast. I don't know. It's like sometimes a fast jig is playing in my head. I like to dance." He laughed. "But you keep up."

"Well, I try."

"Long legs, I guess. Like a colt." He suddenly blushed furiously. "Sorry again. Did not mean to compare you to a horse."

"No prob. I mean, no problem."

Then Mrs. Belson came rushing across the kitchen yard flailing her arms while kicking a chicken out of her way.

"Rose! Get upstairs fast as you can."

"The princess's chambers?"

"If she's there yet. Stop at the chapel. A terrible fight has broken out between the sisters just outside the chapel doors. So go by there first." She glanced at the boots that both Rose and Andrew were carrying. "Doubt if they'll be riding together, but take them anyway." Rose stood still.

The chapel? Which way was the chapel?

"What are you standing there for, girl?"

"The chapel?"

"The chapel!" Mrs. Belson wailed. "Have you never been to the chapel before?" She was rising on her tiptoes, her face coloring bright red. "Off the long gallery. East wing, for heaven's sake. Run, child!"

❋

As Rose ran down the long gallery, she could hear a terrible screeching. The two princesses were surrounded by an assortment of servants in addition to their ladies-in-waiting, and were actually being restrained.

"It's mine," Elizabeth shouted.

"It is the Tudor Rose. It only belongs to the next female in line. Where did you get it?"

"My mother."

"That witch! Anne Boleyn."

A dignified middle-aged woman stood between them, looking furiously at one, then the other. "Both of your highnesses, be quiet this instant. There shall be no more fighting."

This must be Elizabeth's tutor, Kat Champernowne, Rose thought. She had been away with a broken leg when Rose came on her first visit. She walked with a cane that she now lifted up and batted about in the air.

"And to think this outburst is right in the sight of God, just outside his chapel."

"We are always under God's eyes. Even thieves," Princess Mary hissed at Princess Elizabeth.

"You are all under the king's eyes." A tall, dignified man strode up to the gathering. It was the Gentleman Usher Cornwallis, the head of the staff at Hatfield. Rose had met him on the first day of working there. "An order from His Majesty has just been received. You are all summoned to Greenwich to see His Majesty, your father, before he sets out for the campaign in France. You are to begin to prepare immediately for your departure."

❋

Orders flew through the princesses' chambers. Sara and Rose were charged with packing the gowns.

"You'll have to have proper gowns yourself, Rose," Sara said, looking up as they folded gowns into two large trunks.

"Me? Why me? Am I to go too?"

"Of course."

"But I'm a servant. I'm surely not going to a ball."

"When you travel to where the king and queen are in residence, you must wear the proper livery."

"Livery?"

"The proper dress for Greenwich."

"Is it so different from what I wear now?"

"Black, all black, except for a white ruff. There we are expected to just erase ourselves, fade into the background. And not to wear the harsh-spun fabrics of the country folk."

"All right." Rose paused while brushing out one of the princess's gowns. "Tell me something, Sara."

"What might that be?" Sara asked, holding one of the princess's shoes in her hand.

"Why do the two princesses fight? Why do they hate each other so much?"

Sara sighed. "Well, Princess Mary does have some cause not to like Princess Elizabeth."

"What could possibly be the cause?"

"She was born," Sara said, and slapped the sole of the shoe against her palm.

"Born? It's not a crime to be born. How can Elizabeth be blamed for her own birth?"

"It's very sad, really. You see, when Elizabeth was born, her mother, Anne Boleyn, insisted that the king strip Princess Mary of her title. This little baby was called Princess Elizabeth, and Princess Mary was denied her own title and was merely called Lady Mary. She was put aside entirely. Given the worst room in the palace. It wasn't until the king chopped off Queen Anne's head that Mary got her title back."

"That's sad. Very sad," Rose said. She thought of the

older princess's grim, gray face. It reminded her of a tomb-stone. It was as if grief and anger had been permanently engraved there. Did her eyes ever light with laughter? Did her pursed mouth ever draw into a smile?

Rose thought of a guessing game that her mother had taught her. She had called it Animal, Vegetable, or Mineral. One could only answer yes or no, but through deductive questioning one could usually guess the answer. Is it a four-footed animal? No. Is it two-footed? Yes. Is it human? No. Is it a bird? Yes. In Rose's mind, Princess Mary was all mineral. She was made of stone. The hardest stone.

✳

It took several hours to pack up. Rose and Sara were to report to the stables when they finished packing the princess's wardrobe.

Wagons and coaches were already lined up to begin the procession.

Rose spied Franny. "Franny." She waved. "Over here!"

"This is so exciting for you. There will be so many parties and tournaments and masque balls. Even for a servant it can be fun."

"You're going too, aren't you?"

"No. Who'd mind the dairy, churn the butter, do the milking?"

"Oh, I'm so disappointed. I'll miss you."

"And I'll miss you too, Rose, and our scriving lessons. We only just began."

Franny clasped her hand. Rose looked over the array of wagons and coaches. "I wonder which one I'll ride in."

"Ride in? More like ride on, Rose."

"On?"

"On a horse, of course. Had the king or queen been in residence, conveyances would have been sent to collect us."

"Conveyances?" Rose asked.

"Not royal coaches, mind you, but livery wagons. This is much nicer."

"Of course," Rose said meekly. And then she saw Andrew leading a dark bay horse toward her. It had the most peculiar contraption strapped to its back.

That's a saddle? Luckily Rose glimpsed Mrs. Dobkins mounting a squat gray horse. Rose watched as she saw her wrap her left leg around the hornlike thing that projected from the saddle and then saw her foot set on a small rest, not a stirrup. The whole affair looked very odd, as Mrs. Dobkins appeared to be sitting sideways, yet faced forward.

"Ready, Rose?" Andrew said, leading the horse up to her.

"Yes, of course." She felt his hands clasp her waist and in the next second was sitting in the saddle. It felt strange, but oddly comfortable. Rather like sitting in a chair. The saddle was cushioned and there was a padded back piece.

"Rose! Rose!" she heard a voice calling. It was Franny.

She was limping back toward her, waving something in her hand. "I nearly forgot to give you this."

"What?"

Franny shoved a piece of paper into Rose's pocket.

"What's this?"

"A letter." Franny blushed and smiled broadly.

"A letter from who?"

"Me! Who else? My first letter ever."

"But, Franny, we've hardly begun the scriving lessons."

"Yes, but you wrote out those letters so beautifully for me and told me how each one had a name and a sound. I just practiced and practiced into the wee-est hours of the night, until the candle flickered out." She took a deep breath. "So I did it. Wrote you a letter. A short one, and my letters are all wobbly. Like just-born baby lambs trying to stand up for the first time."

"Oh . . . Franny." Rose felt her eyes fill with tears.

"You got me started. And I'll keep practicing."

Rose was left speechless.

"Gotta go," Franny said. "We have a ewe about to birth a lamb out of season. Never a good situation."

"Yes, yes, of course," Rose said, trying to appear somewhat knowledgeable. It was ridiculous, for what she knew about birthing lambs couldn't even fill the smallest Post-it. What in the world would these folks think of Post-its? Or cars, or televisions, or iPhones?

At just this moment in Rose's musings, Mrs. Dobkins rode up to her. "This is always so jolly." She had lost her usually stern demeanor.

"And how long a ride is it, Mrs. Dobkins?"

"Three days if the roads are clear. Enough time to prepare the palace before the princesses arrive."

"Have a good ride, Rose," Andrew said.

"Andrew," Rose whispered, "I'm a bit nervous."

"Why's that?"

"I haven't really ridden that much."

"Oh yes, should have thought of that. Never worked in a palace before. Palace servants know how. Well, all you need to remember is the emergency grip. It's a way of locking yourself in the saddle, especially for jumping."

"Good grief, jumping?"

"No jumping on this route. That's for sport. Just clamp that knee around the saddle horn if you feel wobbly. It will lock you right in." He gave her knee a friendly pat.

OMG, how did I get myself into this?!

There was a sudden blast from two trumpeters.

"Raising the royal badges!" Mrs. Dobkins declared in a clarion voice. Two banners in the shape of a shield were suddenly hoisted. Each banner was divided into four parts with a single emblem in each. There was a rose in one quarter for the royal Tudor princesses. Then in another a falcon, another a sword, in the fourth was a cluster of arrows. "If the king were riding with us, the Tudor Rose would bear a crown," Mrs. Dobkins noted. "Your first time in a progress?"

"Yes, yes, Mrs. Dobkins."

"Best part of the job! And what a day we have for it, a bright summer day. Couldn't be better." She sighed. "See you anon!" she said cheerfully, urging her horse forward.

Then Rose suddenly heard the meow of a cat. "September!"

She looked up to the peak of the stables, and in the hayloft window she saw the tawny cat. She appeared to wink at Rose, then swished her tail as if to say, *See you later.*

They began to trot. Mrs. Dobkins smiled at her. It seemed to be a smile of approval. "You sit well in that saddle, Rose."

"Thank you," Rose murmured. There was just one thing wrong. One thing missing. The pleasant weight of that locket bouncing lightly between her collarbones.

Chapter 12

Untangling Time

It was suddenly pitch dark out, and Rose was definitely not sitting atop a horse. She found herself standing in an alley, and there, sitting atop a trash can, was September. It had turned cold. Rose was freezing, dressed only in a T-shirt and jeans. She looked up. It felt as if it could begin to snow any minute, although it was still autumn. Time—days, nights, seasons—was truly tangled. In a weak attempt to straighten things out, Rose began whispering to herself. "In Hatfield it was summer. Daytime. And it was a Tuesday." How did she know it was a Tuesday? Of course, Franny had told her that Tuesday was butter-churning day. But she was no longer in Hatfield, and it was not day but night. And now it was cold, really cold! "What time? What day?" September meowed very loudly and looked at her fiercely, then scratched the top of the trash can with her claws. Then it came to Rose in an instant, and she remembered. *My diary. My diary is in there.*

"I need my diary, don't I, September?" The gold flash from the cat's eyes seemed to light up the alley. She jumped off the lid and landed perfectly, despite having only three legs. She began rubbing up against Rose's calf. Rose reached down and petted the cat. It was the first time September had allowed her to do this. She purred. Then Rose removed the lid from the can. The red leather diary was waiting for her. She was thankful that she'd gotten back in time before trash was collected.

Shivering, Rose crawled into bed with the diary, untaped the key, slid it into the lock, and opened it. She needed to ponder time, and the shifts in time that took her out of Indianapolis, Indiana, and dropped her across a vast timeless chasm into another country, another century, almost five hundred years before. How had it happened? She began skimming through the blank pages until she arrived at the day. The one she wanted to forget forever. August 15.

She dared herself to face her fears and look at the date of her mom's death, the fatal crash. She bit her lip lightly and felt her chin begin to quiver. How could everything change so quickly? Not just a car had crashed. Her life had too. She felt a wild veering inside, as if she herself were about to fly off the road into a searing nothingness of flames and destruction. Complete annihilation. She stared at the date a long time. Slowly she began to turn the pages forward. Three weeks and five days after that date, she started at her new school. She now began to calculate when she had first fallen out of time and into that distant century. It was the day she had been locked in her locker. September 17 to be exact. And that was when she first laid eyes on Princess Elizabeth. But it was weeks later, during her second tumble through time, that she had met Franny, who led her up to the palace. And now she had just returned from her third visit. She looked at her iPhone. It was close to midnight on October 27. Then she saw that a text message had come in from Anand.

> Four nights till Halloween. Wanna come trick or treating with Myles & Joe and me, and I think Susan? Doctor Who–themed, but you can go as whatever.

Fifteen seconds later, another text message came in. This one from Susan.

> Going with the guys for Halloween. Please come. Guess what! Joe invited me. Do you think this means he likes me? And guess what else! I'm going back to Elsie's and buying the black

lace dress! Don't worry, you don't have to go as a Doctor Who character if you don't want to.

Then there was a ding of a new text coming in. "Lord love a duck!" Rose muttered, one of her mom's favorite expressions. It was a busy night text-wise. Well, the weekend was coming up. This one was from Joe, to both her and Susan.

Would you two like to come to ice-skating rink tomorrow after school?

Susan must be in meltdown mode, Rose thought. Another ding.

Forget black lace dress. I'll call Elsie and put it on hold.

Another ding. Rose quickly texted back:

Excellent decision!

Rose puffed out her cheeks and blew, after her texting marathon. And now she had to sprint back to the text-less, no-smartphones sixteenth century and try to track her time there.

"So where was I?" she whispered, as she focused on the date at the top of the diary page. She unconsciously put her hands to the little hollow between her collarbones to feel for the locket. *Gone! Stolen! But how can I miss something that might not be? It was just a picture!* Then the echo of Franny's voice threaded through her mind. *Why not try to find your father—the real man?*

But what is real? Rose thought. *Is this real, to be caught between two centuries?* Batted about like a stray autumn leaf— a leaf out of season, perhaps, or between seasons. Speaking of which—it suddenly occurred to her—where was September? Was she trapped back there? The last time she had glimpsed the cat, she was in the alley. Her thoughts were interrupted by the ding of another text message. She glanced at her phone. Susan. *Caught between two friends, Susan and Franny!* Franny, who told her to find the real man, and not just the picture. But in that moment when Sara had taken the locket from her neck, when she felt the weight of the locket vanish, she knew for sure that the man in the ruff must be her father.

She got up and went into her bathroom to look at herself in the mirror. She had done this more than a dozen times since she had first had the locket. She would open it up, then glance back and forth between the image of the man's face and her own reflected there. Except now the locket had been taken from her. It was no longer in her grasp. She leaned in closer to the mirror, which was becoming blurry as a scrim of tears filled her eyes. "Stop it!" she hissed at herself. She stomped out of the bathroom and focused on her diary. She forced her hand to stay put and not reach for that haunting spot between her collarbones.

It's October 27 here in Indianapolis, she thought. So, her visit tonight to Hatfield had been days after her previous one, and yet no one at Hatfield seemed to notice that she had been gone. Not Franny. Not the princess. Not Mrs. Dobkins, the head housekeeper. And when Rose had returned to Hatfield, she knew exactly what to do. How to wake up the princess in the morning and where the princess kept her dresses. There had been a few minor errors, yes—like the bedroom slippers—but otherwise she had learned all her duties. Her last memory was Andrew— cute Andrew giving her a tip on how to ride sidesaddle as she set off with Mrs. Dobkins for Greenwich Palace. *Yikes! Hope that went well*. Who knew? She could return to 1544 and discover she'd fallen off the horse and broken her leg. She didn't even want to think about medical care back then—leeches and bleeding. Weren't those the favorite remedies?

But why had no one in that world noticed her absence? What did they do or think when she was gone? It was almost as if she had a double, a kind of stunt double, who cleaned the princess's chambers, was well versed in her wardrobe, and rode sidesaddle perfectly.

Time at Hatfield House in 1544 must proceed at a very different rate. It was still summer there, but here in Indianapolis, winter was just around the corner. It was hard to disentangle past time from present time. She stared down at the diary, which was turned to today's date. Thursday, October 27. At Hatfield it was Tuesday, butter-churning day. A Tuesday in some lost summer month, perhaps July of 1544.

There was no need to go back any further in this diary. Everything before August 15 was too painful. She was tempted to tear up all the pages of the months before. But there was a violence in tearing up a book, even one with blank pages. The pages ahead lured her. They seemed to implore her to write. Her pen hovered over the date of this third visit. Six weeks before, on September 17, her secret life had begun.

October 27. Thursday. Neatly above the date she wrote "Hatfield, Tuesday, Summer 1544." She was determined to record everything that had happened to her in 1544 in the service of Princess Elizabeth. And more important, she was determined to get back what was rightfully hers, the locket, and to uncover its secrets. Franny's words echoed in her head. *Why not try to find your father? The real man; not just the picture in the locket.... Anything's possible, Rose.*

She would try to find her father—her father, the crafter of fine things, as she thought of him. *I shall find my father if it's the last thing I ever do.*

Chapter 13

Nasty Ice

The very next day, *Rose and Susan sat on the wooden benches.* They had just laced up their skates. Joe waved to them from the far end of the ice-skating rink. He had just completed a double axel spin. Susan looked at Rose and in a deadpan voice said, "I don't do that. Just to let you know."

Rose laughed. "You think I do? Forget it."

Brianna whizzed by. She wore a black leotard with a little black satin skirt that flared like bat wings. Her neck stretched out. *No more rodent*, thought Rose. She was a bat on ice, cutting the chill air of the ice rink with her sharp features. Her pointy nose was slightly lifted, as if scanning for prey.

"Hello, girls!" a voice grated behind them.

"Uh-oh!" Susan wheezed. The sound was like a thin stream of air escaping from a punctured balloon. Rose felt Susan deflating as they both turned around and saw Carrie.

"You skate, Rose?" There was an embedded snarl in her voice despite her feeble attempt to sound genuinely curious. "Taking a break from your fashionista life on the internet?"

"I'm not a fashionista."

"Well, what are you?"

A crafter of fine things, she thought. "I sew," Rose said softly.

"How sweet." Now there was a genuinely nasty tinge in her voice.

Carrie went out on the ice and began charging around the ring. "Bulldog on skates," Rose muttered.

"Hi!" Joe said, skidding to a halt just a few feet from the bench where they sat. "Come on, let's go."

"Uh . . . ," Susan said. "You know, Joe, I'm not so great. I kind of look like a scarecrow on ice . . . like someone stuck me up on a post." She gave a soft laugh.

"I've never seen a scarecrow skate, but sounds interesting. Come on, I'll help you out." Susan looked as if she might melt right there. Dissolve with joy into a little puddle with glasses.

"Oh, you guys go. I just got a text from my grandmother. I'll catch up," Rose said.

Liar, liar, pants on fire—a text from Gran? Fat chance. But how could she interrupt this romantic moment? She watched Joe take Susan's elbow lightly and steer her onto the ice. Susan did kind of look like a scarecrow on skates. The cloud of frizzy black hair appeared to tremble ever so lightly. But in another few minutes, maybe three at the most, as they completed their first lap on the rink, Rose saw that Susan was skating with a newfound ease. Joe's hand was still just lightly on her elbow. But it appeared as if he might hold her hand while skating. Rose saw that Susan's face was flushed and tentative. A smile threatened to break through. But just at that moment, a neon-blue streak appeared.

"Watch it!" someone yelled. Then the shrill blast from a whistle sounded. Susan and Joe collapsed in a tangle of skates.

"Okay, blue hair, off the ice now!" someone else shouted.

Then a voice thundered over a loudspeaker. "Reckless skating will not be tolerated!"

"Susan, are you all right?" Joe said as they disentangled their skates.

"Anybody hurt here?" a man said as he skated up.

"I think we're okay, Coach."

"Oh, definitely okay." Susan made a pathetic little okay gesture, but her voice was shaking horribly. Rose skated up to her.

"Are you sure, Susan? And, Joe, are you okay?"

"Yeah, that was just so stupid. Stupid Carrie," Joe hissed.

"It's all right, Joe, don't blame Carrie."

"Don't blame Carrie?!" Joe and Rose both said at once.

"Oh, I don't know. Might have been my fault. I told you I don't skate that well."

Rose looked at Susan. She wasn't okay. Nothing was broken, most likely just bruised. But she was simply mortified. Her moment of sheer happiness had been wrecked. It was as if something within her had been vandalized.

❉

"I should have just gone and got the dress from Elsie," Susan moaned as they walked home.

"Don't be ridiculous," Rose said.

"But it was so embarrassing."

"How can it be embarrassing for you? It *is* embarrassing for Carrie. She was banished from the rink. Sidelined, whatever you call it."

"Time-out," Susan mumbled.

Rose looked at her.

"Time-out. You know, for a foul play in sports," Susan replied.

But the words had a deep resonance for Rose. She pictured the two princesses, Elizabeth and Mary, sitting on a bench—shamed after some fierce referee from 1544 in a waistcoat and a ruff shouted, "Foul play!!" and forced them off the ice. But royalty was probably shame-proof.

"Listen, I'm just not sure about going to this Halloween thing after all," Susan said.

"What? No way! You're going, Susan. Don't be a wuss. You can't let someone like Carrie direct your life."

"I don't know. . . ."

"Don't blow this up into something it shouldn't be. Joe really likes you. I can tell. It's not fair to Joe."

Susan looked at her and blinked. "I guess you're sort of right—about not being fair to Joe."

"I'm completely right!" Rose said, and took Susan's arm in hers.

Chapter 14

The TARDIS

"You see before you the inspiration for this year's Halloween costumes—the box that my parents' new refrigerator came in. Believe me, I rescued this in the nick of time, or the trash man would have taken it," Kevin announced.

"On Friday?" Rose asked.

"Yep, yesterday," Myles said.

"Wow!"

"What's so wow about it?" Joe asked. All three boys and Susan were staring at her. It was because Friday was trash day, and she had almost lost her diary in the trash collection. But there was no other way of keeping track of her time in two centuries separated over a distance of almost five hundred years.

"Oh, nothing, just the same trash day as at my grandmother's house." She realized as soon as she said it that they all thought this was mildly weird. But things were about to get weirder, and there would be no explaining why to her only friends—well, her only friends in *this* world. At Hatfield she had Franny. And Andrew the stable boy seemed nice—she recalled how easily he had lifted her into the strange saddle and placed her just perfectly in the peculiar little seat.

"So," Myles continued, "is this not a TARDIS?"

"Brilliant!" Anand shouted as Joe high-fived Myles.

"So?" Myles turned to Rose. His magnified dark eyes sparkled behind his thick lenses. He clearly had expected her to cheer.

"Uh . . . what's a TARDIS?" Rose asked. "I mean, I don't know all that much about *Doctor Who*."

"What's a TARDIS?" Joe said in disbelief.

Susan stepped forward. "You know *Doctor Who*, don't you, Rose?"

"Yeah, but just a bit, not like you guys."

"The British science fiction show," Anand said. "Between the four of us we have all the DVDs."

"Yeah, but who *is* Doctor Who?"

"He's a Time Lord," Joe said. "He battles injustice, but also explores time and space."

"Time Lord," Rose said, as her voice cracked a bit.

"Yeah, a Time Lord," Susan said. "And he travels in a time machine."

"Time machine?" Rose's voice was a whisper. The boys were all talking at once trying to explain the machine.

"You see," Myles said, "it's called the TARDIS."

"That stands for Time And Relative Dimension In Space. So cool." Anand was jubilant. "And this box is perfect, because it will fit over Myles's wheelchair!"

"We measured it!" Joe said.

They all thought time travel was science fiction, but Rose knew it wasn't. It was REAL. It was nonfiction—and Rose had lived it!

"We have to make it look like a London police box," Myles said.

"What's a police box?" Rose asked.

"In England they have these boxes like old-fashioned telephone booths, you know, before cell phones. Except these were just for cops. They were painted blue and the cops could go in and make calls to headquarters or wherever," Joe explained.

"And what does it do?"

"It transports the Doctor to any time and point in space," Myles said. "Sometimes it's kind of unpredictable."

"But it has this cool thing—called the chameleon

circuit—where it can disguise itself and blend in with whatever's around it." Anand was so excited he was almost jumping up and down.

"Yeah, cool," Rose said, somewhat distractedly. *Sounds like me*, she thought. She had certainly blended in to Hatfield, hadn't she? "Uh . . . where does it go in time?"

"Nazi Germany, sometimes," Anand said.

"Oh great," Rose muttered. "Just where we all want to go."

"Oh, it is, Rose," Anand replied. "That's one of the best episodes. 'Let's Kill Hitler.' They get there. They crash-land in Berlin in 1938. But the TARDIS is highjacked. Its chameleon circuit has broken down. They came to kill Hitler but accidentally save him instead. . . ."

"Okay . . . okay . . ." She put up her hand to stop the yammering. The plot was getting too confusing. "So basically Myles is going as this time machine thing—the TARDIS—and what are you two going as?"

"We haven't quite decided," Joe said.

"We can go as the Doctor's companions."

"I might go as K9," Anand said.

"Who?" Rose asked.

"A robot dog. Get it, K9 as in canine? But you can really go as anything. I mean, it's a time machine. One episode is about Cleopatra."

"And one is about Queen Elizabeth. You know, the old one. The first one."

"What?" Rose's eyes opened wide.

"Yeah, really. As I said, you can go as almost anything. I mean, it's the TARDIS—a time machine," Myles said.

"Susan, who are you going to be?" Rose asked.

"Another Susan. Susan Foreman, also known as the Unearthly Child. She's the doctor's granddaughter." *Unearthly*, Rose thought. Wasn't that exactly the word that had come to Rose when she first saw Susan?

Susan continued. "She's this kind of weird schoolgirl. But her grandfather is the doctor and they live in a junkyard. I kind of thought the black lace could work sort of . . ."

"Oh yes, junkyards can have fantastic stuff. Just like landfills! Terrific source for shoes!" Rose was getting excited.

"Two days," Anand said. "That's plenty of time for painting this box blue to look like a London police box. No problem."

What would they do if I ever told them about my time travels? she wondered. Enter her in the science fair?

❀

Rose's mind was racing as she walked the ten blocks from Myles's house to her grandmother's. She had a piece of brocade fabric that she had planned to make a cape from. But there might be enough for a dress. And of course she would need to make a ruff too. Between her second visit to Hatfield and the time her sewing machine arrived, Rose had ordered two books from Amazon on Elizabethan costumes.

One had even come with several patterns. She had made the sketch of the blue dress, the one with the tiny ruby-red beads that Elizabeth had been wearing when they first met. But she wanted something grander for Halloween. Something that said Queen with a capital *Q*! If she was taking a virtual trip in a virtual time machine, she might as well be a queen with virtual power. Oh, how she wished she had just picked up one of those discarded ruffs that Sara had shown her when they were in the princess's closet.

The thought caught her short. Could she indeed "import" stuff from Hatfield, other than the locket? It couldn't be considered stealing if it was worn-out castoffs like the ruffs Sara had shown her. She wouldn't ever steal jewels or anything of any value, just scraps and royal trash.

It was at this very moment that she remembered she had promised Princess Elizabeth that she would bring back something for her zits.

I make a paste....

With what?

Lavender's part of it, and a little salt and ... and ... ashes.

Rose made a sharp right at Forty-Third Street, two blocks before her house, and headed over to a drugstore on Pennsylvania.

Chapter 15

A Touch
in Time

*B*ack home, with some lavender seeds she had found in the green-house, Rose was in the kitchen working up a batch of her own version of Zitbegone in the food processor. Along with a few tablespoons of ashes from the fireplace, she had thrown in some vinegar for good measure. Vinegar was the opposite of oil, after all, and oily skin was prone to zits. So it made sense.

"What in the world are you doing?" Cook asked as she came into the kitchen.

"Oh, just an experiment, Cook," Rose replied. She turned to look around at her. She was a pleasant-looking, broad-faced woman, but one of those people of indeterminate age. Was she mid-forties? Fiftyish? Early sixties? Her hair was that nondescript hue that could be described as reddish blond or blondish red. "Cook," Rose said suddenly, "what's your real name?"

"Shirley."

"Then how come everyone calls you Cook?"

"Well, my whole name is Shirley Cook, and when your grandmother . . . well." She poked two fingers into her hair and began stirring it a bit, as she might stir cake batter with a spatula. "As your grandmother began to forget, to lose names, she just settled on Cook for me. It was easy, you know. I had this profession that matched my last name."

"Oh, I see."

"You like it here, dear?" Rose shrugged. "I mean, I know it's not the same."

You can say that again, Rose thought, and did a slight eye roll as she turned back to her concoction. "Do you happen to have a small empty jar I could put this in?"

Cook looked around the shelves. "Ah!" she exclaimed, and reached up. "Here's an almost-empty jam jar. Just a tablespoon left in it. I can put it in a plastic container and you can have it."

"Oh, thanks, Shirley."

Shirley tucked her chin and chuckled softly. "Sounds nice to have my name back."

"No problem, Shirley." Rose smiled.

"I'll wash out the jar for you."

"What's for dinner tonight?"

"Chinese."

"You cook Chinese?"

"No, no. Once in a while we order in from Little China. There's a menu pinned to the bulletin board. So tell me what you like. And I'll call it in."

✳

Two hours later, Rose and her grandmother sat in the greenhouse, silently eating their dinner after sowing the last of the winter herbs.

"Try a little of this mint on top of your General Tso's chicken," Rosalinda said as she crumbled two leaves from the seedlings she had just thinned in a tray.

"I'm not having General Tso's, Gran. Remember?"

"I don't remember much, dear."

"I'm having fung yung three treasures with shrimp."

"Oh!"

"You remember more than you think, Gran, especially when you're here in the greenhouse."

"So have you thought about Halloween? It's coming up. Any plans?"

"See, you do remember, Gran."

"I'm looking over there at those sweet peas. I know that in the greenhouse they always bloom right on or a few days after Halloween. So nice after all those pungent smells of autumn and before all the evergreen-y smells of the holiday season. Just a whiff of summer to remind us that it will come round again."

As she poked at her shrimp with her chopsticks, Rose felt her grandmother's eyes settle on her. She looked up. Gran had a way of tilting her head sometimes when she focused on someone, and it was as if she was coming out of a mist of shredded memories and thoughts. One could imagine a sun breaking through her mind after days of fog, and almost see the remnant dewdrops evaporating in the light. A new clarity dawning.

"So, Rose, what might you go as for Halloween?"

"Oh, I don't know . . . maybe something sci-fi."

"Sci-fi? What's that?"

"You know, science fiction, like Star Wars . . . Princess Leia."

"Princess Leia . . . never heard of her. Why not a real princess or queen . . . ?" Rose felt a small jolt, as if her heart had skipped a beat. "There have been so many real ones." Gran spoke softly and tipped her head again. A loop of her hair fell down. She picked up a chopstick she had just eaten with and poked it in her hair.

"Oh no, Gran, don't do that. It's not sanitary."

"What's not sanitary?"

"The chopstick. You just ate off it and there's glop from General Tso's . . ." Rose's voice dwindled. She saw her grandmother's eyes clouding over again. It was as if Rosalinda were dissolving in front of her.

Betty arrived at the same moment.

"Did you enjoy your chicken, Mrs. A?"

Her grandmother said nothing.

"Betty," Rose whispered, "she just stuck a chopstick in her hair. It had General Tso's sauce on it."

"She does that sometimes." Betty looked down at the chopstick now sticking out of the piled hair. "Oh dear. I see a noodle. Well, I can get that out. No problem."

Betty began to lead her away.

"Good night, Gran."

"Good night . . ." Her grandmother paused. A look of confusion swept through her eyes. "Catherine?"

"No, Rose, Mrs. A. Rose."

"Catherine, Gran? What Catherine?" Rose asked.

"Oh," her grandmother replied softly. "Sorry. Someone from so long ago. Very sad story. I think for a long time I was her only friend when her husband began to tire of her. What a heel he was, that Henry." Although the words appeared muffled, there was a terrible regret in her voice. "Henry who?" Rose was about to ask, but saw her grandmother clasp her hands and bend her head as if she were sinking into a deep prayer. Her shoulders shook a bit. *Don't cry, Gran, please don't cry.*

❋

Rose could not quite figure out what had just happened. The sadness of her grandmother seemed to grip the air. It was pitch black outside, but in the greenhouse various lights in certain sections began to blink on. They were all controlled by timers, according to the light needs of the different plants. Night-blooming flowers had their own area. Rosalinda had found a special light some years ago that she called her fake moon for the night bloomers.

It suddenly struck Rose as very peculiar that within the greenhouse, seasons could be reordered; the transits of "sun" and "moon" could be manipulated. Yet she had no control over her own transits to that other world. Rose, as far as she could tell, came and went at the whim of some unseen power. She was a victim of time. Might there be any hope of controlling these visits? What triggered them? The more she thought about it, the more intrigued she was. Why did she have no control over the things that happened in her life? Why did things just happen to her? Her mom died. She was left virtually an orphan. Then she was shipped off to Rosalinda, her grandmother, who didn't even know who she was half the time. She felt as if she were a dandelion flower gone to seed, its fuzz caught and tossed by whatever rascally wind might blow through. Well, she didn't like that feeling. Not at all. The anger she had felt when Sara was removing the locket and handing it to Princess Elizabeth surged within her—my history, my destiny! Mine to control, not yours!

She looked at her watch and found it was almost nine o'clock. Then she slid her hand absently into the pocket of her sweater. She'd forgotten about the jam jar with the lavender acne cream. The jar was perfect. It could have come from any century, really. She had made a little label on it and written *Spotless!* She thought the script looked slightly old-timey. She hoped the mixture worked for the princess, although she didn't know why she should bring Elizabeth anything when the spoiled girl had stolen her pendant. She touched the place just below the hollow at the base of her neck where the locket had rested. She imagined the deep luster of the gold petals of the rose, the outer petals much darker, the center ones almost white gold. And beneath it the picture of the man in the ruff, the man who truly could be her father. She felt a twinge of pain, as if a stitch had ripped in her heart.

A soft summer breeze stirred her hair. As she pushed back a curl that had fallen across her forehead, she was vaguely aware of transferring reins from one hand to another. There was the pleasant sound of hooves and the creak of wagon wheels. *I'm back! Just a touch in time!*

Chapter 16

A Pocket in Time

Rose was posting, posting sidesaddle. It came quite naturally to her, as if she had been doing this all her life.

What a natural! Peter at the Hunter Valley Riding Academy had said during her first lesson as she and Ivy began to trot. *I'm not even going to have to teach you to post. You're doing it already.* She wanted to shout out, "Look at me now, Peter! Sidesaddle no less!"

The road was unfurling before them. Along the way, farm folk and villagers, the local gentry, came out to wave at the procession.

"Let the good king smack those Frenchies to kingdom come!" one fellow shouted.

"Tell Harry to send them to the devil."

"Harry?" Rose wondered aloud as Andrew, the boy from the saddlery, rode up. "Who's Harry?"

Now several voices were calling out the name.

"You don't know?" Andrew laughed.

"No idea," Rose replied.

"Harry's a nickname for King Henry."

"Oh." She was quiet a minute. Mrs. Dobkins had ridden up.

"Andrew, do you think we'll make it to Greenwich by sunset?" she asked.

"Oh yes, Mrs. Dobkins. Long before."

"Good. Those monasteries are not what they used to be. That little room they put us in last night was filthy. That straw pallet was so thin that I might as well have slept on the floor. My back will never recover." *So*, thought Rose, *we slept in a monastery last night*. She must pretend she recalled all this.

"Yes, Mrs. Dobkins, my back hurts too."

"Nonsense, child. You were asleep the second your head hit the straw. Slept like a baby."

"Did I now?" Rose said, trying to conceal the surprise in her voice.

"Of course you did." Mrs. Dobkins sighed. "That's youth for you! I tell you, since the king had the . . ." She coughed. ". . . fuss with the pope, the monasteries have been very neglected. They should keep them up better. If not for praying, there's other uses."

Rose was confused. "Uh . . . what do you mean, Mrs. Dobkins?"

"Oh, you know, back almost ten years ago when the king had his way with the pope. No more monasteries! No more friaries, no more Roman priests. It's all Church of England now, and no money from the crown to keep things up to snuff." She turned and gave a quick smile to Rose. "You were just a babe, of course."

"Yes," Rose said softly.

The progress began to slow. "Must be a horse change station ahead. Thank goodness. I fiercely need to relieve myself." Mrs. Dobkins shifted in her saddle.

"You mean . . ." Rose started to say, "You mean pee?" But she stopped herself in time.

"What was that, dear?"

"Nothing."

"And we'll also get into our court wear."

It all came back to Rose now. The black uniforms and the ruffs. *Great*, she thought. *A ruff*. Maybe she could bring it back for Halloween.

❀

The clothing change was quite a lesson for Rose. She had not realized how many layers she had been wearing, and when she was about to take off her kirtle, she felt something knock against her hip. She reached into the pocket. The jam jar! But not only that, the letter that Franny had stuffed into her pocket was there as well. This was astounding. The acne potion and the letter had both come with her through time and place. One, the acne lotion, was an import from the future; the other, the letter, was an export from the past! She stopped thinking of the jump between the twenty-first century and the sixteenth century as a gap or a chasm, but instead more like a tear or rip in the fabric of time. And somehow the jar got through in her pocket. For the sweater pocket had held the acne potion when she left, and her kirtle had held the note from Franny. This was a literal pocket in time!

"You can keep your same chemise on, but here's a fresh kirtle," Mrs. Dobkins said, handing her a black garment to replace her ochre-colored one. The kirtle had a fitted bodice that laced up the front. "And now for your serving gown." She handed Rose a black gown. It felt very soft compared to the coarse homespun she had been wearing.

"What is this fabric, Mrs. Dobkins?"

"Like it, do you?" Mrs. Dobkins winked. "'Tis a light worsted wool with a tad of silk woven in. Now, don't get too used to it. Who knows how long we'll be in court, and then it will be back to the coarse stuff."

"And the ruff?" Rose asked.

"Right here. Ties in the back."

Rose's heart fell when she saw it. It was rather small compared with the discards she had seen in the princess's closet, with the layers upon layers of stiff ruffles. After she tied it on, she reached for the kerchief and began to wind it back on her head.

"Oh no!" Mrs. Dobkins said. "That won't do at all."

"It won't?"

"No, Rose. This is court. And because you'll be serving in the royal princess's chamber, you must wear this." She held up a French hood. Mrs. Dobkins began fastening it onto her own head. "Now mind you, dear, not a hair must be showing for servants who wear the French hood."

"Is this for hygiene or something?" Rose asked.

"Hy-what?"

"Uh . . . nothing."

"It's just a rule. So mind it."

"A lot of the women in the portrait paintings at Hatfield wear these hoods, don't they?"

"Indeed, but much more ornate than ours. You saw the portrait of Elizabeth's grandmother. She had a cloth with a gold crescent stitched to the top."

"Oh yes."

Mrs. Dobkins nodded. "Before my time."

"Are there any paintings of Princess Elizabeth's mother?"

Mrs. Dobkins looked up in horror. "Of course not, and don't ever mention her. Never, Rose. Do you understand?"

"Yes, ma'am." But was it true? Had Anne Boleyn been a witch like Princess Mary had said? *Of course she hadn't!* Rose knew there was no such thing as witches—except, of course, on Halloween. This reminded her that perhaps there would be some way of sneaking this ruff back to Gran's house. Perhaps she could just add a few more layers of ruffles onto it. No more of this servants' wear for her. She was determined to be a queen! A good queen. Not a Mean Queen.

A Prince

Chapter 17

Greenwich Palace

Dear Rose

This is my furst tri at scriving a reel leter. Be pashunt with me. Lukky you. Grenitch Palus is said to be so grand. But I shall tell you one secrit. In the park at Grenwitch I hurd the princess say that there be a tree with a holow trunk. It be an Ok tree and very anchunt. She and little Prints Edword sumtymes play in the holow.

Luv

Franny

This was at least the tenth time Rose had read Franny's letter. There had hardly been time to write back, but now in this brief moment between preparing the royal princesses' chambers and brushing out their clothes, she had a minute. So she sat down in the tiny bedroom in the chamber that she shared with Sara, and began to write. She had filched a quill pen and a bit of ink from one of the numerous kitchen pantries.

Dear Franny,
    What a great scriver you are! You're right, Greenwich Palace is so grand. The wobbly just–born–baby–lamb letters danced into my heart.

Rose set down her pen briefly and tried to decide what to write next. There was so much that had happened during those first few days she had been there. She wondered how much time had passed at home. What this would add up to in what she thought of as her "home century," the twenty-first. Ten minutes, perhaps? But she had better write fast, as Elizabeth would be arriving in a few days with her half sister, Mary, and there would be no time for scriving then. Writing with a quill was fun. She looked at the feather —possibly from an owl?

    I have glimpsed the king from a distance. He was in the tilting yard. He's quite fat.

She quickly decided to cross that out. It might be treason to call the king fat. She closed her eyes and recalled the scene. They were actually using a sort of crane to get him on top of the horse, and Andrew, along with three other attendants, had to help. She'd heard that in full armor the king weighed nearly three hundred pounds!

She went on, enjoying the scratchy sound of the quill.

I haven't found the tree with the hollow yet. But I plan to try to look for it today. There are so many servants here.

Not just servants, Rose thought, *but all sorts of people purely for the amusement of the king and his court.* Minstrels sang, dwarfs tumbled. It seemed incredibly mean to Rose that people thought people with dwarfism were a source of "amusement."

There were also comedians called "fools," who told jokes and recited stupid rhymes. It seemed like the court had to be constantly entertained. She had not seen these fools perform so far, but when she passed them briefly in a corridor or crossing one of the many courtyards, they always seemed a little bit odd to Rose. There was one called Jane who was completely bald.

Do you know of that woman, Jane the Fool? She's bald—sometimes they call her Jane the Bald. Anyhow, one of her eyes is a bit peculiar. You can never tell if she's looking at you or not. But I guess she can mimic any birdcall. That's her talent. She goes about clucking and cooing, or hooting like an owl or screeching like a blue jay. And people just crack up. I think the whole thing is really odd.

She wasn't sure if Franny would get the expression "crack up" but wrote it anyway.

I have to tell you, Franny, that I am trying to do what you told me—find the real man, not just the picture.

Rose hesitated to come right out and say, "the man in the locket."

You know who I mean. The man with the ruff.

If this letter were somehow intercepted, Rose figured people would be clueless, because of course every man in court wore a ruff. But Franny would know exactly who she was referring to.

I'd better stop scriving now, as there is much to do. I wish Princess Elizabeth could slip you into her trunk and bring you along. I miss you, Franny.
Love,
Rose

P.S. Here is some potion I've included for Princess Elizabeth. Can you see that it gets to her? Thanks a million!

As soon as the ink dried, she tucked the letter for Franny and the acne potion for Princess Elizabeth into the deep pocket of her black gown, then adjusted her French hood so that not a strand of hair was showing. The chamber that she and Sara shared was between the apartments of both the royal princesses. She left and turned into a corridor that took her to a wider hall called a gallery. She went through a door leading to a passageway that was connected to a back stairwell. She had just started down the steps when suddenly there was a terrible cackling noise. From a hidden door at the curve in the stairway, a figure jumped out. Rose yelped and almost tripped.

"Scared you, didn't I?"

The bizarre character stepped out into a single shaft of sunlight that came through a high, narrow window. Her bald head glared like a full moon. One eye winked at Rose while the other, slightly bulged, seemed to jitter in every direction at once.

"What are you doing? Are you crazy?" Rose gasped.

"Of course, Buttercups, I'm mad. Who else could imitate the cry of a Polish Frizzle?"

"A what?"

"Polish Frizzle chicken, dear heart." Rose shivered. She didn't like being called dear heart by this woman. "Introduced to our realm, fair England, by none other than Anne of Cleves. The ugliest of the king's wives brought the prettiest chicken. But I can coo like a dove too."

She immediately started cooing and began a little soft-shoe shuffle on the stone landing. "Taa da ta da . . . lad dee da at ya da da da ya dee dat." She picked up the hem of her very elegant silk dress just a bit. Her shoes were bright pink and had feather tufts on them, as well as elaborate stitching. She might be crazy, but were those shoes fabulous or what? *OMG, I'd die for those shoes!* Jane noticed her attention.

"You like my shoes?"

"Very nice," Rose said curtly. She didn't want to encourage this unpredictable lady. But was she truly mad? Or was that only an identity created by court gossip? Maybe, thought Rose, she just expressed herself differently, like her mom's friend's daughter Judith, who mostly spoke in cartoon voices. Her mom had described Judith as being "on the spectrum." Then she explained that Judith was smart and very kind, and she also had autism. "She sort of doesn't know how to connect socially with people except through those Disney characters. You love Disney characters too, Rose," her mom had said. And Rose had replied, "But not that much. I talk in my own voice."

"Maybe Judith has never found hers. Nevertheless, she has found other things. She is actually quite brilliant—mathematically brilliant," she recalled her mother saying. "And has a kind of photographic memory."

Rose was quite young at the time and tried to imagine Judith chasing about, knocking on doors looking for the voice that belonged to her and each time being disappointed, saying, "Nope, not that one. Not that one either." She would try and be nice to Jane as much as she could. And Jane certainly had good taste in shoes. Rose vowed to make a sketch of those shoes as soon as she got back—whenever that was.

"Not a hair on my head, but feathers on my feet," Jane said.

"I must be going," Rose said.

"Off you go! Off you go!"

Rose zipped past the woman. But she could not help recalling her mother's words about Judith being brilliant. And a photographic memory! Too bad she didn't have the locket. She would have shown Jane the picture of the man in the ruff. The thought arrested her. People were dismissive of fools. Fools were just there for entertainment. They wore stupid outfits like Jane. Or the men, the court jesters, wore pointy hats with bells attached and ugly-colored tights, and of course let's not forget those puffy short skirts! Who would believe a man in tights and a tutu or a bald woman with feathers cackling like a bird? But maybe their foolishness was just a disguise for something else. They often spoke in riddles and nonsensical rhymes. However, they might know more than anyone would dare to believe. Perhaps she should take Jane more seriously.

But then an awesomely embarrassing thought struck her. OMG, what if her father was a fool, prancing around in "motley," as they called those ridiculous costumes. A dad in a tutu! She might have cardiac arrest. Mortal embarrassment. She took a deep breath and continued walking. *No, no! The man in the ruff would never be a fool.*

She found Andrew at the stables.

"Hullo there, Rose." He walked toward her. "Are you all right? You look a tad pink in the cheeks."

"I just crossed paths with that bald woman."

"Oh, Jane the Fool. She's harmless enough. There's a rumor that the king might give her to Princess Mary."

Too bad, Rose thought. Jane might have been helpful on her quest. "Quest" seemed a more appropriate word for finding her father. "Mission," in Rose's mind, seemed rather militant.

"But if the king gives her to Princess Mary, who will he give to Princess Elizabeth? Doesn't she get treated equally?"

"He'll probably give Elizabeth Bettina."

"Who's Bettina?"

"A dwarf."

"What? Why do you people find dwarfs amusing? I don't understand."

"They tumble and are generally good-natured."

"They are human beings. Human beings who happen to be short. I find it frankly horrifying that you take them as objects of amusement and pass them about as one would a toy. It's not only horrifying but very offensive."

Andrew seemed to be studying her in a most thoughtful way. "You know, Rose, I never thought of it that way before. Where'd you get such ideas?"

Rose sighed wearily. "Oh, you wouldn't really want to know," she muttered. "In any case, I have something for you to take to Franny back at Hatfield, since Elizabeth is still there." She slid her hand into her pocket and took out the letter and the jar of Spotless! she had wrapped in the kerchief. "Can you do it, Andrew? I'd really appreciate it."

"Anything for you, Rose! What a lovely name." He drew out her name as he looked at her with dreamy eyes. OMG, was he going to say that Shakespeare quote her mom was always saying from *Romeo and Juliet*? "What's in a name? That which we call a rose, by any other name would smell as sweet." *No, that's impossible. It's 1544 here.* She had a feeling that Shakespeare hadn't been born yet. The play hadn't even been written. She'd google it when she got back and check. But who knew when that would be! She'd mastered getting across, slipping through the time rip, but could she go back when she wanted? She didn't want to. Not yet. And Andrew was sort of cute.

"Thanks, thanks so much, Andrew. That's . . . that's . . . so sweet of you."

"Honestly?" He seemed to glow.

"Yeah . . . honestly. But I've got to go now." She started to leave, then stopped and turned around. Andrew was standing there looking quite dazed. "Hey, Andrew, which way is the park?"

"Straight ahead. Go past the buttery and the rose garden. It's just beyond the maze. You'll see it off to your right. A great sweep of green. The greensward. You can't miss it."

"Thanks, Andrew, thanks again."

She felt his eyes on her back as she sped off.

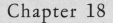

Chapter 18

"Girl, Why Are You Sleeping?"

At the far edge of the greensward she saw a mass of great trees. One of those must be the oak with the hollow, she thought. There was a narrow path that led into the grove. A soft wind began to blow and stirred the branches through which sun filtered. Shards of bright light and shadows did a shifting dance. It was pleasant and quiet. She found it restful. Palace work was not easy. And it would only get harder when the two princesses arrived. Of course she had it easier than the char girls, who seemed permanently crouched over, scrubbing the hard stone floors. But Mrs. Dobkins was always calling on her and Sara for something. And it was heavy work. Flipping the mattresses was very difficult on the high beds. And since Mrs. Dobkins had discovered that Rose had a way with a needle, she was constantly being called upon to repair clothing. Mostly undergarments, as the fine gowns were sent to one of the dozen royal seamstresses in residence. She hadn't realized how tired she was and decided to sit down at the mossy base of a tree stump and rest.

Just a minute, she thought before she yawned and fell asleep.

She found herself walking through a place of shadows and whispers. There was a familiar scent—linoleum. *Linoleum? Not here*, she thought. Not here at Greenwich. Linoleum and mac and cheese.

The whispers grew louder. Three dark figures turned. She could hardly make them out in the shadowy fog, but then she spied something glittering as a blue streak cut through the murk. She was in the school lunchroom. She smelled the disgusting chicken fries piled on a plate with ice-cream-shaped scoops of mashed potatoes. The bologna and cheese stuffed into pita bread. "Yuck!" she cried out in her dream. "Why would anybody do that to pita pockets?"

"Oh, Miss Fashion Plate," said one of the girls. "Too fancy for bologna but full of baloney!"

"We have plans for you—and your kind." A sharp face cut through the gloom. The tip of the pointy nose wiggled, and the mouth pulled back in a diabolical grin to show sharp little teeth—rat teeth.

They're coming for me, Rose thought. And yet she couldn't move. She could not speak or cry out. Her mind was alert but useless, because her body was locked, paralyzed. The teeth grew larger and sharper. All three figures were now approaching, each wearing purple and gold. Their shoulders were draped in weasels, with the heads dangling limply— *ermine fur!*

"Mean Queens!" Rose gasped. "I am being stalked by Mean Queens."

"Girl! Girl, why are you sleeping?" A voice scratched through her dream.

A frail boy was standing over her. He was dressed in a purple velvet doublet, a kind of fashionably fitted, padded jacket, with ermine cuffs. Beneath was a satin vest embroidered in gold thread. The boy appeared to be about seven years old and a living violation of the sumptuary laws. So Rose quickly calculated he must be a prince. In fact, Prince Edward.

"What's MacAncheese?" the prince asked. "A Scottish friend, I suppose."

Rose nodded.

"Well, I've heard of MacIntyres, and MacKenzies, and of course MacIntoshes. Edna MacIntosh was a nursemaid for me. Called her Tosh. Very jolly. But I never heard of a MacAncheese."

"Yes." Rose nodded again and got up. "I'm to curtsy, I suppose."

"Yes, but for the moment—I have escaped."

"Escaped? Escaped what?"

"My guardsman. He is an incredibly boring old sot. He supposedly protects me."

"Supposedly?"

"Yes, but he likes his drink and falls asleep all the time. So escaping is easy."

"Do you plan to return anytime?"

"When I meet with Master Cox, my tutor. He's much more interesting. He protects me from ignorance. You see, I plan to be a wise and informed ruler."

"Sounds good to me," Rose said, and brushed off her dress.

The prince giggled. "You have a funny way with words. I quite enjoy it. Like 'yuck'—what the devil does that mean?"

"Uh . . . kind of disgusting."

"Unpleasant."

"Yes, definitely unpleasant."

"From the Shetland Islands, perhaps?"

"Perhaps," Rose replied cautiously.

"Now where are you from? The Shetlands?"

She was about to blurt out "No, Indianapolis," but caught herself. "Hatfield."

"Hatfield!" The prince clapped his hands in delight. "Then my sister Elizabeth truly is coming."

"Yes, and so is Princess Mary."

"Ugh." He groaned and made a sour face.

"Yeah, she is kind of a jerk."

At this Prince Edward hooted with laughter.

"What's your name? Will you play with me? You know, Elizabeth and I play here all the time. On the other side of this tree, there's a hollow where we take refreshment sometimes. Come, I'll show you. What's your name?"

"Rose Ashley." She studied him. He was a fragile child with none of the vivid coloring of Elizabeth nor the sallowness of Mary. His gray eyes reminded Rose of a calm sea on a misty day.

"Oh, so you must be related to Elizabeth's tutor Kat Ashley."

"Distantly, perhaps." Rose paused. She mustn't let this moment pass. Would there be any chance that this coddled prince would know anything about her father? She took a deep breath and began, "You know, I'm a sort of orphan."

"You can't be a sort of orphan. You either are or you're not," Edward replied crisply.

"Well, I suppose you could say I'm kind of a half orphan. My mother is dead."

"And your father?" Edward's soft gray eyes opened wider. Was it curiosity or wonder? Or most likely neither. Royals had no interest in the personal lives of servants, Rose had realized early on.

"I'm just not sure. You see, my mother died when I was very tiny and I guess my father was so poor he couldn't take care of me." Poor, but he wore a ruff, a sign of a gentleman. "So I was more or less given away."

"More or less? Rose, you must be more precise."

"Well, more, definitely more. And I'd like to find him." She began speaking in a rush of words. "So do you know a lot of Ashleys?" Ones with ruffs? she almost asked, but then realized how truly ridiculous this would sound.

"Not a one beyond Kat. Anyway, come around. I'll show you the hollow."

Chapter 19

Raiding
Gran's Closet

Dear Diary,

When it happens, it just seems to happen all of a sudden. I'm back. I was in my jeans again and I looked at my watch. It was nine o'clock sharp. I remember distinctly that it had only been one or two minutes before nine when I left on October 29th, a Saturday. And guess what. I brought my ruff back with me. I'll have to beef it up for my Halloween costume.

I've made a zillion sketches of the ruffs. They are so cool. I wish they'd come back into fashion here.

As you can see, dear diary, I have been busy. I have less than forty-eight hours until Halloween. I want to be ready for trick-or-treating with Susan and the guys. I made a dress pattern that I found in one of the books on Elizabethan costumes that I ordered from Amazon. Of course I'm not bothering with all the other stuff—no petticoats, shifts, and all that. Tomorrow I'm going to the craft shop that Shirley told me about for a bunch of gold lace ribbon. I want to make a tiara for my hair. Shirley said there's a costume shop that Calvin can take me to where I can probably buy a red wig. I need a really frizzy one—as frizzy as Susan's black hair.

All the pictures of Elizabeth when she is queen show her as having very frizzy hair all piled up. I have to get all this done soon, because on Monday, Halloween, I have a riding lesson. Gran has been so great about letting me take as many riding lessons as I want. I really love it, but there's only one problem. Lisa is always hanging around. She's sort of the darling of the stables. She won some big horse show thing a couple of weeks ago. Nobody sees the totally snarky side of her—at least not as far as I can tell. She's constantly mooning around Jamie. "Oh, Jamie, can you help me with this curb strap? I think it's too tight. . . . Oh, Jamie, I think I lost a barrette when I was brushing Miss Dimples last night. It just fell out of my hair. . . ." Then she tosses her hair and flashes a smile. "Shameless!" my mom would say.

But forget Lisa. Now I'm obsessed with how I was able to get back with the ruff. But what triggered my return? I am trying to remember every single minute of what happened before I left. The prince and I went into the tree hollow, which was pretty big. I mean, the two of us fit there quite comfortably. There was a little makeshift table made from a stump. The prince fetched a piece of cloth. I said something like "I'll do that . . . after all, I'm the servant." And he said, "Oh no, I get to be the servant, because I'm a prince and I get to make the rules. . . ."

I laughed at that, but he insisted. So he spread the cloth, and then he went and fetched two small plates and a tin that had some very stale cakes. So then I said, "If you're the servant, who am I?" He scratched his chin and thought a bit. "Well, you can be a visiting ambassador from another country— like . . . like Spain. They're always sending people from Spain to try to make a marriage between Princess Mary and Prince Philip of Spain."

Then after I got back to the palace, Sara told me that there was to be a banquet that night with minstrels, dancing, and, yes, jesters and fools. She knew a secret place where we could watch the action. Sara is pretty nice. But she's older than me, maybe eighteen. We spied on the so-called merriment, but I did not find it merry or amusing.

First of all, there's the food. Get this: they eat swan. Yes, they had roasted at least a dozen or more swans, and they reattached the wings to the poor creatures when they served them on platters. Next I saw them bring in what I thought were just pies. But then I got a glimpse of little heads poking out of the crust! They were heads. Eel heads! It was eel pie. I thought I was going to barf right there on the balcony.

Soon the "entertainment" started. This is what these royal people and their courtiers consider funny: poop and fart jokes, and Jane the Bald shrieking like a banshee. There was another fool, Will Somers, running around pinching people's butts. It was disgusting. Any kid in the twenty-first century who did this would have been sent from the table. And these weren't kids! Oh, and they even have a special horn that makes fart noises. They sneak up on unsuspecting people and blow a blast near their butts. The higher the ranking, the louder King Henry laughs. But actually, he's a pretty good sport. Even when they sneak up on him with the horn, he laughs. A monarch with a sense of humor is admirable, but this doesn't change the fact that he chopped off the heads of two of his wives!

So, there you have it! Sixteenth-century entertainment is disgusting. It's vile and bizarre and guess what—I want to go back! I have to go back. I don't feel whole anymore. My mom died a horrible death. And my father is lost in time and I feel as if something has been amputated from me. A limb is missing. The pain from missing both my parents is excruciating. I read about this thing once called phantom limb pain. It's about people who have real pain coming from a limb that is no longer there. That's me. I'm not just an orphan. I'm a double amputee. I want to find my father. He's there someplace. I just feel it. Feel it in my bones, as Mom used to say. Was he a courtier? Or a crafter of fine things? Did he live in Hatfield or maybe Greenwich? England is not a big country. Minuscule next to America, but where in that small country might he be?

I remember looking down from the balcony with a mixture of shock and disbelief. It was like a pageant of some sort. I remember the king waving around the drumstick of a swan while singing loudly and belching—yes, both at the same time! And then suddenly I was back—back in Gran's house. How did that happen? When I had left Gran's before, at a few minutes before nine, I had touched that little hollow place in my neck where the locket had rested. Had I perhaps touched that place again and magically been transported back to this century? It might have been hard, as I was wearing that stiff high-neck ruff. And when I got back, the collar lay at my feet in the greenhouse.

Well, it's past midnight. Have to get up early and finish the costume. For me it's only a Halloween costume for a pretend queen. But what is real and what is pretend? If I told people what was happening to me, they'd never believe it. Then again, maybe, just maybe, Franny would. I wonder if Franny would have gotten my letter by now? I mean, here at Gran's house, only a few hours have passed since I returned, but over there it might be days or weeks or even months. For all I know it could be Christmas when I get back to England!

P.S. Had a very disturbing dream—just before I met Prince Edward. I can't remember it very well except that I was in a school lunchroom and there was mac and cheese—that yucky smell—and then —oh yes—

the scent of doom. They were there! It was really creepy. The Mean Queens were planning something.

P.P.S. I wonder if that long ride from Hatfield to Greenwich has improved my riding. Can't wait until my next lesson Monday, October 31. Indianapolis, Indiana, longitude 39.7684° north, latitude 86.1581° west. (In math class we're graphing longitude and latitude on a Mercator map. And while I was at it, I found that Hatfield, England, is 51.7634° north, 0.2231° west, and Greenwich is 51.4826° north, 0.0077° west.) So time might slip around, but places stay put.

P.P.P.S. Just had a super phenomenal idea. I can hear Betty across the hall talking to Gran about clearing out some of Gran's old clothes and sending them to Goodwill. Why have I never thought of this before? I could raid her closet and I might find stuff for my costume!!!

Rose got up and tapped lightly on the door of her gran's bedroom.

"Come in," Betty called out. "We're just getting rid of old clothes, dear."

"Gowns I'll never wear," Gran harrumphed. She was

sitting up in her four-poster bed with a half dozen pillows behind her. She looked quite regal.

"Gran, I love to sew. And I love old clothes—vintage."

"That's me—vintage!" Gran quipped.

"Could I take a look in your closet?"

"Of course. Step right in." She gestured at the open double doors.

It was large—not as large as Princess Elizabeth's wardrobe, but still the size of a small den.

"OMG," Rose whispered. It wasn't the most well organized closet, but there had to be at least thirty evening gowns. And mixed in between the other dresses and coats, there was a pair of riding pants, jodhpurs, and a gorgeous jacket that hung next to them.

"What's this? This is the most beautifully tailored jacket I've ever seen."

"Hermès."

"Hermès the Paris designer?"

"Yes, Hermès equestrian wear—their hunting habits are the best. You know, I used to belong to the hunt club here in Indianapolis. Hard to believe that I used to ride to the hounds on fox hunts."

"It's the most beautiful jacket I've ever seen." It was a tobacco color, and the collar a contrasting navy blue.

"Try it on," Gran said.

Rose slipped into it.

"A tad too big. I could have my tailor take it in."

"Oh, I can do it."

"You're that good?"

"Yep," Rose replied confidently. "But would it be okay with you if I wore it just as a fall coat? It's roomy enough, so I could wear a sweater under it."

"Certainly. You're welcome to it. My riding days are definitely over."

"Thanks!"

Rose ducked into the closet again and came back in half a minute with a gorgeous and quite voluminous ball gown.

"Oh yes, I wore that to some charity ball back in the eighties, I guess."

"You know what I love the most about the dress?" Rose was burbling with excitement. Her gran seemed to be enjoying this immensely.

"What, dear child?" This caught Rose up short. Her grandmother had often called her "dearie," but never until this moment "dear child." It touched her deeply. She felt truly loved in that moment.

"Well, Gran, I'm really crazy for the sleeves. Would you mind if I . . . er . . . separated them from the rest of the dress?"

"You mean cut them off," Gran said mildly.

"Yes, and I would sew them onto something else."

"Fine with me. Just recycling, and I'm a great believer in false sleeves."

False sleeves. The words seemed to resonate in her head. The last time she had heard those words, she was standing with Sara in Princess Elizabeth's wardrobe.

"Thanks, Gran, this will really help with my Halloween costume."

❊

It was almost midnight when Rose kissed her grandmother good night, and it was four in the morning by the time Rose completed her Queen Elizabeth dress. She turned in front of the mirror. *Not bad,* she thought. *Not bad at all.* She scrutinized the entire look. The dress was good. She slid her eyes over to her computer screen, which showed the portrait of Elizabeth as a queen. There were tons of these online. Few from when she was just a princess, however. Rose had bought a bunch of fake pearls to drape around her neck, but there was something missing, and guess who had it? The locket. *My locket!* Elizabeth was wearing a pendant of some sort. But it wasn't the gold rose, the Tudor Rose—or was it? There was so much stuff going on around her neck in the portrait—pearls, lace ruffs—it was impossible to see. She clicked on the mouse and enlarged the image.

Holy moly! This was the pendant. The Tudor Rose with her photo inside—her mom in her mom-kini and Rose in her Little Mermaid bathing suit, her Aguaphile swim goggles, and clutching the Mickey Mouse pocketbook. "Oh my God," Rose whispered as she read that the year of the portrait was 1575, by one "Federico Zuccaro, a fashionable court artist."

It said 1575! Rose quickly calculated. Elizabeth was forty-two years old! Ancient! Older than her own mom. Yet there she was, still wearing that pendant around thirty years after she'd stolen it from Rose! What nerve!

Okay. Okay . . . stay calm, Rose. She began talking herself down. *Time is very screwy here. Yeah, thirty-one years seems like a long time. But hey, time does tricky things.* All within a blink of time. For all she knew, the next time she went back, Elizabeth could be eighty. No! She realized Elizabeth had died at sixty-nine. Nonetheless, she might have wrinkles instead of zits. Speaking of which, Rose noticed a zit just starting on her chin. She went into the bathroom for her industrial-strength cover-up cream. More of a paste than a cream. She never even got to reach for the tube before she emitted a little yelp as she caught her reflection in the mirror.

I'm him! "Dad!" she whispered. It was as if a younger female version of her father was staring back at her. It was the ruff, the way it cradled her chin, that appeared to give her face these clearly recognizable contours. No beard, however, just an oncoming zit. But she now realized that the shape of her face and her cheekbones were his. But who was he? Where was he? She leaned forward until her face was just inches from the mirror. "What is your name?" The mirror fogged with her breath. The reflection began to dissolve. "I need you. Please." The pain was real. The image a phantom.

Chapter 20

A Dream of Friendship

The sheet of paper trembled in Franny's hand as she tried to sound out the letters in the writing. She had never before received a letter, and this one was from Rose. Her lips moved slightly as she whispered the sounds of the letters on the page.

I wish Princess Elizabeth could slip you into her trunk and bring you along. I miss you, Franny. Franny read those sentences over and over again and pressed the letter to her heart. This was so exciting. To receive a letter! And Rose had said what a scriver she was! She missed Rose. What was it about her that made her think that just possibly . . .

But Franny cut off the thought. She could not even dare

imagine such a thing. It was too dangerous. Her parents would be furious. They were safe here. Safe. Her mother had not been hanged, her father not crushed by stones like Uncle Giles. She needed to be happy here. She was happy. Her mum was a laundress at the palace. Franny had her job in the dairy. Her father was a farmer on their small plot. Rose would come back to Hatfield when Princess Elizabeth returned. The king always banished her for one reason or another. Most likely he would change wives again. That always caused him to exile his daughters. Honeymoon time. Of course, little Prince Edward would never be exiled. Being a boy, he was next in line for the crown. But Franny's mum said that King Henry didn't like Elizabeth because she was too much like him. She did certainly look like him with her red hair. Her mum said that it wasn't only the hair. That the royal princess was so smart. "Smartest of the whole lot, Franny. He's jealous of her, I think. He looks at the princess and sees beauty, wit, and cunning. All the while he's getting older and fatter."

Franny tucked the letter away. She headed up to the sheep barn where the little lamb was who had come out of season. The lamb's mother, the ewe, had died. So it had become Franny's job to feed her. She would sop a cloth in cow's milk and, holding the lamb, squeeze the milk into her mouth. She was a clever little lamb, and whenever she saw Franny coming would begin hopping about with excitement in her stall. Today Franny brought a pan of milk, walking very carefully for she was not using her crutch and didn't want to spill the milk. The lamb should be old enough now to lap it up. She set down the pan.

"Come here, dear. You're a big girl now. You don't need me to feed you." The lamb regarded her with startled eyes. "C'mon now. You can do it." Franny sat next to the pan and crossed her legs. The little lamb approached cautiously. "Now now. I won't bite you. Just give it a try," she coaxed, and dipped her finger in the milk. The lamb stuck out the tip of her tongue and licked Franny's finger. "There you go!"

And the lamb did go. She plopped herself right in Franny's lap. Curling up, she peered at the pan of milk. Franny giggled. "You lazy little thing. Come on now. You can do this by yourself." The lamb would soon learn but preferred to lick up the milk while sitting in Franny's lap. It was restful for Franny to sit with this warm fluffy bundle in her lap and dream of friendship. She really had no friends at Hatfield. There was hardly time. And her parents were always cautioning her about "being careful." They had been lucky, so lucky. People didn't talk about witches, not since the king had chopped off his wife's head, Queen Anne. But that was four wives ago. Of course after Anne, the second head to roll was Catherine Howard's a few years ago, but she wasn't considered a witch, just a wanton seductress.

Franny closed her eyes and relived the image in her

mind of Rose sitting so gracefully on that horse. She looked completely at ease in the saddle. Franny herself had never ridden anything but a donkey, and not even with a saddle, just astride with her legs dangling down. She wondered what Rose was doing right this minute at Greenwich.

❃

But Rose was not at Greenwich. She was at Hunter Valley Riding Academy.

"Rose, I think you're ready for a low bar jump."

"Really?" Rose said.

"Yes, I told you you were a natural. So, Jamie, can you help set it up?" Peter called over to the fence where Jamie was watching.

"Sure, Pete."

Lisa had just come up. Rose dreaded having her there.

"Oh, jumping already. I told you she was fast, Jamie."

Jamie gave her a dark look and swung himself over the fence to help Peter put up the jump.

Rose looked over and caught sight of Lisa again. *Why does she have to be here?* It seemed as if she was always hanging around. But still, Rose loved the riding academy. Her grand-mother, pleased with her progress, had arranged for her to take lessons four days a week. Rose had been practicing walking Ivy over poles flat on the ground, then trotting and finally cantering over them. Now the poles would be raised, no more than a foot from the ground. She took the first jump at a walk. By the end of the lesson she was trotting over the jump.

"Beautiful balance!" Peter called out.

Balance, that was the perfect word. Oddly enough, even though she had a foot in two different worlds, she felt somehow balanced. Life was getting better, except when she was reminded of her mom. Then all the memories would come flooding back. But at this moment she felt the hateful stare of one of the three meanest girls in her school piercing her back as she was riding. She was trying her best to keep her balance in the saddle.

She recalled the long ride to Greenwich. Andrew had told her there would be no jumping. She vaguely remembered the trip had been one long flat road in a sidesaddle, so she knew jumping would be entirely different.

At the end of the lesson, when she walked Ivy to the center of the ring, Pete congratulated her.

"I have one question," Rose said.

"And what might that be?"

"Women and girls in the olden days rode sidesaddle, didn't they?"

"Yes indeed."

"How did they do it, especially jumping?"

"Well, the main thing you have to know about riding sidesaddle is something that is called the emergency grip. It's a way of locking yourself in the saddle when you jump."

Andrew's words almost exactly! Rose thought.

"I have a sidesaddle in the back of the barn. After a few more jumping lessons, why don't you try it?"

"Really?"

"Sure, why not visit the past!" He chuckled.

He doesn't know what he's saying! Rose thought.

✽

"You did great out there, Rose," Jamie said as she slid off Ivy. "I swear, you must be taking lessons at night too."

Rose laughed and blushed. She never knew how to answer in these situations. She couldn't even look Jamie in the eye. "Oh . . . no, no night lessons . . ."

"Who knows what she does at night. . . ." Lisa giggled. It was such a weird comment.

"What do you mean by that?" Rose wheeled about, her eyes blazing.

"Oh, nothing. Can't take a joke, can you?"

"What was the joke?" Jamie asked. His voice was flat.

Now it was Lisa's turn to blush. "Nothing." She turned and stalked off.

"So, are you going out trick-or-treating tonight?" Jamie asked.

"Probably . . . I mean, yeah, I think so." It seemed to Rose that the space had contracted between her and Jamie, although neither one of them had moved. But still she could not look him in the face when he spoke to her. So she glanced off to the side. She saw a long shadow cast in a blade of sunlight. Lisa hadn't left. She was listening from around the corner.

"What are you going as?"

"Not sure, really. I'll pull something together. Uh . . . I better go. Calvin is waiting for me."

"Sure thing, Rose. See you soon."

"Yeah, bye, Jamie." *There!* she thought. She had actually said his name!

Chapter 21

Shattered Glass

"Susan, you look fabulous!" *Rose exclaimed when she saw her* in the black lace dress. "And that jacket!" Over the dress, Susan had on a cropped, black tight-fitting jacket.

"And I brought you the spiderweb tights."

"Great! I'll run inside and put them on."

They had met at Myles's house. And because Myles knew every bit of cracked pavement or would-be obstacle to a smooth ride in his wheelchair, he had mapped out a route for trick-or-treating. There was a small park that had perfectly paved bike paths, and by following them they could get to another neighborhood notorious for giving out the best treats. There was one house where they even invited the kids in for cocoa, and they had a ramp for wheelchairs as well. They must have had a disabled family member.

"I'm sort of worried about my gown," Rose said. "It came out wider than I thought."

"How did you make it that wide?" Anand asked.

"Hula-Hoops. It was the easiest way. Just stitched them in."

"Is that collar itchy?" Joe asked.

"Not really. I'm used to it."

"Used to it?" Myles said. "You dress like this every day?"

"Oh . . . no . . . I mean I've just worn a smaller version sometimes for another dress I have. It looks nice."

Anand was making some adjustments to his own costume. He was wearing a creepy silver mask that had lots of wrinkles. On his back was a pair of wings.

"What are you again, Anand?"

"A weeping angel—an ancient predatory race. According to *Doctor Who*, they are the deadliest, most malevolent life-form ever produced."

"And I'm a good guy," Joe said. "An Ood Sigma. Telepathic talents." He put on a creepy monster mask to which he had attached sausages at the chin.

"What's with the hot dogs on your face?" Rose asked.

"Ood Sigmas are supposedly part octopus. Very peaceful for the most part. But see my eyes? Or the eyes in the mask?" He pointed to some eye slits that were actually above the holes he was looking through.

"Yeah."

"Red!" They suddenly lit up. "That means he has linked back to the collective mind of the Ood hive."

"Of course . . . ," Rose said. It seemed that *Doctor Who* was a lot more complicated than sixteenth-century Tudor England.

"I like your crown a lot," Joe said. "Where'd you get it?" Anand reached forward and touched it.

"Old Disney Princess crown. I . . . uh . . . embellished it a bit."

"Oh, points for you. 'Embellished'—that's a spelling word for this week," Myles said. "So I have to say that getting me into the TARDIS time machine box would be easier than getting Queen Elizabeth here in it."

Joe and Anand lifted the box and began to place it over Myles.

"How are you guys doing?" Myles's father came into the garage. "Does it fit?" He looked at Rose. "My, that is some costume."

"Thanks, Mr. Randolph. I mean Captain." Myles's father was in the air force and was still wearing his uniform.

"No need for formality, Rose. These guys just call me Bo."

"Okay, Bo." Rose thought it was a very unmilitary name.

Bo turned to Susan, who had just come out from changing into her spiderweb tights. "And you are . . . Morticia?" Bo asked.

"No, the Unearthly Child. The Doctor's granddaughter."

"I see." Bo walked over to the TARDIS and peeked into the slot.

"Can you see out of there, Myles?"

"Yep, Dad. I see you right there."

"Navigation won't be a problem?"

"Nope, I got my wingmen."

"And wingwomen," Rose said. If there was ever a wingwoman, it was Queen Elizabeth, Rose thought. She adjusted her skirt and headed into the night as the TARDIS began to roll.

✳

"What a haul," Anand exclaimed as they entered the park after trick-or-treating for close to an hour.

"I loved that cocoa that they gave us at the last house. They put peppermint in it," Susan said.

"Wait, stop," Anand said suddenly.

"What is it?" Myles asked through the slot in the TARDIS.

"The sky. I think I saw a shooting star."

"Shooting stars this time of year?" Rose said. "Not exactly the season." She had such good memories of lying out on the lawn in August with her mom on a blanket during the season of the shooting stars, the Perseids.

"I know," Anand said. *Maybe,* thought Rose, *the seasons in the sky are as tangled as the ones in Gran's greenhouse.*

"Look, see, another!"

"And another!" Joe yelped.

"Oh darn! I can't see. Can you take off the box for a second?"

They were just removing the TARDIS box when out of the bushes three figures appeared wearing rubber masks. Disney Princess masks.

A sickening feeling swelled in Rose. Remnants of that confusing dream she had experienced at Greenwich rushed back to her. The place of shadows and whispers. The smell of the school lunchroom and the unmistakable feeling that the Trio of Doom was coming after her. The strange paralysis.

Now, standing before her, was Belle from *Beauty and the Beast,* Jasmine from *Aladdin,* and Briar Rose from *Sleeping Beauty.* They were absolutely ghoulish in this star-spiked night. The very air around them seemed to vibrate with hate and anger.

"Got a new boyfriend, Rose? A cripple?"

Rose gasped and heard a shocked sound from Myles, who was half in, half out of the box.

"You gotta be kidding," Joe said. His voice sounded raw.

"I hear your boyfriend wears diapers." The girls curled

their hands into half fists and started jerking them around spastically.

Rose felt as if she had been punched in the chest. She staggered a bit. She felt Susan clutch her hand. It was the dream all over again. She couldn't move. Couldn't act. She was frozen.

"Of course I wear diapers," Myles shouted. "You would too if you had CP. But I have to tell you something. You need diapers on your brains. All of you!"

Myles slammed his hand on the joystick. The chair blasted forward. There was a screech as all three girls fell backward into the bushes.

"Ouch!" Rose recognized Lisa's voice.

"I'm scratched."

"I have thorns in my hands and legs. Help me, Carrie," Brianna whined.

"Help yourself," Joe growled.

Susan roared. "Yes, help yourself, you sack of pig droppings!"

Rose and the boys were stunned—a roar from Susan!

The attackers' masks had slipped off. Two of them, Belle and Jasmine, were snagged on the brambles. One, Briar Rose, was in the mud by the side of the path.

Myles's wheelchair was off the path in the mud as well, but not in the bushes where the girls were thrashing about. Joe and Susan ran and pulled the chair back onto the path.

"Ludicrous speed!" Myles whooped as he raced ahead. He was grinning like crazy. Rose had never seen him happier. Rose felt her body unlock. She, Susan, Anand, and Joe ran to keep up, leaving the girls to disentangle themselves from the prickly bushes. The last thing Rose heard was Carrie cawing like an outraged crow. "My dad will sue you, Myles. My dad's the best lawyer in the city and you'll be charged with reckless . . ." The voice faded into the night.

❋

By the time they got to Myles's house, they were all laughing.

"Omigod." Joe was gasping with laughter. "How many times has Carrie threatened to sic her lawyer dad on people? She was going to have him sue me for libel when I called her a jerk."

"The funny thing is, her dad is kind of a jerk," Susan said. "My dad told me that he's one of those ambulance-chasing lawyers. He even advertises on the radio and TV."

"Well, now he's a wheelchair-chasing lawyer," Myles said. "Reckless. I'm reckless. Love it!"

"I nominate you, Myles Randolph, for a slice from the quiche of manliness!" Joe said.

This was one of the boys' favorite jokes, and it sent the kids into another round of hysterics. The boys were big on making up awards.

On the sidewalk they all said their good-nights to

Myles, who went back into his garage.

"Want us to walk back to your house with you, Rose?"

"No, it's not far for me."

"Are you sure?" Susan asked. Rose thought how kind it was of her to offer, because Susan lived very close to Joe and most likely was hoping that they could have a romantic walk home. As romantic as one could feel walking next to a boy dressed as an Ood Sigma, with sausages attached to his face.

"Don't be ridiculous. It's just few blocks for me and way out of your way home."

"Okay, see you tomorrow, then," Joe said. "And your costume was great."

"Yeah," said Anand. "Hope it didn't get too messed up. It looks kind of ripped."

"Nothing I can't mend," Rose said.

Susan and the boys turned the corner and walked in the opposite direction. Rose decided to walk up Delaware Street to Forty-Sixth Street, then cut across Forty-Sixth to her grandmother's house. Then, ten minutes later, just as she turned, she felt something hard hit her shoulder. "Try this on for size, Ms. Know-It-All fashion blogger."

A rush of footsteps came toward her and she began running. She heard the sound of more rocks hitting the pavement, just missing her. *Don't look back. Don't look back.* That was what her mom always told her when she competed in swim meets. It takes too much time to look back at who might be closing the gap. She didn't need to ask who. She knew. Her own homegrown Mean Queens. She swerved quickly into the alley behind Gran's house. The cupolas of the greenhouse poked up into the starry sky. She heard the girls closing the distance and shoved an empty trash can that clanked down the alley toward them. Maybe it would slow them down. She heard someone take a hard fall and gasp as if the air had been knocked out of her. There was the sound of shattered glass and at the same time a high-pitched screech. September sailed over her head, her claws spread in attack mode.

Chapter 22

"Shame on You, Princess!"

Rose was inside the greenhouse. *She was panting hard, trying to catch her breath.* She looked down at her feet. There was shattered glass all around. Her dress was torn. It was unbelievable how vicious these girls were. She curled her hands into fists. She wanted to smash their faces. Her heart was racing. Then she felt September brush against her foot and tug lightly on the lace of her shoe. *Lucky I wore my running shoes.* Jane the Bald's feathered footwear wouldn't have gotten her out of that mess. She chuckled lightly and looked down at the toe of her shoe. September was having a fine old time playing with the lace. It was curiously soothing. Then she noticed the shards of glass beginning to dissolve. She found that she was walking on a wide-plank wooden floor, into the presence room. There were young women who attended Princess Elizabeth in the royal court, not for work but to share gossip, take refreshment, play games. Since the princesses joined the king, who was in residence at this palace of Greenwich, other women were here in the royal court.

Rose always had to remind herself that the ladies were not drinking tea. Tea would not come for another one hundred years. So instead they were sipping something called sweet mead—totally gross! She dimly recalled she had taken a sip once. It was one of those half-baked memories that floated up to her, a ghostly feeling.

So she must suppose that she had in fact walked through this presence room before, toward the innermost private chamber of Elizabeth. As she passed between the women bent over their embroidery hoops, she caught scraps of the latest gossip. A fire was lit in the large fireplace and there was a chill in the air. Had summer advanced to autumn in her absence?

"They say that Jane the Bald was wooed by Princess Mary with promised shoes."

There was a sniff of disapproval from a pug-faced young woman who looked alarmingly like Carrie, but without the neon-blue streak in her hair. "Word has it that Princess Mary's stipend was increased and she promised to engage the royal shoemaker to produce six new pairs a year."

But it was not her face so much as the gold pin she wore fastened to her bodice that attracted Rose's attention. It was not exactly a Tudor Rose but some kind of flower, and the workmanship was very similar. She could tell even from this distance.

"What are you staring at, girl?" the young woman snapped.

"Oh, oh nothing . . . uh, just admiring your hairdo."

"Hairdo?" she asked. Peals of laughter broke out.

"You mean dew? Like morning dew, girl?"

"No, sorry, I just mean the arrangement of your hair."

"Aaah . . . coquillage." She smirked. "But then again, I don't suppose you know French." It was all Rose could do to resist giving her the stink eye. She had become truly skillful since having to deal with her Indiana Mean Queens. Rose cast her eyes down and shook her head. "'Coquillage' is the French word for snails. See, little snails." She touched the hair that arched over her brow, and indeed it did look as if a parade of teensy snails were marching across the top of her head. *Yuck!* Rose thought. But instead she curtsied and replied, "Lovely," and then walked on quickly. She had to find the maker of that rose pin, the goldsmith. A goldsmith—possibly an artisan or a crafter of fine things!

✳

The door swung open.

Mrs. Dobkins's face was wreathed in smiles.

"Welcome—the princess will be so happy to . . ."

Then Elizabeth rushed toward her and grasped both of Rose's hands.

"I can't thank you enough. Look!" She pointed to her chin.

"Look at what, milady?"

The princess hunched her shoulders up and giggled. "That's proof enough. No spots. I'm spotless. Your magical cream! And I used it on another one that was threatening!"

"Oh, I'm so happy it worked."

"Now come along. We're going to play quoits with my little brother, Prince Edward. He especially asked that you join in. Said you didn't treat him as a child or a future king." *An equal?* The thought was fleeting, and Rose quashed it before the words could reach her lips. "Imagine that . . . ," Elizabeth continued. "He has such an odd way of thinking."

So, thought Rose, the little prince must have liked her, "taken a shine" to her as her mom would have said, when they played in the tree hollow. But she had no idea what quoits were. Some sort of game?

"And milady, should I join in?" Someone in a corner of the room spoke up. Rose could see quite clearly she was a woman with dwarfism dressed in an identical gown to Elizabeth's. She wore a pale blue kirtle embroidered with a leaf design. Beneath was a pleated petticoat that was revealed by a side slit.

Elizabeth emitted a gasp of exasperation and rolled her eyes. Then she muttered under her breath, "Why would my father think a dwarf would please me?"

"You don't like me, milady?" The woman looked as if she was on the brink of tears.

"No . . . noooo, Bettina. It's not that. . . . It's just that tumbling dwarfs feel so useless." Elizabeth pursed her lips. "I mean no offense."

Rose was boiling inside. How could these people be so insensitive? Wasn't this just another kind of bullying? Sixteenth-century bullying for royals!

"The whole thing is offensive!" Rose blurted out. And it seemed as if the entire chamber had inhaled sharply and was holding its breath. Mrs. Dobkins, the princess, Sara, and a girl from the kitchens clearing the breakfast had all gasped at once.

"What in the world are you talking about, girl?" Elizabeth turned on Rose.

"Pardon me, milady. But I find it very offensive that this short woman is regarded as merely an object of amusement. It's . . . it's . . . it's simply awful to treat a human being this way. Shame on you, princess! Shame on you all!" Rose stomped her foot. Mrs. Dobkins staggered a bit and grabbed the edge of a table. Sara fled the chamber. The princess's face swam with a peculiar mixture of emotions. And Bettina looked up in awe with shining eyes at Rose.

It took several seconds, but the princess's face finally settled into one expression—curiosity. "Everyone leave my chamber save for Rose."

When the door shut, Elizabeth turned to Rose.

"Who are you that you dare to say 'shame on you' to a royal princess?"

"I am an ordinary girl."

"You're not ordinary. I know it. I saw you reading a book of mine. One that Kat Ashley, my tutor, had left for me. I asked Kat about you. She said she knew of no relative named Rose Ashley. At least no one nearby."

"I'm not from nearby."

"Nearby or not, you are definitely not an ordinary girl. Ordinary girls do not know how to read." She inhaled sharply and continued. "And mathematics? You know how to do simple sums?" Rose nodded. "Beyond simple sums?"

"A bit."

"A bit of what?"

"Geometry?"

"Isosceles triangle, perhaps?"

"Two equal sides." Rose's eyes had fastened on the pendant at Elizabeth's neck, the Tudor Rose locket that held her picture with her mom and her dad inside. It made her seethe.

"An equilateral triangle?" Elizabeth asked as she angled her chin somewhat defiantly.

"All sides equal," Rose snapped.

Elizabeth narrowed her eyes.

The princess then unleashed a battery of questions, demanding that Rose give the definition of an obtuse and a right-angle triangle. Rose answered them all correctly. Geometry was her strong point in math. She hoped the princess wouldn't venture into algebra too deeply.

"You see, Rose Ashley, I like clever people around me, not dwarfs for amusement, or idiots like Jane the Bald."

"Is Jane an idiot? Really? She seems in her own way very clever." Dared she use the word "autistic"? Better not.

"Well, yes, she can read and write, but that aside, my father the king does no favors by sending such . . . such . . . humans." It seemed to pain the princess to say the word "human," but Rose counted it as a small victory. "And the problem with Kat Ashley as a tutor is that I have out-grown her." Rose said nothing. "She's proficient in Latin and French, and a smattering of Italian."

"I'm not!"

"Of course you're not conversant in such languages. You are a complete commoner. So much of mathematics is— dare I say—common sense. But not in the coarse, vulgar way of your class."

Oh great, thought Rose. *That's supposed to be a compliment, I guess.*

"But . . ." The princess resumed scratching her chin

lightly. "You might have a gift for alchemy."

"Alchemy! You gotta be kidding!"

The princess now tapped the middle of her chin. "Not turning spots into gold—for heaven's sake, no! You think I want a gold pustule on my skin? Making them go away with your magic lavender potion. That is certainly a kind of alchemy."

"Oh, you mean chemistry."

"Chemistry? Never heard of it. Is that a branch of science?" Elizabeth paused and now scratched her ear. "I suppose that makes sense. 'Chemistry' must derive from the Greek word 'khemeia,' which means a transmutation. You changed my pustule into normal-looking skin."

I'm a chemist, Rose thought proudly.

Normally kids didn't take chemistry until they were well into high school. She had had a chemistry set once. She had rubberized an egg by soaking it in vinegar, and dissolved the shell. She had made a crystal from the kit and also made slime with a small vial of sodium tetraborate and a bottle of glue. With baking soda and vinegar she'd created a small volcano. Vinegar was a key ingredient. And she had certainly been very liberal with the vinegar in the Spotless! mixture.

"So I won't be punished?" Rose asked.

"No. But you shan't say ever say 'shame on you' to me again. I am royal. Don't forget it." She lightly tapped the pendant.

Tap that pendant all you want! thought Rose. *I'm going to find the man who made it—the goldsmith, a goldsmith for the court.* But as this thought streamed through her mind, Rose cast her withering gaze to the floor and muttered beneath her breath, "Whatever!"

"What? What did you say?"

"I said thank you."

Now there was a rap on the door.

"Enter," the princess called out.

It was the lady with the snail hairdo.

"Ah, Lady Margaret," the princess said.

Snail Head! Rose thought. She oozed the slime of treachery.

"Your brother, Prince Edward, awaits your presence and hers at quoits."

"Hers?" Elizabeth replied, hiking one minnow-like red eyebrow into her very high forehead.

"That girl who serves."

"Her name is Rose, Rose Ashley. That is her Christian name. I suggest you address her as such." Lady Margaret looked somewhat confused, but no more so than Rose. *Mercurial.* The word popped into Rose's head. It was another word her mom often used. A few of her clients were always changing their minds as to what actually was their dream house. They were mercurial. One minute they wanted a colonial-style home with pillars and all, and the next something log cabin–y, and then they might go from log cabin to super-modern all-glass house. A lot of her mom's clients were constantly changing their minds.

Rose followed the princess out to the quoits court. Snail Head came too, much to her regret. It became immediately clear to Rose that quoits was just another name for tossing horseshoes. There were pegs set in the ground at the end of a closely clipped strip of grass.

"I think I should go first," Prince Edward announced.

"But you went first last time, Edward," Elizabeth protested.

"But it doesn't matter. I'm first in line for the throne."

"But I'm first in order of birth."

"Well, actually, Princess Mary is," Edward said slyly. Princess Mary had just joined them and could hardly conceal the smirk that began to squirm behind her lips. The prince then turned abruptly to Rose. "What do you think, Rose?"

"Me?" Rose squeaked.

"Why ask her?" Snail Head huffed.

"Mind your tone, Lady Margaret," Elizabeth scolded. All eyes turned toward Rose. Rose felt she was in dangerous territory. Snail Head would blame her for the fact the royal princess had corrected her for speaking rudely about Rose.

"Well, let me think. Maybe we should do eeny meeny," Rose offered.

"Eeny meeny?" Edward said with delight. "What's that?"

"It's a rhyme that makes it easy to decide who should go first."

"Do it!" Edward clapped his hands gleefully.

So Rose began. "Eeny meeny miney moe . . . out goes one . . . out goes two . . . out goes another one and that leaves you!"

"You" was Princess Elizabeth. To Rose's great relief, Edward did not seem to mind.

Between turns, Rose observed how attentive Snail Head was to Prince Edward. Fussing over a buckle that had come undone on his boot. Fetching him a goblet of cider when he said he preferred it to the honey mead. Then insisting that he get an extra turn because a strong wind had come up during his last toss. Rose sidled over to Bettina.

"So, Bettina, what's with Lady Margaret and her obsession with Prince Edward?"

"*What's with her?* I don't understand this phrase."

"I mean why is she fussing so about him?"

"Fussing—oh yes. Now I understand. She wants to marry him."

"Marry him! He's only seven years old, for crying out loud."

Bettina blinked. "Nobody's crying, Rose."

Rose shook her head. These people were very literal.

They needed a little metaphor in their lives. "I just mean that he's seven and she's at least fifteen."

"It won't happen. He's already promised to a Hapsburg princess in Austria anyway."

Chapter 23

A Question for Edward

Rose *had arrived on the quoits court with one thing in mind. She* wanted to pull the prince aside and asked him about the pin that Snail Head wore. It seemed impossible to get him off by himself. Finally, when more refreshments were brought out and the prince was clearly fatigued, Rose offered to fetch him a goblet of cider.

"How kind of you," he said as Rose handed him the goblet. "Do sit by me a moment."

"Of course, Your Highness." Rose sat next to him.

"We really beat them, didn't we? Twenty-five to . . . ? Who scored the second highest?"

"Sn . . . I mean, Lady Margaret."

"And who scored the lowest?"

"I believe your sisters, the royal princesses."

"Oh yes, they are disastrous as a team. Always were . . . always shall be."

"How sad," Rose said.

"Not really. I mean honestly, Rose. Mary is so impossible—a jerk, as you said." He giggled. "And Elizabeth is a thousand times more clever. I wish she would succeed me and not Mary."

"But Your Highness, you're younger than both of them. You'll live a very long time." *But he won't!* Rose suddenly remembered. She had googled Prince Edward and found that he had become King Edward VI in 1547 when he was only nine years old. He ruled for barely six years and died at the age of fifteen. But how could she tell him this? He was just a boy, a boy of only seven. A second grader.

"You're nice, Rose. I like you. And you speak so well, if in a slightly odd way. You have the most peculiar accent I've ever heard. What do they call it?"

"Uh . . . Yank?"

"Yank—sounds Dutch almost. My father, the king, has a councillor named Horace Janke. But although it is spelled with a 'J,' it's pronounced with a 'Y'—like this Yank accent of yours."

Time was slipping by. Rose knew she had to ask the question. "Your Royal Highness," she started hesitantly.

"Oh, don't call me that, Edward will do, or even Ned. Some call me Ned."

"Edward, then. I do have a question."

"Well, pop it out, Rose. Just pop it out."

"Edward, you see Lady Margaret over there?"

"Oh yes, not one of my favorites. Did she do something awful to you? I can have her punished, you know."

"No, nothing at all. She's been very polite. But she is wearing a pin in the design of a rose, similar to the rose pendant your sister Elizabeth is wearing."

"Yes, of course. The Tudor Rose. I wear one on my belt buckle." He stood up and drew back his striped tunic, revealing his doublet. He then hiked up his doublet to reveal his cambric shirt, which appeared to be tied to his breeches with several bows. *Clever*, Rose thought. She would have to make a sketch of that in her diary. But there was the belt with a rose, seemingly identical to the one that his sister Elizabeth now wore. "And look, the top clasps on my boots are the same rose, only smaller." Rose felt her heart beating wildly.

"So there is a jeweler."

"Oh, not just any jeweler. A goldsmith."

"And who might that be?"

"Nicholas Oliver. Why do you ask?"

"I'm just curious. Is he always at court, like right now? Is he here?"

"Not sure, most likely not. You see, there's dozens of artisans connected to the court. But they don't like to live at court. They're artists. All the foolishness of the court distracts them. My father understands this. The painter Master Holbein only comes when the king commands a portrait. Holbein did one of my mother the year I was born. I think Oliver lives near Hatfield actually."

"Near Hatfield." Rose had to suppress her excitement. "And when might he be coming to court again?"

"I don't know. Perhaps if my father has ordered some jewelry for my stepmother, Catherine Parr, or a medallion for a councillor."

"I see," Rose said as the prince pulled his cloak tighter around him.

"Are you cold, Edward?"

"Oh, I always get cold at summer's end."

"Summer's end?"

"We're a week into September. September tenth. Officially summer ends in another twelve days."

"Oh," said Rose softly.

"Oh what?"

"Nothing, really." But she began to calculate quietly in her head. *So here it's September 10, 1544, and at home it is October 31—my two worlds are shifting again.*

Chapter 24

A Cruel Game

Following the quoits game, Elizabeth had dismissed her and said
that she would not be needed until later that evening
to help her prepare for a grand banquet. She was free to
wander. Wander and wonder about this jeweler, Nicholas
Oliver. When might he be coming to court again? This palace was so vast. She wondered where visiting artisans stayed.
Were there special quarters for them? She should have asked
Edward. As she passed by the many-walled gardens, she
heard squeals of laughter coming from one. It sounded as
if some game was taking place. Then she spied one of the
palace gardeners peeking through a crack in the wall. He
heard her footsteps on the gravel path and turned around,
beckoning her with a nod.

"What's going on inside there?" Rose asked.

"Just a game of tag that the ladies-in-waiting to Princess Mary like to play. Come take a look. They call it Slap Dash."

Rose walked up to the wall. She pressed her face to the crack. Of course, the first thing she saw was Snail Head dashing by.

She was holding something in her hand as if she was about to throw it. Rose turned to the gardener.

"I thought you said it was just Princess Mary's ladies-in-waiting?"

"Oh, some of the others joined in as well," he said. "But not Elizabeth. She doesn't care for this sort of thing. Take another look."

So Rose peeked through again. She gasped as she saw the shining bald head of Jane the Fool.

"What are they doing?"

"Chasing the fool."

"But they're throwing things at her!"

"Just eggs—nothing that can harm her. Her head—like an egg itself—makes a great target, don't you think?"

"No!" Rose turned toward him. Her eyes were blazing.

"You're a little spitfire, ain't you?"

"You bet I am!" she shot back, and stomped off.

❋

It was not long after the terrible scene that Rose was climbing the spiral stairs of the turret when she heard a familiar singsongy voice. "Taa da ta da . . . lad dee da at ya da da da ya dee dat."

There ahead was Jane sitting on the stone steps. Her head was still splattered with egg yolk. She was holding a cloth and dabbing at one of the shoes.

"Oh, hello there," she said kindly as she looked up from the shoe.

"Hello," Rose replied. "I'm sorry about your shoe."

"Oh, don't be. Comes with the job, you know."

"The shoes or the bullying?"

"Bullying?" Jane tipped her head to one side. A look of confusion passed over her face.

"Teasing," Rose said.

"But I'm a fool. Fools are born to be teased. And the shoes are part of my pay. I'll get new ones—all paid for by the king. The only problem is . . ." She paused.

"What?"

"The cobbler who made these died. The feathers are ruined. I can get new feathers but not a new cobbler, and I fear these stains are forever."

"Maybe not. May I take a look?"

"Sure, Rose."

"You know my name, then?"

"I make it my business to know everyone's name, everyone in the entire royal court. I'm a fool, but I'm not stupid, you know," she said, handing over the shoes.

"I'm sure you're not, Jane," Rose replied firmly. As a matter of fact, Rose felt she had glimpsed something deep inside Jane's very bald head that made her think once again that this so-called fool might be the brightest and the slyest person in the court. *Cunning*, Rose thought. One had to be cunning to survive in the court of Henry VIII.

Rose looked at the shoe. There were stains all over it. "What about the other one?"

"Not as bad. And egg isn't as bad as dung."

"Dung?"

"Cow dung, or sometimes horse or sheep dung."

"They chase you with . . . with . . . poop?!"

"Poop!" Jane threw back her egg-stained head and laughed raucously. "That is completely delightful. I love that word. Let me think now. How might I work that into one of my performances . . . ?"

"You know, I might be able to help you with these stains," Rose said, examining the shoe.

"Truly, miss?"

"Yes. Lend them to me for a little bit . . . well, actually, it might take a while." Rose was thinking of the dry cleaner's close to her gran's house. Their now-unforgettable slogan *We Mean Clean* was too true! *Yikes!* thought Rose. The perfect place to deal with stains made by the cruel game of an up-and-coming Mean Queen, Bloody Mary.

"Oh, how wonderful! Take them away! And I'll get the feathers!"

As Rose was leaving, she had a thought. She turned on the steps. "Jane? If I might call you that?"

"Certainly, Rose." That one eye seemed to jitter a bit.

"You said you knew everyone in the court. But some are not always at court. Some artisans and craftsmen. Do you know a man by the name of Nicholas Oliver?"

"Of course! I know of him. The jeweler. Very favored he is by the king."

Rose felt her heart race. "Do you know when he might be coming?"

"Oh no, dear. I'm not the keeper of the king's calendar. Seems like whenever he has a new bride, Nicholas Oliver comes quite a bit. You know he'll dress her out in precious jewels and gold. They say no jeweler can set a sapphire like Nicholas Oliver. He is a true artist, just like . . ." Jane's eyes seemed to grow misty. "Just like my Sidney."

"Your Sidney?"

"Sidney Garston, the royal cobbler."

"The one who died?"

"Indeed." Tears had begun to stream from one of her eyes, the one that didn't jitter. "And you know what?"

"What?"

"I can't even cry enough tears for him. Only one eye works for tears."

"Oh dear" was all that Rose could think to say.

"Oh, don't 'oh dear' me, sweet girl. I cry sometimes all night with this one eye to make up for the other eye. A crying fool! Ever heard of such a thing?" She giggled, then jumped up and began to dance a barefoot jig.

Chapter 25

When You Made
Me the Rose

*I*n the tiny hamlet of Stow-on-the-Wold, a few miles off the old Roman road, the goldsmith had put away his tools for the day. Scissors, pliers, cutters all lined up, slanting against the rack like tiny soldiers at ease. But Nicholas Oliver was not at ease. He was haunted by what he had seen when he was called to Hatfield a few days before, summoned to deliver a piece of jewelry the king had ordered for his bride, Catherine Parr. There had been a small royal progress setting out with Princess Elizabeth. He had arrived shortly before the progress left. The princess was already mounted on Aureole, a roan pony whose coat matched her own red hair. She sat erect and proud and looked every bit the Lion's

Cub, as she had been called, since she resembled her father in so many ways, in particular her hair and coloring.

Nicholas was just approaching Master Parry, the royal treasurer, when a blade of sunlight struck the princess's bodice. For a moment he felt as if he were caught in a quivering spiderweb of golden light. He felt a dizziness beset him and staggered a bit before he recovered himself. Princess Elizabeth was wearing a pendant, and not just any pendant—a locket, the locket that he had made for his beloved Rosemary. Within that locket was his picture—rather a photograph that Rosemary had taken with a bizarre device called a camera. The other side of the locket held a picture of her and their darling little Rose on a beach, both of them dressed in the oddest and most immodest costumes he'd ever seen. From the wrist of the little girl, a pocket purse hung by a strap with the picture of a peculiar sort of mouse that had enormous ears.

A terrible thought seized him—what if the princess found the secret pin and opened the locket? She might think the photographs were some sort of magic. It would be dangerous for him and dangerous for the princess. The witch talk might start up again. He could just imagine Princess Mary brewing that cauldron of lies. It was witch rumors that had cost Anne Boleyn her head, with a bit of help from the king. Nicholas had made Rosemary promise to take the pictures out of the locket before she left that last time, in case they were discovered. She had agreed and told him that he too must destroy the other pictures she had brought to show him of their daughter, even though he kept them safe in his locked box where he stored precious metals for his work. However, he couldn't destroy them—it would be too hard. And when Rosemary left and did not come back, he was glad he had not destroyed the pictures. But why had she never come back, and how had she managed to leave the locket behind? She wore the locket always. How long had it been since she'd left? Seven years? Eight? Rose must be nearing thirteen, for she was a couple of years older than Elizabeth. Princess Elizabeth was not yet three when her mother was beheaded. And now she was almost a young woman herself. But the witch talk had started when she was just months old.

Nicholas Oliver had tried to reconstruct the timeline of the events before Rosemary had left for good. Anne Boleyn had been crowned queen in May of 1533. The baby princess had been born in September of 1533. The former queen, Catherine of Aragon, had already been banished to an obscure palace. She was to be moved again, and this time her daughter, Princess Mary, had been attending her. But unbeknownst to either of them, Mary was to be dropped off at Hatfield to help tend the newborn Princess Elizabeth. The humiliations devised by Anne Boleyn were unending.

Rosemary had served in the royal household for some

time. Perhaps five years. She had begun in the confectionery making sweetmeats—candied fruits, decorative treats and delicacies. It was a small kitchen that was one of several connected with the main kitchen. Her handiwork was exquisite, and she soon was moved to the wardrobe, where she worked on the delicate stitching required for Anne Boleyn's extravagant gowns. Queen Anne insisted that stitchers for the drab previous queen had no idea how to work a fine fabric with gold thread. "It looks as if it's been gnawed by a goat," she had declared. And thus Rosemary was sent for.

"She's quite impossible!" Rosemary had fumed once to Nicholas. "But hey, I'm a Realtor. I deal with impossible clients all the time."

By that time, of course, Rose had been born in that other world of the unimaginable twenty-first century, on the distant continent of America. She was a toddler back in Haverford, Pennsylvania. Rosemary had hired a nanny for little Rose because of her busy real estate business.

A "Realtor" was what Rosemary's profession was called, one who sold homes. It was hard for Nicholas to imagine a vocation like this—a woman actually working not as a servant—but apparently the money was quite good. Of course, in that odd way in which time tangled for such travelers as Rosemary, when she was gone from him it might be weeks in her world when only a few minutes had elapsed in his.

But then one time the minutes stretched to hours, and the hours to days, then months and years. Nicholas knew she was gone for good.

They had not planned on conceiving a child. But she had. They were both thrilled, of course, though there was no way that she would have dared bring a child into his world. However, she kept him apprised of all the major events. When little Rose began to crawl, then walk, make her first scribblings, she had documented it all with this strange device, the camera. She even brought him one of the first pictures Rose had drawn of a person. Just the head, of course, with a big wobbly smile and a scribble of hair on top. Rosemary had written "Mama" across the top. He had tucked it away in his safe with the other mementos—more pictures of Rose. Rose on her first day of school. Rose ice-skating. Rose on her bike. He'd never seen such a contraption as a bike before. Rose in something called her Brownie uniform, and then her Girl Scout one. Rose midplunge from a rope swing over a pond. He could almost hear her scream of delight. How odd things were in that distant twenty-first century. But Rosemary helped him imagine it. He also imagined that the reason that Rosemary had never returned was that she had met someone in her own time and fallen in love. Although she swore she never would. He only hoped he was a good man who would take care of and love his little Rose, the daughter he had never met.

The image of that gold rose locket suspended from the neck of Princess Elizabeth flared in his mind again. Rosemary certainly would have taken it with her when she left. She felt it had a power through which she could control her visits. Her comings and goings. He thought it was nonsense. He asked her how she had first come to his world, and the conversation came back to him now.

All I can remember, Nicholas, is that I was working in my garden. I was transplanting a damask rose. They're delicate. You have to be careful. The soil temperature has to be right. Perfect if there's a warm, gentle rain falling. This rose came from a cutting of a very old one my mother had that she gave me. I planted it at midnight—an old gardener's trick. Midnight on a full moon. I just remember the silver light of the moon shining down on my shoulders, and then suddenly I was no longer at 35 Ashbury Lane. I was at Richmond Palace. Elizabeth hadn't been born. Queen Catherine of Aragon and the king were in their rose garden and I could hear them quarreling fiercely.

And then you met me, Nicholas had replied.

Yes, and then I met you. We fell in love, but I still often had trouble controlling my time travels. I couldn't just come and go as I pleased. But once you made me the rose locket, it all became so much easier.

But now the rose no longer hung hidden beneath the bodice of his beloved but swung brazenly from the princess's neck, the Lion's Cub, Elizabeth. How had that happened? He felt a rage begin to simmer within him.

✳

Franny was no more at ease than Nicholas had been three days before, but she was jittery for a somewhat different reason. When the gentleman had come striding toward her, she had stopped in her tracks with the milk pail. She could hardly believe her eyes. It was the man whose picture she had seen in the locket! He approached her directly. "Child, can you direct me to the palace cofferer, Master Parry?" She could hardly speak and simply stared at him. He bent over a bit. His face filled with concern. "Did you hear me, child? Are you deaf?" he asked gently.

"No, no, sir. I believe Master Parry's round the other side of the stables. He's traveling with the royal princess to Greenwich."

"Thank you, child." He slapped a farthing into her hand and rushed in the direction she had told him. Franny stood fixed to the spot, as if her work clogs had been bolted to the ground. "I can't believe it!" she murmured. "It's him! And he looks so much like Rose."

She had tried and tried to write a letter to Rose.

Dear Rose,
    Something very strange happened today. I seen a man . . .

The man . . . But she always paused at this point. She knew what she wanted to say, but she was actually almost frightened to write the words: "The man whose picture is in the locket." It seemed dangerous to even mention the locket. She wasn't sure why, but the locket was part of a deep secret. She recalled those moments after she first met Rose. She had begun to wonder if Rose was like some of what she and her family called the Others. The Others were just like her own family, except for the fact that they all had eventually disappeared. It was a dangerous thought to even have. Her mum and father would be angry. It was their secret. It must never be found out. And if she told Rose that she had seen her father . . . She could not complete the thought. It was just too frightening.

It was Franny, of course, who had urged Rose not to worry about the locket but to find her father. Her own words clanged in her head like the sound of the loudest church bells. *Why not try to find him—your father? The real man, not just the picture in the locket. . . . Anything's possible, Rose.*

Well, she'd found the real man for Rose. Or rather, he'd found her. And now she was frightened. She'd asked Andrew about him and he'd told her the man's name was Nicholas Oliver and that he was the king's goldsmith. He was not certain where the man lived. So many times Franny had tried to write this letter. But she could never get the words exactly right. And she worried that if Rose did find her father, she might leave, leave like those others before her. Her mum had warned her to be careful about making friends with the wrong people, people like themselves. "Such attachments can't last, Franny. Simply too danger-ous." But then just four days before Rose left for Greenwich, she had said something. She had whispered it to Franny. "Every time I see the princess and that locket, it still makes me mad. I don't think she's discovered the pin that unlocks it yet. I hate to think of her looking at those pictures of . . . of . . . of my father . . ."

Now Franny would be brought to Greenwich. She had been sent for by the Gentleman Usher, Master Cornwallis, the head of the Hatfield staff. A scullery girl was needed. So Franny would now be able to tell Rose in person. It would be better than sending a letter, as there were always spies about. A letter could be stolen. There were already rumors about the spies of Princess Mary. Jane the Bald was said to be one. *Really odd.* Wasn't that what Rose had said about her in the letter? She smiled when she thought of Rose's letter, knowing she would see her again soon.

Chapter 26

The Marks of September

Dear Diary,

    First things first: sitting on my desk, in front of my very own eyes, are the shoes of Jane the Bald! And tomorrow I am going to take them to Berks Dry Cleaner's and see what they can do. They are stained with egg yolk from September 10, 1544. That was the date of my most recent visit to England. When I got back and carefully made my way around the shattered glass of the greenhouse, it was still October 31. I hadn't looked at the clock when I left, but I think it was around 9:30 when I got back after trick-or-treating. As soon as I was back, I ran upstairs to Shirley's room and told her about the broken window.

But the point here is that I was gone to Greenwich for about three minutes tops tonight. The first time I was at Greenwich, when I met the prince, I was whisked back here for a few days, yet nobody from that old world seemed to miss me at all.

My question now is, how can I control my comings and goings? I am at time's whimsy. I feel as if I am like a ball of yarn a cat might play with—but not September! I trust her. She is the least whimsical creature I know. What was the word Mom always used? "Capricious." Mercurial, capricious. My mother's vocabulary seems to have been enriched by crazy people buying and selling houses.

Rose sighed and closed the diary, her eyes shut tight. Would she ever stop missing her mom? Did she want to stop missing her mom? She had better get some sleep. Tomorrow was a math test. Undoubtedly there would be some geometry on it. Her conversation with the Princess Elizabeth drifted back to her.

"Isosceles triangle, perhaps?"
"Two equal sides."

"An equilateral triangle?"

"All sides equal."

Soon she was fast asleep.

❊

"Well, that's a miserable, rotten trick." Rosalinda's voice scalded the air the next morning as Rose entered the sunroom, or as her gran called it, the "conservatory," where breakfast was served. It was a circular, pleasant room with tin-lined troughs for plants beneath every windowsill. This was where her grandmother proudly displayed her favorites from the greenhouse when they were in full bloom. The air now swirled with the summer scent of sweet peas. Gran took enormous delight in these "tricks" of the season as she called them. The troughs were spilling with the delicate little blossoms in summer colors of pale pink, lavender, and white. Rosalinda smiled sweetly toward an especially robust explosion in one trough as the sun streamed through the arched window.

"Pastels! Such a relief. Far too much orange this time of year. By the way, is Calvin able to fix the broken glass?"

"Oh yes," Shirley said as she came in with a plate of scrambled eggs. "He came early this morning, but I was telling Mrs. A, Rose, how you and I did the temporary fix with the cardboard."

"Well, that could have been dangerous," Rosalinda murmured somewhat breathlessly. "You could have cut yourself."

The old lady seemed to struggle slightly for a breath. "In my day, children who indulged in mischief on Halloween merely soaped windows."

"And in mine it was shaving cream," Shirley offered.

"Harmless fun stuff," Rosalinda said. She turned sharply toward her granddaughter. Rose felt her gaze settle on her. "No mean girls at your school who might be bullying you, are there? Bullies are everywhere, you know, through every age in time and place."

"Oh no, no, Gran." She crossed her fingers under the table, thinking of the Mean Queens, that wicked Trio of Doom. "Everyone's been very nice to me."

"Any clues at all as to who might have done this?" Shirley asked. Rose shook her head. Another lie. There were clues all over the place. She'd spotted them when she took dustpan after dustpan of shattered glass to the back-alley trash cans. The first clue was a sprinkling of glitter on the pavement in the alley. You-know-who's calling card. Then there were the smashed Disney Princess masks. But she would say nothing.

❄

When Rose arrived at school, most of the kids were still outside and had sorted themselves into their usual clumps of friends. She saw Lisa, Brianna, and Carrie in their huddle, a very tight huddle at that. Their backs were turned on the rest of the schoolyard. Some wannabe sixth-grade Mean

Queens, the remoras, were circling but keeping a wary distance. Sibby was trying to get Brianna's attention.

Rose headed toward her three buddies, who were with a couple of other kids, including Susan. "Have you seen them?" Joe tipped his head toward where Carrie, Lisa, and Brianna huddled.

"Well, yeah. Not that they ever talk to me."

"No, I mean up close. Their faces."

"What about their faces? That thornbush?" Rose asked.

"Worse than that," Anand said.

"What?"

"Claw marks. Lisa looks like she tangled with a tiger," Myles replied.

Rose blinked. *More like a cat*, she thought. *September! My feline in shining fur.*

At that moment the three turned toward her. She felt as if she were caught in the crosshairs of a rifle. There was an angry-looking scratch that ran diagonally across Lisa's face.

"Oh dear!" But the words came from Susan, not Rose. Rose felt only a surge of anger. She turned away.

Joe stepped closer and whispered to her and Susan almost conspiratorially. "The good news is that I made the cut for the Snow Show."

"The ice skating show?" Rose asked.

"That's great, Joe," Susan said, but his face turned serious.

"But there's bad news too . . ."

"What could be bad news?" Rose asked.

"Brianna did too."

"But still, Joe. I bet you'll beat her." Susan stammered a bit and blushed furiously. "I . . . I . . . I mean, I saw you do that double axel when I was at the rink last week. You were great."

"Thanks, Susan, but we both have to do a final audition for the lead."

"But wouldn't the lead have to be either a boy or a girl?" Rose asked.

"Gender neutral."

"What do you mean?"

"The choreography is the same. If it's a boy, he's a prince. If it's a girl, she's a princess. It's an adaptation of the story of Saint George and the Dragon. They'll either call it Saint Georgia and the Dragon or Saint George. You know—why shouldn't gender equality be part of fairy tales?"

"So you get to fight a dragon on ice?" Susan asked.

"Yeah, actually it's pretty cool. I don't mind the idea of a girl in the part. Just *that* girl."

"I agree," Rose said, and Susan nodded vigorously.

"Me too!" she whispered.

❋

School was uneventful. The math test went exceedingly well. The Mean Girls kept their distance. She supposed the rock through the window—indeed, the whole Halloween attack—would qualify as a Trio of Doom special-ops effort. What would these evil girls dream up next? Rose was nervous about seeing Lisa at her riding lesson that afternoon.

Everything was great when she got to the stables. She looked around, confident that she would see Lisa getting her horse, Miss Dimples, ready. But no Lisa. At that moment Jamie came up instead.

"Hi, Rose. Have fun on Halloween?"

"Oh yeah. Hey, where's Lisa?"

"Her mom called and said she wasn't feeling well."

"Hmm . . ." *It's her face that isn't feeling well*, Rose thought. September had done a number on her face.

"Okay, well, let's get you up." Jamie said, giving Ivy a pat.

It felt good to forget. Forget Halloween, though it had been fun in its own way. Forget the Mean Girls, the Trio of Doom, the snotty Lady Margaret, Snail Head. Forget the imperious young Elizabeth and the treacherous Princess Mary, whom history would come to call Bloody Mary. Forget that Edward was going to die so young. For ahead of her a new, higher jump loomed. This was what she must focus on. First she had to look ahead and pick out a tree, anything to center her attention on. As the jump neared, she must squeeze with her legs to keep Ivy going. Then she must begin stride counting and know when she was three strides away from the jump—that would be the take-off mark. At the same time, she must relax the reins so Ivy could stretch out her neck. Keep her heels down. Lower leg straight, with her knee in line with the ball of her foot. There was the thrilling sensation when she could feel Ivy gathering her muscles for the jump and then the magical moment when Ivy's hooves left the ground and they sailed. Yes, sailed into the air, sailed toward the sky. Together, just the two of them, Ivy and Rose, and finally Ivy's gentle yield to gravity. And together they would land as softly as a ballerina completing a grand jeté.

Rose was only halfway through her lesson when she suddenly saw Jamie heading to the ring. He signaled Peter, who began walking toward the fence. She saw Peter look at her with a worried expression.

"Rose, can you bring Ivy to the center?" What was going on? She still had another thirty or forty minutes left.

He came up to her. "Rose, we just got a call. I'm afraid your grandmother isn't well. She's been taken to the hospital, and she wants to see you."

"Is . . . is . . . is she going to die?" She remembered what Calvin had told her about the "little episodes" when her grandmother would faint and had to go to the hospital.

"Oh, Rose, I'm sorry, I don't know anything about that, her condition. She just wants to see you. Needs to see you. I think that was the message. Calvin is on his way to pick you up."

"Okay."

It wasn't a long trip to St. Vincent Hospital. But Rose kept going over Peter's words in her head—*wants to see you . . . needs to see you*. Want and need, what was the difference? There was a difference. Of that Rose was certain. If her gran was really dying, did she need to tell her something? Some secret about her own mom?

Chapter 27

A Confession

*G*ran's eyes were closed when Rose entered the room. She had oxygen tubes poking into her nostrils.

"I think we have a visitor, Mrs. Ashley."

Gran opened her eyes. "We?" she croaked. "What do you mean 'we'? Me. I have the visitor."

"I stand corrected." The nurse nodded at Rose and winked.

Yuck! Rose thought. She couldn't bear that patronizing voice. She turned to the nurse. "I think Gran and I need to be alone."

"Of course, dear. Just ring the buzzer if you need me."

Rose nodded.

She pulled a chair up to the bed and took her grandmother's hand. The skin felt papery. Her knuckles were knobby and hard as rocks.

"Hey, Gran," she said softly. "You've got dirt under your fingernails, you know that?"

"Oh yes. I was transplanting some Italian radish seedlings when I started to feel a little whiffy."

"Whiffy?"

"Short of breath. Happens to me occasionally." She paused for the better part of a minute. Then she opened her eyes wide and clutched Rose's hand tightly. It was an amazing grip for a whiffy old lady on oxygen. "I'm trying to think of how to put this, Rose."

"Put what?"

"You know." She nodded slightly, and Rose felt a sudden relief. Gran knew! "You've been there, haven't you?"

"Been where?"

"Cluelessness is not your strength, dear. You have no talent for it."

"Hatfield." Rose whispered the word.

"Hatfield, you said?" Gran replied. Rose nodded. "Richmond was my first visit. Hung about there for quite a while." She paused. "You see, you got the gene." She snorted now. "Genes, they didn't even know what genes were back then. Mendel wouldn't start fooling around with his peas for another three hundred years or so. Darwin? Forget about it."

"My mom had the gene too, I think."

"Yes, she did. It's why she and I had a falling out. I tried to stop her from going back. All I could imagine for her was heartbreak. It was a mistake."

"But it wasn't heartbreak for you?"

"No, it saved me. You see, once, long ago, I had a really bad husband."

"A husband from then?" Rose asked.

"You mean from five hundred years ago? The sixteenth century?"

"Yeah."

"No, no, he was from now—well, the twentieth century." She took a deep breath. A film of tears covered her eyes. She began to speak haltingly. "He . . . he . . ."

"He what, Gran?"

She sniffed and wiped her nose briskly. "He left."

"Left? He just left?"

"Left with some of my money after your mother was born. Left us both." She sighed again. "Some people can fall out of love as quickly as they fall in love."

"But was your husband's name Ashley?"

"Good heavens no. I took the name Ashley for myself and your mother because I met some Ashleys from way back when at Richmond, and they already had a reputation for being intelligent, kind people. Learned people for those times."

"So that man who left you was my grandfather, but who was my father?"

"I don't know."

"You don't know, Gran?" Rose narrowed her eyes and drew her face very close to her grandmother's. It was amazing. Rose felt as if she were getting a bird's-eye view of a landscape. Tiny purple veins webbed across her cheeks like the streamlets pouring out of river deltas. There were so many wrinkles, some deeply gouged. Others spread like silken spiderwebs across her face. There were age spots and a scar, a tiny one above her bristly left eyebrow. It was a remarkable landscape, a vast expanse, a cartography of Rosalinda's life on Earth. "Are you sure, Gran, that you don't know who my father is . . . or was?"

"I don't know his name, but I think yes, he was from that time. If I knew his name I would tell you. You see, your mother went away before she became pregnant with you."

"Didn't you ever see Mom again?"

"I did. But it was always very tense. I didn't want to pry. Your mother was very smart. Went to an excellent college. Then a fine business school and did well."

"So will you forbid me to go back?"

"No. Never. I learned from my mistake. I don't want to lose you too, Rose. You are the best thing that ever happened to me. And, of course, the death of your mother was the worst thing. When she died . . . well, it was too late."

"So you'll still love me if I . . . I . . ."

"Go a-wander?" Rose nodded. "Rose, I shall love you through all time and place. Through every century imaginable. But now we are here. And I love you so very much." Her voice cracked. Tears slid down Rose's face and dropped onto that old veined hand. Rosalinda smiled and, still holding Rose's hand, lifted it with her own and kissed the tear.

Chapter 28

Radishes and
Jane's Shoes

Rosalinda was home from the hospital within three days. She seemed perfectly fine. She and Rose resumed their evening suppers in the greenhouse. Gran complimented her on finishing the transplanting of the Italian radishes. "They grow lickety-split. We'll be eating them in a week."

The subjects of Hatfield, of her father, of time travel were carefully avoided, or so it seemed to Rose. She was dying to ask her grandmother if there was any way she could control her journeys. Could she ever come and go as she pleased? Must she always be in the greenhouse to leave? And what triggered her returns to her gran's house? She also wondered why no one seemed to miss her in the old world of England when she was gone. How it was as if she had left a shadow self behind who did all she was expected to do. But she pushed these thoughts away for now. She mostly wanted her grandmother to regain her strength.

❃

The Mean Queens' scratches healed quickly. Not their feelings, apparently. A month later, when Rose went to her locker, she found a note undoubtedly composed by Carrie but signed by all three.

> I just want to inform you that on behalf of the undersigned, my father, Neil Harrison, is filing a personal injury lawsuit.
> Carrie Harrison
> Brianna Gilbert
> Lisa Woodson

"Gimme a break!" Rose gasped.

At just that moment Myles rolled up with Anand and Joe. "You got one too?"

"A lawsuit threat? Did you get one, Myles?"

"Yep, for reckless operation of a vehicle."

They both started to laugh.

"No way they're going to do this," Anand said.

"And attacking a CP kid in a wheelchair." Myles made a slightly huffy sound. "Puleeze."

"I can say they threw a rock through my grandmother's greenhouse window."

"They did?" Susan asked, walking up to them. "They are the worst."

"But why? I just don't understand."

"Why? Power. Look, my dad's a lawyer. He says a lot of crime has to do with power. Take it from me, the Mean Queens want power. You know, last year Carrie deliberately sat on my glasses when we were in the locker room getting ready for gym."

"I don't see how breaking your glasses gives her power."

"Do you know how nearsighted I am? Take away my glasses and I'm stumbling around. She could laugh at me. She's a bully. Bullies love laughing at people weaker than them."

"What did you do?" Rose asked.

"I . . . I . . ." Susan seemed to be summoning all the breath she could. "I told her to get her big fat butt off my glasses." Except for Halloween, when Susan had called the three girls a sack of pig droppings, that was the loudest any of them had ever heard her speak. "But they were already broken."

"Well, good for you anyhow," Joe said as he gave her a

pat on the shoulder. This set off mild internal tremors in Susan. About a three on the quake-of-joy Richter scale.

❋

Rose stood in the schoolyard with Anand and Myles, waiting for Calvin to pick her up, watching the buses line up. The number one was already beginning to pull out onto the street.

"Uh-oh . . . here comes a remora looking desperate."

It was Sibby Huang. She was carrying a pair of skates. "Has the number two bus left yet?"

"Nope, but about to," Anand answered.

"I . . . I . . . have to get Brianna's skates to her." There was a desperate squeaky sound in her voice.

"Man, Brianna has big feet!" Anand commented.

A look of panic swept across Sibby's face. Just then Brianna came tearing off the number two bus. "At last!" she said, seizing the skates.

❋

That evening, Rose and her grandmother were sampling the first of the Italian radishes.

"It's amazing, Gran, that these radishes grew so quickly. I only transplanted them a week or so ago." They were both munching the Italian radishes with butter and salt. "These are really good. I never thought of butter on radishes."

"Learn something new every day," her gran replied. She

looked around. "This is my favorite time of year in the greenhouse. Summer in December."

"In Australia it's summer now too."

"But we're not in Australia. We're here in Indianapolis."

"Not exactly rooted, though," Rose murmured.

"In time or place?" Rosalinda said.

Rose had almost been ready to ask her grandmother a few more questions about her possible father. She had been thinking how she might phrase it. *Gran, did you ever have a . . . a kind of crush on any guy—sixteenth-century dude?* Or *Gran, what kind of man do you think Mom would have gone for?* She was posing these questions silently in her head when her grandmother interrupted her thoughts with great excitement.

"Oh, will you look at the damask rose over there, dear? Quicker than you think, it will be ready to burst into full bloom. Ready to transfer in two days to the conservatory. It must wake up to sun, real sun, not the artificial light in here. You must bring them out near dawn. It opens at dawn. The bewitching hour for a damask."

"You make it sound like Cinderella's pumpkin turning into a coach for the ball."

"Oh, but I don't like orange. Be sure to get it out to the conservatory by dawn. You plant them, however, at midnight—always."

"She'll have to get up early for that, Mrs. A," Betty

said as she came into the greenhouse to take Rosalinda up to bed.

"Oh, she will." Then Rose heard her whisper in a lower voice. "Who is that girl, Betty? I always forget her name."

Rose winced. How could her gran forget her name? Her gran, who had kissed Rose's tear off her hand. The only one who understood the magic of the other world Rose had come to know so well. She went to the table where she always put her laptop and googled dawn, December 2, Central Standard Time. It would be 7:01. No problem. She usually woke up several minutes earlier, but on cold mornings she loathed getting out of bed. She'd put woolly socks and her down vest on the table next to her bed so she could slip right into them.

She realized when she looked about the greenhouse that not only were the ragged robin and the damask roses ready to open, but so were a multitude of other flowers that Gran said had their peak bloom time in December. Peak, that is, for a greenhouse flower, carefully nurtured and cultivated to bloom in this time out of time.

Rose had become most comfortable doing her homework in the greenhouse, and she was working on an essay for language arts. It could be any subject, but she had to do three things: A) define the theme and central idea; B) use source materials and select facts from a literary or informative text; C) interpret these facts using background knowledge.

Surrounded by this blooming garden on a cold winter night in her gran's greenhouse, Rose had been tempted to write an essay about gardening or flowers. She had learned a lot, and there were four shelves of "source materials" crammed with her gran's horticultural books. But then those fabulous shoes of Jane the Bald's had dropped into her life. She had just picked them up that day from Berks—the Mean Clean Dry-Cleaning Machine! And they did a wonderful job. So she was now about to begin writing an essay entitled "Jane's Shoes." With her iPhone she had taken a picture of them, all nice and clean now, and then begun googling Jane the Bald. There was very little about her, but a lot about the shoes worn by women in that century. Rose began to download some images of other sixteenth-century shoes and printed them out on the color printer her gran had bought her.

Sixteenth-century ladies' shoes were fantastic. Made of all sorts of fabric, they were heavily embroidered in silken thread, encrusted with jewels just like Jane's. She could have gone on for ten pages! Jane was an inspiration on so many levels. Most of all she was a riddle—an "enigma"! A word on the spelling list for this week. And now that she thought of the word "enigma," what could you get out of those same letters? IMAGINE! Not quite. It had one more letter, but nevertheless she tried to imagine Jane living her life not as a fool but possibly a fashion designer! She was so hip. Hip before the word was, well, not a word but just a body part. That was Jane—ahead of her time by about five hundred years or so. A fashion designer or perhaps a spy?

JANE'S SHOES
By Rose Ashley

Chapter 29

A Blade of Light,
a Rose Blooms

I t was almost midnight by the time Rose finished her essay. She fell asleep the minute her head hit the pillow. But it was at dawn that the damask rose would bloom. So she was careful to set her alarm in case she overslept. A soft purring in the night awoke her ten minutes before the dawn broke. She sat straight up in bed. "September," she whispered. But nothing stirred. She must have dreamed it. Nevertheless, she got out of bed and put on her woolly socks, her sweater, then her down vest, all over her pajamas. She stopped in the front hall and got a stocking cap for her hair. She noticed it was snowing lightly. She hoped the sun—the real sun— would shine through for the damask rose. She began to walk toward the greenhouse. There were no grow lights on, no false moon for the moon-loving flowers, just darkness. She felt as if she were crossing a vast, dark sea. She found her way to the damask rose. It was so close to opening. The black of the night began to fray and grow threadbare as she took the rose and walked back through the house to the conservatory. She had this strange sensation, as if the furniture were floating in a shadowy sea, that the Oriental carpet she was walking across had become unmoored and she was somehow adrift. There was an eerie stillness. In this moment she seemed to be a trespasser in the dawn as she walked away with the damask rose.

Entering the conservatory, she gently set the rose in the trough. Was there a glimmer staining the sky? She watched as a gray light began to leak over the edge of the window-sill just as she felt her cell phone vibrate in her pocket. She must have left it there from yesterday. She checked the time: 6:58. Three minutes to go. She'd missed a text message from Anand from several hours ago—eleven o'clock the night before, just when she was working on her essay.

Joe broke ankle. Out of competition. Skates messed with.
Time to slay a dragon or two or three.

She read it again twice more. How could that be? What bad luck. She kept staring at the phone. Two minutes past dawn now, and in the next second a blade of sunlight sliced through the windowpane, striking the damask rose. Rose's eyes opened wide. The petals were unfurling, huge petals. But at the very center were pale ones that were almost white. She had never seen anything more beautiful. And then she felt it. *I'm not in the greenhouse . . . but I am going back . . . back on a rose . . .*

❋

And she was back. Running across a courtyard between the east and west wings of Elsyng Palace, not far from Hatfield, as she carried a pile of black cloth. She knew exactly where she was going. She had picked up the fabric from the clothier and was delivering it to the tailors' workshop. Fifteen stitchers were working away on mourning clothes and drapery for the royal escutcheons, coat of arms, seals, and various emblems that were hung in all royal residences because King Henry VIII lay dying in Whitehall Palace in London. Prince Edward was soon to arrive at Elsyng, where Princess Elizabeth was already in residence. The Earl of Hertford, Jane Seymour's brother, was bringing the young prince. It was felt that he should be near his favorite sister, the one closest to his heart.

So, thought Rose, the bad news was that a king was about to die. But a new king, Prince Edward, who liked her quite a bit, would soon be crowned. That, she supposed, was good news. However, the best news was that Franny was coming with the retinue from Hatfield. She had been promoted to scullery maid. This meant she would now work in the same palaces as Rose did.

Once more it was as if Rose had never been gone. There was just one thing that troubled her. For the longest time, Rose had felt that Franny had something important to say to her but was never quite able to get it out. Rose didn't want to pry. Everyone had secrets, no one more so than Rose! She sensed that Franny would tell her when she was ready. But right now she couldn't wait to see her old friend again.

It wasn't until she came into Elizabeth's presence room that it really hit Rose how long she had been gone. Elizabeth had grown. She was as tall as Rose and her figure had become quite shapely. But then again, almost three years had passed in this century, although it had only been a couple of months that she had been in Indianapolis. It was now January 1547. She knew it because she had googled Henry VIII, and all his family for that matter. Indeed, everyone had changed quite a bit. Kat Ashley had certainly aged. Her face had grown drawn and wrinkled. Mrs. Dobkins's hair had turned quite white.

Rose looked about slowly. Even Bettina, the woman with dwarfism, looked older, with more wrinkles and gray streaks in her hair. She too was dressed for mourning. Would anybody notice that Rose had not aged? Of course, she was quite tall for her age to begin with. Now Elizabeth, at fourteen, was almost two years older than her.

"Aah, here you are, Rose," Sara said. "You put in the order for a second formal mourning dress."

"Yes, Sara. And here's the one for Mrs. Ashley."

"Oh, thank you, dear." She paused and looked at Sara and Rose. "Now, when the dreadful news arrives, both of you shall have to swap your white French hoods for black ones."

"Of course, ma'am," Sara said, and curtsied. "They have already been made."

"Good girls!" Kat Ashley responded.

❋

And by ten o'clock the next morning the news did come to Elsyng Palace. A messenger had been sent from Whitehall. He had ridden through the night and demanded to see the prince. A hush fell on the room as the messenger, sweating and somewhat disheveled, dropped to his knee and bowed his head in front of Edward.

"The king is dead. Long live the king."

Rose gave a little gasp as she saw Edward sway a bit. It was as if the weight of the crown had already been placed on his head. Instantly everyone in the chamber dropped to their knees and a chorus rumbled through the chill air. "God save the king, Edward the Sixth!" *He's only nine years old. Just nine.* That was all Rose could think.

Edward steadied himself. "And can you tell me, sir, when did the end come and who was with my father?"

"His majesty left this world at two o'clock this morning. He was alone except for Archbishop Cranmer."

It would be another three days until the announcement was made in Parliament and the news swept the land. Those three days were the busiest Rose had ever known in her life as a servant. Franny was called up from the scullery to help with the packing, for the new young king and his sister Princess Elizabeth were to move to Whitehall Palace in London.

Chapter 30

The King, Minus
a Few Parts

The servants were the last to pay homage to their late king in the presence chamber of Whitehall. As they filed in, Princess Elizabeth walked out pale and trembling. Kat Ashley was by her side and appeared to be supporting her. Rose caught a fragment of her mutterings.

"Never, Kat, never let them do that to me if I rule."

"What is she talking about, Sara?" Rose was standing between Franny and Sara at the far end of the chamber. Draped in blue velvet and cloth of gold was the lead coffin in which the king's body now rested, embalmed with more than fifteen different kinds of herbs and wrapped in wax.

On top of the coffin lay a wax effigy of the king clad in crimson velvet trimmed in fur. Dozens of burning tapers surrounded the coffin.

"You see the box at the foot of the coffin."

"Yes."

"That's the evisceration box," Sara whispered.

"The what?"

"Before the embalming of kings and queens, the royal physician opens the body and removes the heart and the entrails. They are to be buried separately."

"Oh yuck!" The words just escaped. Rose couldn't help it.

Sara looked at her with alarm. "What did you say?"

"Oh, just . . . just that I think that sounds awful, vile."

"Well, so does Princess Elizabeth. I heard her fuming to Kat last night about it. She says if she dies a queen, she wants no part of her to be removed."

"So where will they bury all these parts of the king?"

"His body will be buried in St George's Chapel in Windsor and the other parts at the chapel of the Palace of Westminster."

Rose clamped her eyes shut. She could not help but think of her own mother, the snippets of that phone call she had overheard—*engulfed in flames . . . died instantly . . . no remains.* But here there were remains and they were scattering them all over the countryside.

"I don't blame Princess Elizabeth one bit. It's absolutely savage."

"Hush, Rose," Franny hissed.

"Our turn now," Sara said. The three girls joined a line of servant mourners who were filing toward the coffin. When they arrived, they were to fall to their knees and pray for the soul of their king. Rose tried to keep her eyes down, or at least not look at the dreadful box that held Henry VIII's heart and guts. This was not difficult, as the effigy was so lifelike. She had not realized the detail. She had seen the crown, but beneath the crown was a black nightcap set with a dozen or more precious stones.

"The nightcap of forever sleep," Sara whispered.

The wax hands of the effigy were gloved, and rings adorned the fingers.

❊

Two days later, Kat Ashley entered the wardrobe chamber of Princess Elizabeth, where Sara and Rose were arranging the mourning clothes.

"The king has been buried at Windsor," she announced. *The king, minus a few parts*, thought Rose. The thought still gave her the creeps. "The chief steward, Master Barrett, has informed me just now that Elizabeth is to proceed to Hatfield directly following the coronation."

"But the coronation? Is it not to be in four days?" Sara asked.

"Yes, Sara, do you have some objection?"

"May we attend?" Sara asked. "We so want to see the young king crowned."

"Nonsense. King Edward will arrive tomorrow from Windsor and shall enter the gates of London. He will then proceed from the Tower of Westminster in a grand procession so that his people may see him and celebrate."

"But we are his people," Sara whined.

"You are in service to the royal princess and must prepare for her return to Hatfield when she leaves the coronation."

A perplexed look crossed Kat Ashley's face. She did not answer. Turning her back, she walked out of the room.

It was nearly midnight when Rose and Sara finished the packing. They both went down to the servants' kitchen. On her way, Rose tapped on the door of Franny's tiny little chamber, hardly bigger than a chicken coop.

"What are you doing up so late?" Franny rubbed her eyes and yawned.

"Packing. We're going back to Hatfield."

"I know."

"Sara's in a snit because she wanted to see the coronation."

"Yes, so does Princess Mary."

"She's not attending?"

"Already gone!" Franny announced this with some glee.

"How do you know this?"

"You'd be amazed how much gossip one picks up in the scullery. You see, the new king and Princess Mary have had a falling-out."

"Well, they never really liked each other that much."

"True, but he is as fanatical a Protestant as she is a Catholic. I heard a horse guardsman say that the Privy Council wants to get Mary as far away from London as possible. She is said to be quite popular in the city and the surrounding countryside. So she has been already sent off to Beaulieu Palace. What do you think of that? Is this a gee-whiz moment, Rose?" Franny had loved it when Rose blurted out those two odd words recently about one of the antics of Jane the Bald.

"Well, yes, it is. Come, let's go to the kitchen and get something to eat. I'm starving."

"Me too."

Sara was not there when they arrived. She must have already taken something to eat upstairs in the room they shared.

They were alone at the table. Franny was fiddling with her bread.

"You going to eat that or you just going to look at it morosely?"

"Morose? How do you spell that?"

"M-O-R-O-S-E. It was on my . . ."

"On your what?"

"On my mind." That was sort of a lie . . . as she was about to say it was on last week's vocabulary list for language arts class. Rose could tell that Franny wasn't quite buying it.

"What does it mean?" Franny asked.

"Morose? It's just another word for feeling sad, gloomy."

"Oh, and here it has part of your name in it—Rose."

"Well, I'm not sad, Franny, but . . ."

"But what?" Franny said, shoving the bread toward Rose.

"But I think something is bothering you. You seem a little sad." Franny flushed. The color crept up her neck above her ruff until her entire face was quite pink. Franny turned her head away from Rose and rested her chin in the palm of her hand. "Whatever is wrong, Franny?" Rose reached across and touched her hand. "You can tell me. Really. That's what friends are for."

"I haven't been a very good friend, Rose." Tears had started to slide down her cheeks.

"No, you've been the very best of friends I've had here."

Here! The word echoed in Franny's head. So where else might she have friends? She couldn't think about that now. "Rose, I think I saw your father," she blurted out.

"What? Where? When?"

"A while ago. Quite a while ago, actually, at Hatfield."

"But why didn't you tell me?"

"I . . . I was afraid he might take you away. And . . . and I couldn't really think how to tell you exactly. I tried ever so many times to write you a letter."

"Take me away? Away to where?"

"Uh . . . I don't know." There was so much she was not saying. Would this be considered lying?

"Was his name Nicholas Oliver?"

"Indeed it was, Rose. How did you know?"

"When I first met Prince Edward—I mean King Edward—I asked him about my pendant that Elizabeth wore. You see, I saw one of the young women at Greenwich, Lady Margaret, wearing a pin that was similar. I asked Edward who made such lovely jewelry, and he told me that a certain Nicholas Oliver did. So if you saw him, he must live close to Hatfield. Oh . . . oh . . ." Rose began to sputter. "Wowzer!"

And now Franny giggled for the first time. Sometimes the words that Rose came out with were quite amazing.

"Yes, Franny, this is a genuine wowzer, gee-whiz, OMG moment." Then Rose's expression changed suddenly. Her forehead crinkled. Her voice became cold. "But why didn't you tell me? We're supposed to be friends. Friends tell each other the truth. And you are the one who told me to look for my father and not . . . not . . . just think about the locket."

"Are you angry, Rose? Please, please don't be angry."

"I'm not angry, but I'm confused." She paused. "And yes, to be honest, a little bit angry."

"I was fearful you'd leave with him. It was selfish of me, I know."

"But where to?" Rose asked her again.

"I don't know, Rose." She cast her eyes down. She was afraid to look Rose in the face.

She's holding back something, Rose thought. *She isn't exactly lying, but she's not telling me the whole truth.*

"I just want to find him, Franny. That's all. I told you that my mother died. I don't really have anyone else."

"I'm sorry, Rose."

"Don't be sorry. Help me find him."

"I will! I will! I promise." And now Rose believed her. They were best friends, but in that moment, as they peered into each other's eyes, they each sensed that the other had an even deeper secret that she dared not reveal.

"I can't believe it. My dad, my very own dad, might be near."

"Dad?" Franny asked. "Is that the same as father?"

"Yes, yes. Do you know where he lives?"

"Andrew, the horse master's son, told me. The goldsmith had come to Hatfield with some jewelry to be delivered to the royal court. That's when I first saw him. So I asked Andrew and he said that he thought Nicholas Oliver lived over near Stow-on-the-Wold."

"Never heard of it. Where's that?"

"About a day's ride from Hatfield."

"So you're saying I could ride there?"

"Yes. I'd be happy to go with you."

"But how could we get away? And would there be enough time?" Rose suddenly thought of her gran's words: *Some people can fall out of love as quickly as they fall in love.* What if Nicholas Oliver had fallen out of love with her own mother? Would he accept her?

"There's time, Rose. Princess Elizabeth is not to come back for another four days at the earliest. We go to Hatfield tomorrow and work hard. Get all the dusting up done, the wardrobe organized. There's a rumor that the upstairs steward . . ."

"Master Stanhope."

"Yes, Master Stanhope. The rumor is that he's being promoted to King Edward's household and is to become Groom of the Stool."

"What's that?" Rose asked.

Franny blushed. "You know."

"Know what, Franny?"

"The stool, the garderobe where we go . . ."

"To the bathroom."

"Oh yes, that's what you call it, isn't it—going to the bathroom. Well, the king has a special one. Very fancy, and the Groom of the Stool helps him with . . ."

"Pooping!" Rose burst into laughter.

"Yes, his bodily functions. And bathing as well."

"This is unbelievable."

"Only kings have them. Never queens."

"Is that supposed to make me feel better?"

Franny shrugged. "It just means that there's a reordering of our household going on, and while the cat's away, the mice will play. Speaking of cats, I saw that orange cat I spied when I first met you. The three-legged one."

"September?"

"Is that what you call her?"

"Yes." Rose chuckled. "She's a dear old thing. A stray, I guess. Very shy but has developed a fondness for me. She's very independent. Comes and goes as she pleases."

Chapter 31

"Imagine That, September"

*F*ranny had been right that the household staff was shifting, with several staff members being ordered to attend the new king. Thus there were fewer servants. But the workload had dwindled since there were no royals to serve at the moment.

September had deigned to join "the staff" and had distinguished herself as a superb mouser. Mrs. Belson, the cook, could not sing the cat's praises enough. And while the human "cats" were away, certain mice did play. On this particular morning there was time at last for Rose and Franny to set out on their expedition to Stow-on-the-Wold. They left at dawn. It was the end of February, and it seemed as if there might be more than a hint of spring in the chill air. The trees were about to bud and had that slightly shy look, as if to say, "Dare I?" The leaves were still furled tight as babies' fists, but eager to grasp at the sunlight as it spread across the land.

"Why did Andrew let you ride astride and me side-saddle, Franny?"

"I ain't a lady like you, Rose. And it's easier for me with my leg."

"I'm not a lady."

"You serve upstairs. I'm downstairs, beneath the stairs, really."

"Astride is much more comfortable," Rose said.

"Have you ridden astride?"

"Uh . . . once or twice."

"Do you want to now?"

"I'd love to, but what would I do with the saddle?"

"Up there in that little shed. Looks like a sheepfold to me, a lambing shed really. But no sheep or lambs around. This croft has been abandoned for years. Nobody will find it. But you'll have to ride bareback like me with just the blanket underneath your bum."

They stopped and dismounted, and Rose walked over with the saddle to the shed. It was very low. Definitely made for sheep and their lambs, as Franny had said.

Rose laughed as she stooped to walk inside and saw September perched on an upside-down wooden bucket. "Now whatever are you doing here?" The slit of light flashed in her eyes, as if to say, "What do you think? Guarding your saddle until you get back."

Five minutes later, Rose and Franny were trotting along in a companionable silence. The sun had risen and was gilding the field, which spread out like a cloth of green and gold. Snowdrops bowed their heads shyly as if they were beginning to curtsy to the two passersby. A bold daffodil trembled in the light breeze. Rose couldn't help but wonder when spring might appear in Indianapolis. Gran had said by the end of April, when there was no chance of frost, they would move many of the plants out of the greenhouse to the walled garden.

"Look, Rose." Now late into the evening, Franny drew her pony to a halt. "Stow-on-the-Wold."

"That's it?" All she could see were two or possibly three thatched cottages.

"Well, it's not exactly London."

They rode on for another ten minutes or so as the road began to bend down a slight incline, winding into the village. There were actually four houses, and a woman with a staff came out from behind one, escorting a rather large pig. "This way, Tonks. This way, dearie." She looked up and caught sight of the two girls. "Don't worry, girls, old Tonks won't bother you. What brings you this way? No one comes to the Wold, save with messages from the king to Master Oliver."

"Yes!" Rose exclaimed.

"You have a message for Master Oliver, do you?"

"Not exactly," Rose said.

"Now what the devil does that mean?"

"It means," Franny said firmly, "that we don't have a message . . . uh, we just have a question."

"Well, he ain't here."

"Where'd he go?" Rose said, trying to disguise the disappointment in her voice.

"He left last night for London. Official business. Royal business."

"Oh!" Rose's shoulders slumped.

Franny reached across and squeezed Rose's hand. "When might he be returning, good lady?"

"Oh, one never knows, my dear. He comes. He goes. No rhyme nor reason. Very much in demand, you know, by the court, and the only one by royal permit allowed to fashion the Tudor Rose. King Henry most likely needs some new jewelry for his love, Queen Catherine Parr."

Franny and Rose exchanged shocked looks. Franny leaned forward over the withers of her pony.

"Madame, I am sorry to bring you this news, but the old king, King Henry, has died. There is a new king now, King Edward."

The woman wobbled a bit, then grabbed the neck of the hog and fell to her knees, making the sign of the cross.

"I didn't know. It takes a long time for news to get to the country this far away from London. Master Oliver didn't mention anything. But I expect they need new jewelry, new adornments for this new king. He be a Protestant, I understand. Not like his dear sister Mary, of the old faith."

Franny and Rose looked at each other and decided to stay silent.

"Thank you for your help, ma'am," Rose said. "Might we just walk about his yard? I think I'd like to leave him a message. Do you by any chance have any paper and pen?"

"Me, girl?" the old lady cackled. "What do you take me for? I don't do no scriving. Never learned my letters or how to read. Ain't you a funny little thing." She looked at Rose more carefully now. "You know, you do bear a wee likeness to Master Oliver."

"Oh, I doubt it," Rose said quickly.

"Well, no harm in walking about, I s'pose, but the cottage is locked up tight as a drum, and even if you had a message to slide under the door, probably couldn't squeeze it through. He's a goldsmith, after all. Precious things in there."

"Yes . . . yes . . . I'm sure, precious things," Rose whispered to herself.

The woman and her pig toddled off. As soon as she was out of earshot, Franny said, "You see, even she said you looked like your dad." Franny loved that word, "dad." She called her own father Pa, or Papa, but Dad was . . . well, debonair. It certainly fit Nicholas Oliver, for he was a debonair, handsome man.

"Come on, let's look around," Rose said, sliding off the horse. There was a post by the front door of the cottage to tether horses to. The cottage was a squat little affair with very small windows. But it did have two chimneys.

"I suppose he needs two chimneys if he's a goldsmith. He must have one fire to melt the gold and another fire for cooking his food," Rose said, pressing her face against a small windowpane. It was almost impossible to see anything. The back part of the cottage had been built out, and as she peered through that tiny window, she saw a workbench and could just make out a row of tools and a very small cast-iron wood-burning stove, on top of which was a pot. It must be for smelting the precious metals.

Franny could tell that Rose was bitterly disappointed that the goldsmith was not home. "Try not to fret, Rose. You'll catch up with him soon. I think the old lady was right. He was probably called upon to make new medals and decorations for the new king."

"Yes, I suppose," Rose said.

They mounted their horses and headed back to Hatfield.

"There's the shed ahead. Better stop and get my saddle. Won't do for me to ride in bareback."

Rose wondered as she slid off the horse if September would still be there, guarding the saddle. She was, and she seemed to sense Rose's disappointment. She leapt into Rose's arms and licked Rose's cheek with her warm pink tongue. Rose looked into the cat's lovely green eyes. She could see her own reflection. "The old lady said I looked like my dad," she whispered. "Imagine that, September." The cat looked up at her and seemed to almost speak, to say, "Yes, imagine that!" And just then she felt a strange gravitational pull. She knew instantly that she was going back, back again. But she didn't want to. She wanted to stay. Stay and find her father. *Dad!*

Chapter 32

Dragon Slaying and Other Sports

"**O**h my goodness, Rose. Aren't you up early!*"

"Hi, Shirley. Uh . . . I came down to bring the damask rose into the sunroom here." She'd just set it in the trough and was now looking at the text message from Myles:

Joe broke ankle. Out of competition. Skates messed with.
Time to slay a dragon or two or three.

That was the last thing she remembered before she had been whisked away to Elsyng and had learned that the king lay dying. The time on the cell phone when she had read the message about Joe had been 6:58. Then she remembered the sunlight piercing the grayness of the dawn at 7:01. Now it was 7:03 in the morning. Two minutes, that was all the time she had been gone. But within these two minutes, a king had died. A new one had been crowned and a father almost found.

"Oh dear," she whispered as she read the text about Joe again. *Slay some dragons.* Obviously Myles felt the dragons were the Trio of Doom. How had this happened? Rose was torn. On one hand she felt horrible about Joe. This would mean that Brianna would get the lead role in the ice show. But on the other hand, she didn't want to be part of some middle school warfare anymore. She was desperate—yes, desperate—to get back to England and the year 1547 and find her father—Nicholas Oliver.

Was there any way she could will herself back to England? What if she just cut school today, pretended she was sick? She hadn't missed any days so far. Maybe somehow, some way, she could get back.

Shirley was busy setting the breakfast table.

"You know, Shirley, I'm not feeling so well this morning. I think I'll stay home from school."

"No breakfast?"

"No thanks, my stomach feels a little queasy."

"All right, dear. I'll tell your grandmother."

"Think I just want to sleep."

"Then run along upstairs."

She was just about to walk out of the conservatory when she thought of September.

"Shirley, you haven't seen that cat around, have you?"

"The three-legged stray?"

"Yes."

"No sign of her, dear."

"Okay. See you later." She looked at the damask rose, which was perhaps one-third open. She wondered what her grandmother had meant when she had spoken of the bewitching hour for this rose.

She crawled into bed, pulled her covers up, and reached for her diary.

Opening the diary, she crossed out the current date, December 2, the time which she thought of as her home century, the twenty-first, and wrote in February 27, 1547, for that was the day that she and Franny had ridden to Stow-on-the-Wold. She began writing.

I want to go back. I need to go back. But I've absolutely no clue as to what triggers my tumbles through time. I call them "tumbles." To merely call it time travel doesn't seem right. The word "travel" makes it sound as if there is a schedule. Like it's a train I can catch, or a plane, if I just make my reservation and show up at the station or airport.

But as you and I know, dear diary, it's not that way at all.

One thing seems important. When I left this last time, I was not in Gran's greenhouse. I was in the conservatory at what Gran called the bewitching hour. I had just set out the damask rose.

The rose, she thought. The word lingered in her mind. Was a rose, that rose, in some way the key? There had been another time when the rose had played a part in her transport, had launched her right back to the sixteenth century. That had been almost one month before. The moment came back to her. Vividly. She had stooped down to look more closely at the tiny bloodred seams in the bud. And at the same time she had heard September meow; September, who had not been around for days. The rose had appeared to unfurl that evening, but of course it hadn't yet. It wouldn't until dawn of this very day, and yet at the time it had seemed to engulf her. She remembered her exact words to the cat that evening. *But it's not December yet.*

What was it about that cat? And what was it about the rose? The rose that her father had made for her mom with the secret pin that unlocked their own strange histories. And when she had gone back this last time, September had leapt into her arms and peered so deeply into her eyes, and she into those pools of green. Then within seconds she was back—back in her own home century. Those might be the links, the clues to her travel, but how could she gain control?

She came downstairs for lunch. Her grandmother was already at the table in the conservatory.

"Well, my dear, you might not be feeling well, but look at our damask rose. Thank you for getting up that early. I declare you must have hit the bewitching hour right on the nose!" She paused for a second. A mischievous light flickered in her eyes. "I wonder if time has a nose." She chuckled softly.

"What exactly is the bewitching hour, Gran?"

"Oh, I don't know. Just an expression I use for when something—how should I put it—achieves its destiny in life. Yields its beauty and its scent to the world at large. Becomes one, I suppose, with the world."

"That's a nice way of thinking about it, Gran."

"There are many such moments in life, I think."

"You mean bewitching moments?"

"Yes, that's what we've been talking about, isn't it?"

"Yes." But for some reason she didn't believe her gran was referring to her own tumbles through time.

"I'll tell you one such moment," her gran said with new energy. "Reading."

"Reading?"

"Yes. You try and try to figure out all those squiggles on

a page when you're a little tiny child. They mean nothing to you. You might know their names and know the sound each letter makes, but to slide them together into a meaningful word seems impossible. But then there is this moment. This bewitching moment when you see it. You break through the code that has been shutting you out and you land softly in this beautiful world of meaning and stories."

"That's wonderful, Gran."

Rosalinda was growing very excited. "I'll tell you another such moment. Swimming. Same thing. You know there's that moment you've been trying to imagine what it's like to float. To float and not to sink. It seems like a foreign language for your body. You come so close but you just can't quite do it. And then one day it happens. You float off. You move your arms, kick your feet, and you're at one with the sea. This brand-new element that seems made just for you. I think the secret is that you just relax. You yield to the extraordinary. So much of life is yielding to the extraordinary."

"The extraordinary," Rose said softly. "I know what you mean." Rose was thinking of those first moments when she had really learned how to jump with Ivy. When the pony's hooves left the ground and together they sailed into the air, sailed toward the sky. They were fused for those fleeting moments—girl, pony, sky.

Rose went back upstairs, climbed into bed, and took a nap. She dreamed of Ivy; she dreamed of damask roses and September with her sea-green eyes, cuddled in her arms.

There was a soft tap on the door.

"Yes?"

"It's me, Rose, Betty."

"Oh, sure, come in."

"Feeling better, Rose?"

"Yes, much better."

Betty held up an envelope. "This just came for you. Someone slipped it through the mail slot."

She reached out her hand. "Thank you, Betty."

Rose opened the envelope. She could tell it was a kid's handwriting. She skimmed to the bottom. It was signed "Sibby."

"Sibby Huang," Rose murmured. One of the remoras. Her eyes went to the top of the page.

Dear Rose,
    I need to tell you something . . . something very important. I can't tell you in school. We can't be seen together. Can you meet me at the corner of Delaware and Hampton Street at 4:30? Please please please.
        Sibby Huang

Was this a trick? Sibby was one of the most ardent of the remoras, a super suckerfish if there ever was one. Rose felt she had to be careful. At the same moment, her cell phone rang.

She looked at the number. It was Susan. "Hi."

"Where were you today?"

"Uh, sort of sick. How is Joe?"

"Well, not happy, you can bet that . . . but, Rose . . . they're saying you did it."

"Did what?"

"Messed with Joe's skates."

"Me, mess with Joe's skates? How would I do that? And why?"

"They're saying you had a crush on him, but he liked me better and you were mad."

"You have got to be kidding me."

"I'm not."

"You don't believe them, do you?"

"Of course not, Rose. How could you ever think such a thing?" She sounded hurt.

"I'm sorry."

"Don't worry about it. I'm just worried about you."

"Me?"

"Look, Rose, just stay alert. I think the Trio of Doom aren't settling for a broken ankle. They want to break you too."

Suddenly the meeting with Sibby seemed more important than ever. But she didn't want to say anything yet. "Look, Susan, I've got to go right now. But I might need your help soon. Yours, Myles's, Anand's, and Joe's if he can."

"All right, but look out for yourself."

"I will."

Rose quickly got dressed. Just as she was stepping out the door, September appeared.

"Wanna come?" September cocked her head slightly and jumped into her arms.

It was a fifteen-minute walk to the corner of Delaware and Hampton. She spotted Sibby slouched on a bench as she crossed the street. There didn't seem to be any Mean Queens around. But there was a teenage boy. He looked a lot like Sibby. He must be her older brother. He stood up as Rose approached and so did Sibby, slowly. She had been crying. Her face was puffy and tearstained.

Her brother gave her a slight nudge on her shoulder as if to urge her on. "Uh, Rose, I'm Michael Huang, and Sibby has something to tell you." Sibby began crying harder and sniffling.

"I . . . I . . . I did something awful, Rose."

"Does this have something to do with Joe Mallory breaking his ankle?"

"Uh . . ."

"Louder, Sibby," Michael prompted.

"It does." Sibby blurted it out with a wail. "Those skates. Well, you were right. They were too big to be Brianna's. They were Joe's."

"Did you take them?" Rose asked.

"Yes, but it was all Brianna's idea. Well, Brianna, Carrie, and Lisa's idea. They knew about Michael's metal bender for speed skates. Because, you know, my brother is a champion speed skater. She sputtered. "I . . . I bent them."

Rose looked at the sniffling, shaking little girl. "You bent the blades?"

"I . . . I . . . made Joe fall. I bent his skate, and it made him fall."

"You bent them? You're so little; how could you bend a metal skate blade?"

"I used the bender in my brother's shop in the garage."

Michael began to explain. "Speed skaters often have to customize their skates for certain events. We use it so the blades can grip the ice at just the right angle for high speeds. But bending a blade for figure skating is disastrous. As we can see from Joe. It's not something you'd notice to begin with. You'd have to take a few jumps and turns. Which Joe did during practice."

"So why exactly are you telling me this, Sibby?"

"They're going to try to blame you."

"Blame me?" So Susan was right.

"Brianna is at the club right now with her parents," Michael said.

"Blaming me?"

They both nodded. How stupid was that! Joe, Anand, and Myles were all her friends, not potential boyfriends. If there were any potential boyfriends, it was that cute guy Andrew, the horse master's son. But he was an ocean away, both in time and space, in the sixteenth century. But jeez! It dawned on her that there was also Jamie at Hunter Valley, and guess who had a huge crush on him—Lisa! Things were starting to make sense.

"But," Michael said, "to my sister's credit, she told me the whole story this afternoon. She confessed. And if you'll drive with us over to the club right now, we'll tell Coach Feynman."

"I'm sorry! I'm so sorry," Sibby wailed, and flung her arms around Rose's waist. She was hiccuping now and had managed to smear snot all over Rose's down vest. "I wanted to be like them. I wanted to be included, but now I see . . . I'm awful. I'm a horrible person."

"No," Rose said.

All she could think of was how much she wanted to get away, to go back to Hatfield, to Stow-on-the-Wold, to find her dad. But now was not the moment. Not the bewitching moment. Still holding September in her arms, she climbed into the car with Sibby and Michael.

*

"And just so you know. There was this little mix-up and . . . and . . . Rose Ashley said something about wanting to skate, and she had these old skates . . ." Brianna was talking very fast and very breathlessly.

"I did? I said that?" Rose roared as they entered the office of the head coach at the Indianapolis skating club.

"That cat. Get that cat out of here. It's . . . it's . . . ," Brianna screeched.

"Coach," Michael said, "my sister has something to tell you."

"You wouldn't dare, Sibby," Brianna hissed.

Sibby seemed to have recovered.

"Oh yes I would." She squared her shoulders and began to explain the whole story, plus the plan to place the blame on Rose.

The coach, a mild-looking man, seemed to turn gray as stone.

"Thank you, Sibby," he finally said. "I think for now it would be best if you not participate in the Snow Show. But it took courage to come forth with the truth.

"Now, you, Brianna. You're another story."

"What do you mean?"

"You are banned from the club for the next month. And your friends, they are never to come here again either."

"You . . . you can't do that!" Brianna gasped.

"I can do it. Not only that, I'm calling your school and reporting you and your two friends. I'll explain how Sibby came forward and told the truth. But, Sibby, is it understood that you are not to be in the show? And I think perhaps you should take a week off from lessons and reflect on what you've done. I'll have to inform your parents. And needless to say, inform Joe's parents as well."

"Yes, Coach."

The coach then turned to Rose. "And you, Rose? That is your name, right?"

"Yes, sir."

"I'm sorry that you got dragged into this mess. I think Brianna owes not only Joe an apology, but you as well, Rose."

"No way!" retorted Brianna.

"That's it!" the coach said in a quiet voice, sharp as a blade's edge. "You are banned from the club forever."

Michael drove Rose home. "Sibby, I hope you've learned your lesson." He then glanced over to Rose, who was riding in the passenger seat. "And, Rose, I suppose there is some satisfaction that Brianna got the worst punishment a competitive skater can get."

"Yes," she said softly. *One down, two to go,* she thought. *Three, if you count Princess Elizabeth. Oh, and Mary. Can't forget Princess Mary!* And then of course Lady Margaret—yes, Margaret, with those disgusting little snail curls. Elizabeth, Mary, and

Snail Head, that would make the perfect sixteenth-century Trio of Doom. An abundance of bullies!

Then Rose's mind drifted far away into that distant century, to the thought of her father. What might she say to her father the first time she met him—if that time ever came? Would he recognize her? How would she tell him about her mom and the terrible accident? He probably didn't even know what a car was! She wondered what her father was doing at this very minute. . . .

Chapter 33

A Heartbeat
Skipped

Nicholas Oliver was displeased. He had been called to London by the uncles of the young king, Thomas and Edward Seymour. Edward Seymour, the Earl of Hertford, had been appointed the "Lord Protector" of the king, who was considered, at the age of nine, too young to rule. Nicholas thought he had been called to review the state of the king's jewels, but found himself in the midst of a hornet's nest of jealousy. The Earl of Hertford's wife, Anne, was an arrogant, grasping woman. Since the day of Edward's coronation, she had been scheming to get what she felt was her fair share of crown jewels since her husband was the protector of King Edward. What had begun as "skirmishes" were mounting into battles, especially when Thomas Seymour began to openly court the newly widowed queen, Catherine Parr, the stepmother to the young king and to Princesses Elizabeth and Mary. Courting aggressively to the point that Nicholas had been summoned on this day to discuss a wedding ring for Catherine. Her late husband, Henry VIII, had been in the grave not yet three months!

But perhaps worst of all was that he felt haunted— haunted by the beautiful gold rose pendant that he had created for his beloved Rosemary. He had been shocked to see Princess Elizabeth wearing it, and he prayed that she had not discovered the pin for the locket. And now the princess had moved into Catherine's home. The dowager queen felt it was her duty to care for Elizabeth. He had arrived at the appointed hour on this late-March day for yet another discussion about the wedding ring and a necklace.

"Ah, Master Oliver, the dowager queen is in the knot garden awaiting your arrival," the gentleman usher of Chelsea Manor greeted him.

The knot garden, how fitting, Nicholas thought. Every time he visited, he felt as if he were at the nexus of jealousy, politics, jewels, and intrigue—a veritable knot.

A small table had been set near the center of the knot garden, where there was a ring of snapdragons that were almost in full bloom.

The dowager queen and her soon-to-be husband, Thomas Seymour, were sitting at the table holding hands and whispering to one another.

"Ah! Master Oliver." Thomas Seymour jumped to his feet. "You brought the sketches for the design."

"Of course, My Lord."

Nicholas drew the furled drawings from his portable case.

"The Seymour coat of arms with the wings of a hawk rising out of the coronet of a baron," the goldsmith explained as he pointed with his finger to the drawing.

"Yes," Thomas Seymour murmured. "But then again, she is a queen." He clasped the dowager queen's hand and gave it a kiss. "Perhaps some reference is needed, yes?"

"Well, yes," Nicholas replied.

"I have an idea," Queen Catherine offered brightly. "Perhaps we could have atop it the badge of the Tudor Rose? Wouldn't that be wonderful, Thomas? If we are to wed in May, the damask roses are in full bloom. Only symbolic, of course, as in truth there is no such red rose with a white center."

No, thought Nicholas. *She's wrong. At dawn on the first day of its bloom, it can have for a brief few moments a white center.* Rosemary had taught him that, and for that reason he had created the locket. The center petals were not the darker gold of the outer ones but pale gold. And now it seemed every time he came here, he caught glimpses of Princess Elizabeth wearing it. How had she come by it? She had not even been born when he had made it for Rosemary. Perhaps a better question was how had Rosemary lost it?

The goldsmith and his clients concluded their conference. It was decided that the design for the wedding ring would have elements of both families' badges—the wings, the coronet, the rose. To Nicholas Oliver it seemed a rather overwrought design, but he would do it. He picked up his drawings, packed them into his portable case, and set out winding his way through the knot garden and into the rose garden. Though it was still a month from full bloom, it was lovely any time of year. He found the damask roses, their buds still tightly sealed. He reached out his hand and touched one. At that same moment, he heard the giggling of young girls coming down a path. Through the thick tangle of rose vines he saw a flash of gold, gold and red. Princess Elizabeth out for a walk with her ladies-in-waiting. Their gowns grazed the pebbled walk. He watched them for a minute, then heard the sound of feet running up the path toward them. "Your Highness! Your Highness. A message from your brother, His Majesty the King."

He did not have a clear view now, as the princess's companions drew close around her. The figure in a servant's black dress handed her the dispatch. "It came from Hampton Court." The voice intrigued him. An odd accent, yet like a distant echo that was vaguely familiar. He could not see the servant clearly, but as she walked away, there was something about her posture, her gait, that made his heart skip a beat. Nicholas Oliver began to walk as quickly and quietly as possible. Like iron filings to a magnet, he was drawn to this figure. The sky suddenly clouded over, the air turned chilly, and a light drizzle began to fall. He quickened his pace. He heard the princess and her entourage squealing.

"How could it!" demanded the princess, as if only she could call off the sun and invoke the rain. "Rose! Our cloaks. Our cloaks!" At this point the servant in black paused, seemed to laugh, and turned around.

"Rose!" Nicholas Oliver gasped. *My Rose, our Rose.* Her face was nearly identical to her mother's, but he could see a bit of himself as well. There was a flash of orange as a cat crossed the path and a mist engulfed them. Then they simply dissolved into the thickening fog.

Chapter 34

"Just Say Her Father"

Rose and Susan, *along with Anand, Myles, and Joe, leaning on* crutches, watched as the Mean Queens and Sibby trooped out of the principal's office. Sibby looked positively ghostly. Her chin trembled. Rose's heart went out to her. She walked over to her and took her hand.

"It'll be all right, Sibby. You did a brave thing."

"No." Carrie glared. "It's not going to be all right."

"We aren't done with either of you yet!" Lisa spat.

Susan stepped forward. She stood in front of Lisa. She inhaled deeply. Everyone fell silent. Her voice was no longer a sandy whisper, nor was it a roar. But it cut, cut like a finely honed blade.

"You're wrong. You are done. All three of you. One more trick like this and I report you under Public Act 11-232, which makes it a violation of IC Title 42. Criminal Law and Procedure." She paused and took another breath, then continued. "Title 42 basically clears the way for criminal prosecution in bullying cases. And that means that my father, Samuel Gold, as attorney general of Indiana, can prosecute the three of you! So Carrie, you can just forget about your ambulance-chasing dad busting Myles for reckless driving in a wheelchair. You'll be up for a hate crime." Rose looked at Susan in awe. She was as commanding as any monarch, and Carrie, Brianna, and Lisa seemed to almost shrink before their eyes. Then they all three turned and walked away.

Joe gasped. "Susan, how did you know all that?" His eyes were shining with admiration.

"I didn't really." The sandy whisper had returned. "I mean, the only part that is true is that my father is the attorney general. And I know that there were obstacles in the way of prosecuting hate crimes that are slowly being cleared. But that's all."

"Well, it sure worked with them!" Myles said.

❋

The news had rolled through the school and was the cause for an "intervention." This meant that an outside consultant was to be called in to give workshops to teachers, parents, and students on strategies for everything from sportsman-ship to combating bullying. Essays had to be written by students as well as teachers. "Implementation programs" for building a safe environment, for encouraging respect and positive behavior, were to be explored and discussed. The Mean Queens were not singled out as criminals, much to Rose's disappointment, but as having "aberrant behavior."

"A synonym for being a jerk," Myles said.

"They aren't going to change," Anand said, shaking his head.

"Put them in the Tower," Rose muttered. The boys looked at her.

"Huh? What tower?" Myles asked.

Rose paused. "Um, I'm not sure why I said that." It was as if a fragment of a dream had blown across her mind. "Forget it."

But Rose didn't forget. All day she felt as if she had been haunted by a dream. Even during her riding lesson after school, where she did in fact jump sidesaddle on Ivy. "Beautiful!" Peter called out as she floated over the jump. *I'm yielding,* she thought. *Yielding to the air.*

She had her usual dinner with Gran in the greenhouse. They planted some seedling bachelor's buttons and trans-planted some pansies that would eventually be put along their front walk in April. Rose asked if Gran had any plans for snapdragons.

"Never!" Gran growled.

"I guess you put them in the poinsettia category."

"Worse. Snarly little things. Ugly as sin in my mind. Freakishly gaudy." *Hmmm*, thought Rose. *Sort of like Lisa.*

"I get the picture, Gran. You don't like them."

"'Abhor' is a better word."

Rose went to bed before Gran for the first time. She wasn't sure how long she had been asleep when she woke up, suddenly, not from a dream but from the memory of one that had haunted her all day. There had been fog. Chill, damp air, and she was standing in a rose garden that was not yet in bloom, a grand house in the distance. She had just delivered a message to Princess Elizabeth when she spied the figure of a man. She had turned around. Or was it that the man had turned around? It didn't matter. In an instant she knew that it was her father. She had to get back. She just had to.

Climbing out of bed, she pulled on a pair of leggings, woolly socks, and her down vest. It never seemed to matter what she wore, since by the time she was back serving Elizabeth, she was always dressed in her proper servant's dress and French hood.

She would go to the greenhouse. Perhaps she should go to the conservatory, for the rose was still in full bloom. She looked at the clock. It was almost two o'clock in the morning: 1:57 a.m. Long before dawn and hardly the bewitching hour, but maybe. As she entered the conservatory, the rose was dazzlingly beautiful even in the dim light. She must remember what her grandmother had said when she had described the moment she learned how to swim so long ago.

To float and not to sink. It seems like a foreign language for your body. You come so close but you just can't quite do it. And then one day it happens.... So much of life is yielding to the extraordinary.

"Yes, Gran," she whispered, and then imagined herself back on Ivy, and felt just as she had that afternoon while riding sidesaddle—girl, sky, pony!

And now once more she yielded to the extraordinary.

Chapter 35

A Glimpse

"**H**uzzah!" *Prince Edward cried out as he watched Rose sail* over the hedge on the pony. It had been Edward, of course, who had insisted that Rose join Princess Elizabeth and Princess Mary on a ride through the countryside. "How well you took that jump, Rose."

"Thank you, Your Majesty," Rose said.

"Completely improper," Princess Mary sniffed, and cut a disapproving glance at her brother.

"I think not, dear sister," Princess Elizabeth said. "Rose is like a playmate for Edward. He enjoys her thoroughly."

"Kings do not have playmates," Princess Mary said, and urged her horse on.

"What a jerk!" muttered Elizabeth. She had picked up the word after hearing Rose use it once under her breath in reference to Lady Margaret. Lady Margaret had been trying to impress the king and praising him in a most outlandish and ridiculous manner.

Rose herself, although happy to be riding, was eager to get back to Hampton Court, the most lavish of all the palaces. Edward had told her that with the upcoming May Day celebrations in mind, he had commissioned medals in honor of his late father. Medals meant that Nicholas Oliver might be coming to deliver them. She couldn't wait to get back and share the news with Franny. She and Franny now shared a room at Hampton Court, as Franny had been officially promoted from scullery to the kitchen proper.

When they finally returned to the horse yard and the stables, Andrew was waiting for her.

"You sit well, Miss Rose. I saw you canter out." He flashed her a grin and his dimples grew deeper. Oh dear, he was cute. She was tempted to bask in that smile of his. It was warm as sunshine, though the day had turned suddenly cloudy.

"Over here, boy!" Princess Mary cawed. "Since when do you serve a servant before a royal princess? That's punishable, you know."

"Sorry, Your Highness. I thought her saddle looked loose and was about to slip." He turned, and just as he dashed to aid Princess Mary, Rose heard him mutter, "Fiendish thing!"

Rose's eyes followed him. Again she was struck by the

similarity between the way Andrew and Jamie both walked.

Then she headed off to change out of her riding clothes and into her servant ones.

A few minutes later she burst into the kitchen, where Franny was on her knees, scrubbing the stone floor. Rose dropped to her own knees, seized a rag, and began scrubbing.

"Rose, you can't scrub in your serving kirtle. You'll ruin it."

"I don't care," Rose whispered. "I have news, Franny!"

"What news?" Franny rested back on her heels.

"He's coming!" She paused. "Or I think he might be."

"Your father?"

"Yes. Prince Edward told me that he has commanded some medallions to be made and presented on May Day." Franny seemed unusually quiet. "Aren't you happy for me, Franny?"

"Yes, yes, of course," she replied in a subdued voice. The color had drained from Franny's face. Her lower lip began to quiver.

"What is it, Franny? Looks like you've seen a ghost."

"Oh, no, nothing. Nothing at all." But the smile she flashed was more of a grimace, and there was something. Rose was sure of it. Again Rose felt that Franny had a secret, a deep and very dark secret.

"Come on, I'm done here," Franny said quickly. "Let's go

back and take a rest. I've got to be down here to help Cook pluck the geese and the swan."

"I hate that," mumbled Rose.

"Hate what?"

"Eating swan. They're so beautiful. And haven't you ever heard the story of the Ugly Duckling?"

"Never."

Oh right, thought Rose. *Hans Christian Andersen hasn't been born yet.*

❉

Rose and Franny walked through the shadowy halls of Hampton Court toward their room off the kitchen, just as Nicholas Oliver was riding from the north on the King's Highway. He had two missions: the medals, and to see if his daughter might be there in service to Princess Elizabeth. May Day was a favorite holiday of the young king's, as there were jousts and masques and acrobats. It was also his favorite time to bestow medals. The court, of course, had been consumed with the festivities.

Whenever Nicholas came to court, especially if Princess Elizabeth was there, he always wondered if he might see the girl Rose. But in full court there were hundreds of people occupying the palaces. They were, in fact, like small cities.

He often felt he had almost caught a glimpse of her, but

then she seemed to vanish. His trips had been infrequent, however, as these had been dangerous times and the king feared that the Seymours would suspect Nicholas Oliver was up to something more than simply hammering gold into royal medals for the court.

That poor young king had been through a devil of a time with those mad, power-hungry Seymours. Nicholas would never forget the night that a messenger came to him from Windsor Castle just three years before with a short note. It was in a code known as the Cardan grille, which involved shuffling the letters of the alphabet in a particular sequence and then placing a sheet with punched holes over the message so that only the relevant letters would be revealed. Nicholas was able to quickly decode it. The message from the young king read, *Methinks I am a prisoner here in my own castle.*

In fact, his protector, Edward Seymour, now the Duke of Somerset, had issued a proclamation that insisted on the protection of the king's safety, and had removed him to Windsor Palace without consent of the Privy Council. That had been the beginning of the end of the Seymours. The goldsmith had ridden like fury to alert the Duke of Warwick and other members of the council. Within twenty-four hours, Edward Seymour was arrested and imprisoned in the Tower of London. Within a very short time, Nicholas

Oliver had become King Edward's favorite and most productive spy. He had the ideal cover—goldsmith to the royal court.

Now he had been summoned again, under the guise of delivering new designs for medals, but in fact to report as well on Princess Mary. The rise in her popularity alarmed King Edward, who was fiercely Protestant. He worried about those who were perhaps wobbling in their devotion to his father's creation, the Church of England.

When Nicholas Oliver arrived the following day, he took his horse to the stables and then walked through the main gate of Hampton Court. He could see that the entire west courtyard was festooned with flowers and no fewer than four maypoles. In the center of the courtyard, a throne had been set up for the king. In the Clock Court, jugglers and acrobats were practicing, and fools and dwarfs were indulging in their usual antics. As the clock struck ten that morning, trumpets began to blow the royal fanfare, announcing the arrival of the king. Edward was now almost fifteen, but he had the stature and size of a boy much younger. As he walked up the steps of the throne and seated himself, the slight king seemed swallowed by the throne. But he appeared happy. His cheeks were rosy and he appeared in good health.

Perhaps this was wishful thinking on Nicholas Oliver's

part. He lived in dread of the possibility of Princess Mary's ascension to the throne if anything happened to King Edward. She was a peculiar woman. Her religious beliefs were not simply fanatic but bordered on violence. He had witnessed too often the flogging of a servant whom she suspected of heresy. Dressed in fine gowns but with bare knees, she would crawl on stone to offer her prayers to the Virgin Mary. She was so proud of those knees if they were bloodied by the end of the ritual. It was rumored that she beat herself on Good Friday in penitence for Christ's crucifixion.

Nicholas Oliver had had enough of Princess Mary, and his heart lightened as he saw Princess Elizabeth take her place with her own ladies-in-waiting at the maypole nearest to the king's throne, her red hair flowing over her shoulders. She first curtsied deeply to the king and then gave him a jaunty wave. The air rippled with the multitude of colored ribbons fluttering in the light breeze. The May Day dancers arranged themselves, as many as twenty at one of the poles. At another pole were the wives and children of the king's Privy Council. Another was for the royal servants, those who were part of the lord chamberlain's office and those of the lower household. The dancing began, and the dwarfs and the fools commenced cartwheeling between the poles.

Oh, there's the bonny girl
And there's a bonny boy
And in the middle a bonny tree
The finest tree you ever did see
Oh hidee hee, hidee ho
And on this limb there was a branch,
The finest branch you ever did see,
The branch was on the limb,
Oh, there's a bonny girl ...

"There *is* a bonny girl!" Nicholas Oliver gasped. It was Rose. His Rose. She was dancing at the servants' pole. Her French hood had slipped back, and the rich copper curls flowed free. She was here! Here in the courtyard. He must see her. He had to find a time to speak to her alone. There would be feasting and dancing throughout the day and far into the night. He watched her as she gaily danced around the pole, braiding her ribbon with the others. Princess Elizabeth was considered pretty, but Rose was lovelier. Her eyes sparkled in the morning sunshine. She moved with an ineffable grace.

Nicholas Oliver could not help but remember Rosemary at a similar celebration at Greenwich. All seemed joyous that day, but the very next day Queen Anne Boleyn, wife of Henry VIII, mother of Princess Elizabeth, was arrested and taken to the Tower of London. Seventeen days later, on

Tower Green, her head was chopped off. The king, in his unending thoughtfulness, had imported a French swordsman. They were said to be quite skilled, and the sword rather than an ax was said to be more humane. Those were dangerous times, and by summer Rosemary left.

He had not seen her since then. Rose would have been six, for she was born in that world of Rosemary's three years prior to Princess Elizabeth. And now the princess was older than Rose. For in that peculiar flow of time between these two distant centuries, those of his century aged while the travelers, the visitors from that future time, never did. Would his Rosemary have some gray in her hair now, as he did? So much time had elapsed. The princess was now close to twenty, but Rose would only be thirteen at the oldest. Nicholas kept track of such things. Early on, Rosemary had brought him a calendar from her world. In her world it was now the twenty-first century. Five hundred years ahead of his world and the Tudor Court.

He put these thoughts aside. The only intention he had now was to meet his daughter. He would make himself scarce for the rest of the day until evening, when most of the people were well into their cups and might not notice if he carefully approached her.

He watched her, followed her discreetly. Rose seemed to be constantly in the accompaniment of a slight, blond girl who walked with a limp and often used a crutch. From the girl's clothing he guessed she was a kitchen worker.

He lost both the girls just as darkness began to steal the daylight. They had seemed to go separate ways, with the blond girl headed for the kitchen yards. But where was Rose heading? Was this going to be like the first time he spotted Rose at Chelsea Manor, when she seemed to magically dissolve into the fog? He continued searching. The palace was huge. He was unsure of where Princess Elizabeth's apartments were in the vast complex. He was now alone in the gallery that was said to be haunted by the late queen Catherine Howard. With some sixth sense he had developed as a spy, he became acutely conscious of someone following him. He heard a scuttling sound. Not a rat. But shoes. Small shoes on small feet. He wheeled about. There was nothing.

Then suddenly a shadow slid out from behind the statuary of a rearing lion with a crown atop its head. The shadow melded with that of the lion—Kynges beasts, they were called, and this one was modeled after Henry VIII's favorite lion in the royal menagerie. Nicholas caught his breath. A dwarf he'd seen many times before was standing in the shadow that devoured her own. He recognized her. It was Bettina, dressed in the same pink silk gown as her mistress had worn, with an overlay of broad stripes in several colors suggesting the ribbons of the maypole.

He caught his breath, shocked by the vision of the little

woman, then addressed her sharply. "Why are you following me, dwarf?"

"My name is Bettina. She would have never called me 'dwarf.' She knows I am more than my size."

"What? Who knows what?"

"Your daughter. Rose Ashley."

Nicholas closed his eyes tight. He took a long, deep breath and then began to speak slowly. "How do you know she's my daughter?"

"She looks so much like you."

"Do you feel anyone else knows?" They had begun walking side by side. The tiny woman hardly reached his waist, and he had slowed his pace.

"No, no one pays attention to servants. They have a blind spot when it comes to us. We are like air. They just move through us, never giving pause."

"But you did."

"I gave pause because she gave pause for me."

"What exactly do you mean?"

"The court regards people like myself as a curious little aberration that was created by God for the sole entertainment of royalty and court. Your daughter, Rose, sees things differently. I'm not sure why. I'm not sure where she comes from that she should have been . . ." Bettina hesitated. "Blessed with this kind of vision of seeing things differently."

"And how do you know this? Are you a close friend?"

"Not really." Bettina was thinking back to that day when Rose had dared chide the princess for her remarks on how useless dwarfs were. "The Princess Elizabeth does not actually care for the entertainment dwarfs provide. The princess had declared that tumbling dwarfs were so useless. I apologized for not being more entertaining. The princess said she had meant no offense."

Bettina went on. "I could see that Rose was carefully listening, for she was absolutely seething with anger. And do you know what that saucy girl did?"

Bettina continued to answer her own question. "She cried out on my behalf. She said very loudly, 'The whole thing is offensive.' I tell you, Master Oliver, the entire room went silent. Everyone was stunned. And Rose was not finished. She turned to the princess and said, 'Pardon me, milady. But I find it very offensive that this short woman is regarded as merely an object of amusement. It's . . . it's . . . it's simply awful to treat a human being this way. Shame on you! Shame on you all!' Then she stomped her foot."

"Good gracious. And she kept her head? Wasn't sent to the Tower?"

"No, sir; I think the princess secretly admired her boldness. Her boldness and her wit." She inhaled deeply. She raised a hand to her eye and wiped a tear. "She showed me respect. Nobody in my life has ever shown me such kindness. My parents were embarrassed and hid me away, but when times were bad and we'd come near to starving on our small croft, my mother heard that they were looking for dwarfs at court. So she took me to Richmond Palace. I was given as a gift to the king's new bride, Queen Anne Boleyn, and my parents were give ten bushels of groats a year, a dozen chickens, and a lamb every spring. I was worth a lot, they told me, and pinched my cheeks. I was 'valuable,' but I was not human."

"I'm sorry, Bettina. I do remember you from Queen Anne's court."

"No need to feel sorry. Your daughter has more than made up for so much."

"Would you help me meet with her? Could you perhaps take a message to her?"

"Certainly, sir"

Nicholas rubbed his chin as he thought about how he should do this. A note? No, notes had a way of getting lost, then found by the wrong people. As a spy he sent only coded notes. "Tell her to meet me when the clock tower chimes midnight in the rose garden. She must know the rose garden."

"Oh yes, sir, she walks there every day with the princess. She especially likes the circle of the damask roses. They attract the loveliest hummingbirds."

"She likes the damask ones, does she?"

"Indeed, sir."

"Then tell her to meet me at the damask circle."

"But whom shall I tell her she is meeting?"

"Just say . . ." He paused. "Her father."

Chapter 36

The Damask
Circle

Rose's heart was racing as she wrapped the shawl more tightly around herself and walked into the kitchen gardens, then around to a lane leading to the rose garden. Ever since Bettina had crept into her bedroom, tapped her shoulder, and awakened her, Rose's mind had swirled with a zillion questions. How had she not seen him herself? What if he didn't like her? What if she was a disappointment to him? And if they did like each other, what kind of life could they have? Could she go back to Stow-on-the-Wold and live with her own dad? It struck her now most forcefully that in fact she was no longer an orphan! But should she live here with her father, Nicholas Oliver, or—she hardly dared imagine it—was there any possibility he could somehow pass through that rip in time and go back to Gran's house with her? But what would a goldsmith from Stow-on-the-Wold, England, in the year 1553 be able to do in modern-day Indianapolis?

Her mind began to buzz with all sorts of difficulties he would encounter. He couldn't drive a car, for one thing. He'd have to get inoculations—polio, flu shots, tetanus. And his clothing. She tried to imagine this father whom she'd never met in, say, jeans, a plaid flannel shirt, and a North Face parka!

She had just passed a pathway to the tiltyard when a spray of moonlight illuminated the gates of the rose garden. A shift in the wind brought the heady scent of the pink tea roses that clambered over the brick walls of the garden. She ran through the gates. A few petals swirled about her ankles. She turned down a path where immense yellow blossoms burst like a gathering of suns in the shadows of the night.

She stopped and caught her breath. There at the end of this row was a figure standing by the circle of damask roses. He was very still, his hands clasped behind his back. She couldn't quite believe what might happen. Should she call out to him? Run to him and embrace him? She suddenly was frightened, nervous—like an actor waiting for her cue to stride onstage, yet worried about forgetting her lines. She began to walk slowly toward him. He turned and leaned forward a bit, peering into the darkness. Now the moon had completely vanished behind clouds.

"Rose!"

"Dad!" She tore down the path. She felt herself embraced. He was picking her up; her feet left the ground. He was a tall man. Much taller than most of the men of the court.

"Rose! Rose!" he kept saying.

"Dad!"

"Your mother said that's what you would call me if we ever met. She's right, she's always right." He took a step back and, still holding her hands, seemed to almost inhale the vision before him. "She's right about your eyes too, green like hers. But you're tall like me. I guess you got your height from me, though precious little else." He looked at her through the scrim of tears in his eyes.

"Well, I can't make jewelry, Dad. But I sew."

"Oh, your mother sews so beautifully."

Then it struck Rose. *He doesn't know she's dead.* "And how is she, Rose?" The words came out in a rush now. "She left that last time. It was a dangerous time, but she promised to come back. She will now, won't she? Now that you've come."

"Dad, Dad." Rose lifted her hand to her father's lips to gently stop this storm of words.

"Rose, why are you crying so?"

Like waves crashing on a beach, sobs were breaking from her, racking her whole body. "Come come, dear, let's sit on the bench right over there." He helped her to the bench. "She's still not worried about those times, is she? Times are better now. Safer. At least as long as King Edward lives."

"Dad, it's not that. It's not the Tower. It's not beheadings. There are other dangers in our world." Nicholas Oliver's mouth began to quiver. It was almost as if his mouth could not find the shape of the word he wanted to say.

"Whh . . . what other dangers? The sweating disease. Did she catch the sweating disease?"

"No. Cars."

"Cars," he said vaguely.

"Dad, Mom is dead. She was killed in a car accident."

He crumpled forward, grasping his knees. His eyes seemed to twitch with a strange look of incomprehension. "Cars," he said. "Automobiles."

"Yes, Dad. Did Mom tell you about them?"

"A little. She drove one. It was hard to imagine."

"I suppose so. But sometimes there are accidents. Bad accidents where the car crashes and catches fire."

"Fire!"

"Yes," she said in a small voice. She couldn't tell him the horrible part, the "no remains" part. "She died."

"Oh my God!" His broad back heaved and a most awful

sound escaped from the deepest part of his chest. Rose wrapped her arms around him. He buried his head in her shoulder. She was uncertain how long they remained clasping each other. Finally, the quaking sound of his weeping subsided. He drew out a large cloth and wiped his nose. She could see the effort it took for him to speak again. "And where have you been living?"

"With my grandmother."

"In Indianapolis?" Just the name of that city coming out of her father's mouth somehow shocked Rose.

"You know about Indianapolis?"

"Yes, a Midwestern city in the state of Indiana. She said it was bordered on the west by Illinois, east Ohio, south Kentucky, north Michigan."

"Jeez, you're good. I mean with geography."

"Well, what can I say? It was always hard for your mother and me to locate ourselves in time. Luckily our paths occasionally crossed. But I always wanted to locate myself in space, on Earth. I've heard about what your century's done in space. The moon and all."

"That was actually the last century, Dad."

"Oh, the mere twentieth century. Yes, the moon landing! What's his name, Neil Armstrong? Your mother told me about it." He took a deep breath and looked at her again. This time taking in her every feature, every freckle. "So you like it, living there with your grandmother?"

Rose shrugged. "It's . . . it's all right, but . . ."

"But what, dear?"

Rose started to cry again. "I'm sort of a half orphan, you know. I'd like it better if you were there too."

"If I were there? But how could that work? I know so little about your century, your culture. I'd stick out like a sore thumb."

"No, you wouldn't, Dad. Look at me. Do I stick out here?"

"No, you don't. Nor did your mum, except perhaps for her accent."

"But Dad, wouldn't you at least consider it?"

"Of course I'd consider it. You're my daughter. The only child I have. But what would I do there?"

"You'd be a goldsmith, like here."

"But how would I get there? When you go back, how does it happen?"

"It doesn't seem to be in my control, Dad. Just kind of a whim. A whim of time."

"Yes, your mother couldn't exactly explain it to me either."

"Tell me one thing, Dad. When she did leave, did it seem as if she were gone a long time?"

"Not exactly. One minute she was there. Then she'd be back, and it might have been in her time, twenty-first-century time, days or even months since her last visit. But the most peculiar thing was that I was never exactly aware of her being gone." He bent down and picked up a rose blossom by his feet. "It was almost like this rose. The scent lingered. I didn't seem to be fully conscious that she was gone—until these last few years."

"Years, you say?"

"Yes, years."

"Interesting, because in truth, Dad, Mom only died a few months ago."

"Really?"

"Yes. If there is a way, will you come back with me?"

"How can you ask? Would I not follow the only thing on this Earth that I love? You are all I have left. Of course, dear child. I'll go with you to the end of time, to the end of space, and place. I'd cross oceans and borders—borders between centuries and between Kentucky and Indiana or Ohio or Michigan."

These ordinary names sounded almost magical now in Rose's ears. But most magical of all was that she was here, sitting in this rose-scented garden with her very own father. She was no longer an orphan.

Chapter 37

Three Awful Girls

*T*hat same night, close to dawn, Rose crept into their bedroom and wakened Franny. One look at Rose's face told Franny everything.

"You found him!"

"I did. He's here now. At least for a while. And he thinks that Princess Elizabeth is moving back to Hatfield soon. Then we'll be even closer. I want you to meet him, Franny. He's so . . . so wonderful."

"Aaah . . . ," Franny said sweetly. "I'm happy for you, Rose. Too bad your mum isn't here. You could be one happy family." Franny immediately noticed the change in Rose's face. "What is it, Rose?"

"It's about my mother, Franny. I had to tell him she was dead."

"He didn't know?"

"No."

"But she died a long time ago, right?" There was a shadow of anxiety in Franny's voice. They both seemed to sense that they were approaching a difficult, possibly perilous subject.

"Well, sort of a long time ago, Franny. But not exactly."

"What do you mean?"

"Franny, I don't know how to say this . . . b-b-b-but . . . b-but . . . but I have a secret."

"You do?" Franny said in a barely audible voice. She looked down as if to avoid Rose's gaze. Rose reached out and grasped Franny's hands. Franny shifted her gaze to the floor. It was as if she were evading Rose's eyes at all costs. The color was creeping up her neck to her face.

"Franny, might you have a secret too?"

"Maybe," she mumbled.

"Franny, I'm going to tell you mine, but you don't have to tell me yours." There was only silence. "Franny, my secret is that I . . . I come from another time."

"What time might that be?"

Rose took a deep breath. "A time almost five hundred years from now."

"So you are a traveler, a time gypsy." Franny raised her

head. Her blue eyes were clear and wide with wonder.

"A time gypsy?"

"Yes." Franny paused several seconds. "And so am I."

"You are?"

"That is my secret."

"From what time?"

"From 1692. Salem, Massachusetts," Franny said softly. Rose felt a coldness course through her. That was a terrible date and a terrible time. The Salem witch trials. This was unbelievable. She was sitting at a table with a girl from Salem, Massachusetts.

"You were a witch?"

"Not me; my mum was said to be one. You know about that?"

"Of course. Every kid knows about it. It's a terrible part of our history. We learn about it in school."

"It all started with these three awful girls." *Three awful girls.* The words tolled like a death knell in Rose's head. She knew three awful girls. Not much changed in four hundred years. "Their names were Abigail Williams, and her cousin Betty Parris, and her friend Ann Putnam. The meanest girls in the colony."

"Yeah," Rose said softly.

"You know mean girls too?"

"Oh yeah." Rose rolled her eyes.

Epilogue

*S*hortly *after Rose and her father had found each other and after the* court had moved to Greenwich for the summer, word flew around the palace that King Edward was suffering from a congestion in the chest that the physicians called a *catarrh*. The mood at court became somber and then anxious. The king was not improving but getting worse. A steady stream of doctors and councillors filed into the king's bed-chamber.

Princess Mary, who'd been far away at Hunsdon House, which she had been given upon the death of her father, suddenly appeared at Greenwich. There was a palpable chill between the two princesses.

On the afternoon of July 6, the two princesses were called to the king's bedside by Sir John Mason, first gentleman of the king's bedchamber. Elizabeth grasped Rose's hand before she left.

"Pray come with me, Rose. He likes you and I'm fearful of going alone. I have no stomach for death." It was the only time Rose could recall seeing Elizabeth fearful. But was it death she feared, or was it her sister, Mary?

Rose had no stomach for death either, but they proceeded to the king's chamber. At the door they met Princess Mary, who was clutching her rosary beads. Elizabeth nodded, and then her eyes fell on Mary's beads.

"You think it wise, dear sister, to enter your brother's chamber clutching the beads of the faith he has rejected?"

"He should thank me," Mary replied. Elizabeth said nothing.

They proceeded into the chamber. The stench was terrible.

A nurse carrying a pan of vomit passed them. "It's not the vomit you smell, dear. It's the suppurating tumors," she said, and rushed on.

The king was in a feverish state, but when one of his attendants whispered that his sisters, the royal princesses, had arrived, his mind seemed to clear a bit.

"Ahh, and did she bring the girl?"

Elizabeth and Mary exchanged glances. "Whom do you

mean, dear brother?" Mary asked.

"Not you, sister."

"Me?" Elizabeth asked.

"Yes, did you bring the girl? The one named Rose."

"Indeed, sir, she is here."

Rose stepped forward. She was shocked by his appearance. His skin was erupting in boils. His face was gray. His hands were bloated, and it appeared his fingernails were falling away.

"You remember the tree hollow where we first played, Rose?"

He gasped as his voice grew weaker, but he struggled to continue. "And when you and Elizabeth and I went riding? I insisted that you go. And my goodness, Elizabeth and I were surprised at your skill when you dared to jump that high hedge."

All these faded memories began to tumble through Rose's head. Like a tapestry, these scenes began to kindle in her mind.

"And when we played quoits, you taught us the eeny meeny miney moe . . . out goes one . . . out goes two . . . out goes another one, and that leaves . . ." Then his eyes rolled back into his head. Rose looked up at Princess Mary. A smirk had begun to crawl across her face, and Rose could have sworn that the princess said, "And that leaves me!"

Princess Mary narrowed her eyes and shot darting

glances around the chamber. Glances of expectation. There was a terrible stillness, and then Sir John Mason dropped to his knees.

"The king is dead," he said. "God save the queen."

❊

A message arrived for Rose early the next morning.

> *Following Mass, at which your attendance is required, the queen requests you in the presence room.*

At precisely half past eight, following the morning Mass, Rose entered the presence room of the new Queen Mary. Her back was turned as she gazed out a window. She was a stumpy woman but had the regal bearing of a queen. When she turned round, Rose gasped as her eyes fell on the rose pendant. Her rose pendant! Mary must have demanded it from Elizabeth. What else would she demand?

"Rose Ashley, we hear you are excellent in the wardrobe, have a way with a needle, and can do fine and delicate work. You shall from here on be our mistress of the wardrobe."

"I . . . I . . ."

"Out with it, girl."

"I shall no longer serve the Royal Princess Elizabeth?"

"No, you shall serve me, queen of this realm, and swear loyalty to me above all others save God. Do you swear?

Down on your knees and swear."

Rose must have hesitated for a moment.

"DOWN!" barked the queen.

Rose fell to her knees.

"I swear, Your Majesty."

But Rose crossed her fingers in the deep pocket of her dress.

Never, never, never!

KATHRYN LASKY is a *New York Times* bestselling author of many acclaimed children's and young adult books, which include her latest historical fiction novel, *Night Witches*. Her picture book *Sugaring Time* was awarded a Newbery Honor. She has twice won the National Jewish Book Award, for her novel *The Night Journey* and her picture book *Marven of the Great North Woods*. Her book *Elizabeth I: Red Rose of the House of Tudor* was the most popular book in Scholastic's bestselling Royal Diaries series. Her bestselling series Guardians of Ga'Hoole was made into the Warner Bros. movie *Legend of the Guardians: The Owls of Ga'Hoole*. She lives in Cambridge, Massachusetts, with her husband.

www.kathrynlasky.com

⌒ Author photo by Jean Fogelberg and Fran Forman ⌒

Read on for an excerpt from
Tangled in Time 2: The Burning Queen!

Chapter 1

Fingers
Crossed

"*Never . . . never . . . never!*" *Rose muttered in her head.* Her fingers were crossed and still jammed in her pockets, but the pockets were different—not the deep ones of her kirtle but tight shallow jeans pockets. The floor was hard beneath her knees—not wood, but stone or cement. And the scent. Fresher. And yet she still had her eyes clamped shut. She was almost afraid to open them. The last thing she had been aware of was a slight smell. Yes, Queen Mary, who now wanted to enslave her, did have a little body odor problem. Why didn't they have real deodorant in the sixteenth century, instead of those stupid little cloth bags filled with dried flower petals?

But the scent that swirled about Rose now was not of

dried flowers but fresh, just-blossoming flowers. A sweet, alluring fragrance suffused the air. Slowly Rose opened her eyes. She looked up. A fifteen-foot vine with beautiful pink blooms fell through the darkness. The vines could have been fireworks mutely exploding in the night. But they weren't. They were hibiscus, and they were cascading from the central cupola of the greenhouse. She was back! Back in her grandmother Rosalinda's greenhouse. Back in Indianapolis, Indiana. Back in what she now called her home century.

But was she *safe*? She uncrossed her fingers. She looked around. The words of the nasty queen, Mary Tudor, still rang in her ears. *Rose Ashley, we hear you are excellent in the wardrobe, have a way with a needle, and can do fine and delicate work. You shall from here on be our mistress of the wardrobe.... You shall serve me, queen of this realm, and swear loyalty to me above all others save God. Do you swear? Down on your knees and swear.* That was when Rose had crossed her fingers and lied to this new queen.

Rose had previously served Princess Elizabeth, who, although very demanding and imperious, was not the nasty piece of work that Queen Mary was. However, when their half brother, King Edward—barely fifteen—had died, Mary had ascended the throne, to everyone's horror.

That was the bad news. Not just for Rose, who would have to serve this vile piece of royal nastiness. But also bad news for Princess Elizabeth. Mary liked to take things that belonged to Elizabeth. She was insanely jealous of her half sister—of her youth, for one thing, since Queen Mary was seventeen years older. But she was also envious of Elizabeth's beauty and her smarts. Elizabeth was the smartest kid Rose had ever met. She was insanely smart—spoke French, Italian, Latin—yes, she actually spoke Latin! If she had lived in the twenty-first century and been in Rose's school, she could have been a mathlete and gone to the state championship.

Elizabeth was already doing trigonometry when she was just eleven years old. In Rose's home century, you didn't do that until high school. When Rose had once asked Elizabeth if she knew calculus, the princess's face turned blank. And when she asked Rose to explain what calculus was, Rose's mind turned blank. She almost blurted out, "How should I know? That's not until high school." But she stopped herself in the nick of time. As soon as she got back to her home century, she googled calculus and found out it hadn't been discovered until the seventeenth century! By Isaac Newton, no less.

Well, no matter how you looked at it, Queen Mary was definitely bad news. This was in fact a typical bad news/good news situation. The good news—Rose was back. The bad news was that her father, Nicholas Oliver, was not with her, nor was her sixteenth-century best friend, Franny. Then, just as she was reflecting on all this, she felt something brush against her leg. Good news! September! She gasped and reached for the bright orange cat. Picking her up, she pressed her to her chest. The cat wiggled and began head-butting Rose. Head-butting was the supreme expression of affection for cats. Sometimes September did not return with Rose to their home century but lingered in the sixteenth instead. Better mousing back then, due to lousy housekeeping habits. All the palaces had stables chock-full of mice and other less charming rodents.

As she walked upstairs to her bedroom, Rose felt the sudden vibration of her cell phone in the other pocket of her jeans. She took it out and looked at it. The time was 8:45 p.m. and it was Susan calling, of course. Susan Gold was Rose's best friend in her home century.

"Hey, Rose, what's up?" Susan said cheerfully.

Rose was always a bit disoriented when she first returned to the present day. "Uh . . ." She couldn't answer immediately.

"Whatcha been up to?"

"Uh . . . French homework." A sort-of lie. She had been doing it before she'd left. But the fact was, none of her friends knew about this. This . . . was there any other word for it? Rose had a definitely weird skill, this *ability* of hers. She could travel through time. Was it a skill or her fate? Rose often wondered.

"I thought you'd be sewing with all those new bow tie orders. Not to mention the costumes for the Snow Show."

Rose glanced over at the costumes piled on a futon in the corner of her bedroom. They were awaiting their final touches, which meant glitter and glitz. Skaters loved the glitz—sequins, feathers, whatever. The costumes were designed to dazzle AND accentuate the skater's motion. A jump was all the more beautiful with a fringe of glittery spangles sewn to the hem of a skating skirt. Fake feathers attached to sleeves suggested flight. Seams were often accentuated with rhinestones. To study up on all this, the Indianapolis Skating Club had given her tickets for her and two friends (Joe and Susan) to see the *Disney on Ice* show. They even got to go backstage and look at the costumes. The wardrobe mistress gave a few old ones to Rose so she could study them. Apparently a single costume only lasted for a couple of weeks during show season.

"The costumes are almost done," Rose said. "Just have to sew on some fringe and stuff. Then I'll get to work on this last order of bow ties." She yawned.

"You sound tired, Rose."

"Hmmm . . ." She was about to say that you would be too if you'd traveled back five centuries and watched a prince die and a complete rat get the crown, and then were made to get down on your knees and swear to serve that rat queen. Not to mention—Dad! *I miss my dad.* Tears started to run down her face. She couldn't cry on the phone with Susan. There was no way she could explain it all to her.

"Listen, I have to go. This French is hard. I don't really get the difference between the *passé composé* and *passé antérieur.*" Rose sighed.

"Oh, one is really for speaking, like 'We went to the Louvre.' *Nous sommes allées au Louvre.* The other is *nous eûmes au Louvre,* and that's just for literary use, you know, in books. The first one is kind of regular time. The second is when you're in a literary time zone."

"Oh," Rose said. That was, of course, her problem. She seemed to slip between time, between tenses and time zones. There wasn't exactly "regular time" for Rose.

"Get it?" Susan asked.

"Sort of," Rose replied.

"The Mean Queens have been back for two weeks now. It seems like forever, doesn't it?" Susan said. Rose caught her breath. Susan wasn't talking about Mary Tudor, Queen of England. She was talking about Carrie, Brianna, and Lisa—also known as the Trio of Doom. The Nemeses on the Premises. They had all three been suspended from school for two days after playing a terrible trick on Joe, Susan's sort-of boyfriend. They basically sabotaged his skates, so that he fell and broke his ankle. Meaning he was out of the Snow Show. But Brianna was out too—not only out of school for two days, but also banished from the Indianapolis Skating Club for good. Served her right. Sometimes Rose felt as if she were caught not just between two centuries, but between two sets of Mean Queens as well.

Well, Princess Elizabeth was not a queen, of course, but she could be mean too. Not as mean as Mary, but kind of spiteful. Like the time she took Rose's locket. The locket that her father had made. The rose-shaped locket that had the photo of her and her mom in it . . . and that of her dad, Nicholas Oliver, the goldsmith to the court! It was downright mean that Elizabeth had snatched that locket from her, with the lame excuse that only royals could wear the Tudor Rose. Rose crossed her fingers again and sent up a little prayer.

Oh please, don't let Princess Elizabeth figure out the secret to opening that locket!

Chapter 2

Fish Sticks and Other Lunchroom Atrocities

"*Good morning, students!*" *It was the voice of Ms. Fuentes, the* principal of Lincoln Middle School. "'Tis the season to be merry, but also grateful. And we are grateful to the Bow Tie Team—Susan Gold, Rose Ashley, Joe Mallory, Anand Preet, Sibby Huang, Kevin Ellsworth, Sayid Nassim, and Myles Randolph—for their extraordinary efforts in raising money for Indianapolis's most needy children. They have all been awarded certificates of community service from the *Indianapolis Tribune*. They will be presented today at morning assembly."

"Myles." Carrie's snarky voice slithered through the air. "Your hands can barely move. How can you sew? All you can do is push the button for your wheelchair with one finger."

Rose turned around in her desk. "Myles happens to be our chief financial officer, Carrie. He does all the math and bookkeeping for this project."

"Please! No talking, young ladies," ordered Mr. Ross, the homeroom and language arts teacher. Rose felt her skin prickle. She hated it when Mr. Ross called them "young ladies." Did he think he was making them feel grown up? He wasn't. Rose had always felt that there was something belittling about addressing middle school girls as "young ladies." There was certainly nothing ladylike in Carrie's remarks. It was pure bully.

Myles shot her a glance from his wheelchair. Even though he could only move one hand because of his cerebral palsy, his eyes said it all. "Let it go, Rose."

The irony of Mr. Ross calling them "young ladies" hit her squarely as she looked at the words of the week on the greenboard. In five minutes Mr. Ross would erase the words on the board and then they would begin their spelling review. The students would be required to write out each word after Mr. Ross said it, then write it in a sentence. The words for this week were: chimera, egotistical, superior, condescend, betray, maniacal, belligerent, lackadaisical, and . . . ta-da! PATRONIZING. That was exactly the definition of calling a seventh-grade girl "young lady."

Quiet descended on the homeroom as Mr. Ross said the words and the students wrote them down. Mr. Ross was very pale with red-rimmed eyes, and he kept a huge box of tissues on his desk. It seemed to Rose as if he were always on the brink of a sneeze. He appeared hyperallergic to something. After the class had written down all the words, they spent the next twenty minutes writing sentences. You got double points if you could use more than a single word within one sentence. Rose felt her brain rev up as she began to write the last sentence.

To address seventh-grade girls as "young ladies" is not simply condescending but in truth patronizing, and although it might suggest apparent kindness, it actually betrays the sense of superiority of the speaker.

There! thought Rose. She ground in her pencil tip for the period at the end of her triple-whammy sentence.

When they finished the spelling review, Mr. Ross collected the papers.

"Now please take out *To Kill a Mockingbird* and we'll discuss the first chapter."

He turned his back and used his laptop to project a sentence from the book on the screen.

Maycomb was an old town, but it was a tired old town when I first knew it. In rainy weather the streets turned to red slop. . . . Somehow, it was hotter then . . . bony mules hitched to Hoover carts flicked flies in the sweltering shade of the live oaks on the square.

"This, ladies and gents, is PERSONIFICATION!" He shouted the word as if he had invented it. *Jeez,* thought Rose, *what a way to ruin a wonderful book.* Rose must have made a face, for she'd caught Mr. Ross's eye.

"Do you have something to say, Rose?"

"No, no . . . just a random thought."

"Oh, please share it."

"No, I'd rather not." *Mr. Ross does not like me.*

Susan's hand shot up. "I think it's interesting to note that Harper Lee spent more time in New York City than she did in Monroeville, Alabama. Because she became so famous, she liked the anonymity of a big city."

"Well, yes, Susan, that is interesting, but I was going to ask if any of you understood what I mean by personification?"

"Uh . . . ," Susan said. "I think it's describing something in a human way that is not human—like the town of Maycomb."

"She wanted to get out of Maycomb and go to New York 'cause it was just too boring," Tom, the boy who sat behind Susan, offered. "I know about small, boring towns. I lived in Kokomo until last year—really boring. Indianapolis is like New York compared to Kokomo."

"Whhhaaaat?! Are you kidding?" said Joe.

A boisterous argument broke out. Mr. Ross flushed, the

way he always did when he lost control of his class. Someone made a fart noise in the back of the room. Or maybe it was a real fart.

"Ladies and gentlemen. Ladies . . . ."

Oh, just shut up! thought Rose. But she saw the look of near panic in Mr. Ross's eyes and almost felt sorry for him.

Almost but not quite. . . .

Rose was sitting at lunch at her usual table with Susan and Joe, Anand, Kevin, and Myles.

Rose cast a glance over at Joe's plate.

"Barfaroni," Joe said. "But better than fish sticks in a taco with cheese on top . . . I just couldn't." He paused and looked at Marisol, a new girl who was making her way toward their table. But then, within another second, she tripped. Her tray went flying. Her own barfaroni splattered on a sixth grader's sweater. The sixth grader, Jenny, began wailing and jumped up from her chair.

"My grandma gave me this sweater. It's cashmere. You . . . you . . . clumsy girl. You've ruined my heirloom sweater!"

"Heirloom," Susan muttered. "Give me a break."

"Stupido!" Jenny shouted.

Marisol turned pale. Her eyes darted around the room like a trapped animal looking for escape.

"I can't believe she just said that!" Rose gasped.

"Look at them! Look at the Trio of Doom." Joe leaned over and whispered to Rose. "They're trying not to laugh."

"Duet of Doom. No Brianna," Rose said.

Indeed, Carrie's and Lisa's mouths were locked between smirks and howls of merriment. Meanwhile Jenny was giving an Academy Award–winning performance of outrage. "Do you know how much this cost? This sweater?"

Anand, who was sitting next to Joe, jumped up to help Marisol salvage what she could from her lunch. She had arrived only a few weeks ago. Rose scooted over and made room for Marisol. "Don't listen to them, Marisol. They're just a bunch of jerks."

"Hey! Look over there—seismic shift," Kevin said suddenly.

"What are you talking about?" Rose asked.

"Okay, don't be obvious, but look who's sitting in the corner—alone."

They all slid their eyes around to steal a glance.

"Brianna alone?" Joe said. "Impossible."

"Then it *is* a duet," Myles said. It was difficult for him to turn around in his wheelchair.

"Who will replace her?" Anand asked.

"Someone, I'm sure," Rose said. "Power vacuum."

"Power?" Marisol whispered. She appeared frightened. Very frightened.

"Oh, don't worry, it's just an expression," Rose said.

"A law of physics, actually," Anand said. "Any space in which the pressure is lower than the atmospheric pressure. I'll demonstrate." He began sucking on his straw. The liquid rose in the straw. "See?" he said, looking up at Marisol. "I reduced the pressure by sucking and the milk flowed up. Same thing over there." He tipped his head toward Carrie and Lisa, who were sitting at a table with a couple of sixth graders. "One of those kids will fill in for Brianna."

"I'd put my money on the cashmere sweater heiress, Jenny," Rose replied in a scalding voice.

Jenny was quite tiny, more the size of a fourth grader than a sixth grader, and right now she was looking up at Carrie with adoring eyes. Was she seeking approval? Jenny's once almost white-blond hair now shimmered pink and had a spritz of glitter as well.

"What's with the pink hair?" Joe asked.

"Well, look at Carrie with her blue streak. Obviously, she is worshipping at the altar of the Mean Queens—the glitter like Lisa, and the pink hair. What more do you need to know?"

"Looks like a wad of bubble gum," Rose muttered.

Jenny had a tiny turned-up nose and she very much reminded Rose of Tinker Bell since she wore her hair in a little knot on top of her head. Her bangs fell in a slant across her forehead. It was the exact same hairstyle as Tinker Bell had in the Disney movie. *Perky!* Rose thought. *Perky with a capital P!* There was a rumor that Jenny's mom was grooming her for the tryouts for the next season of *America's Next Top Tween Model*.

"Hey, Rose," Myles said. "Look over there; Mr. Ross is trying to get your attention."

Rose looked up and saw Mr. Ross waving at her.

Uh...oh..., thought Rose, and got up from her seat and walked over to him.

"I didn't mean to interrupt your lunch, Rose."

"No, it's okay. I was done." *Lie.*

"Well, I'd rather discuss this in homeroom."

"Fine."

When they got to the homeroom, Mr. Ross pulled out the spelling papers. "I want to apologize."

"For what?" she asked, and dipped her head. She could not face those watery translucent eyes that looked as if they were on the edge of tears. She heard him sniffle.

"For this." He slid a paper toward her.

Her own handwriting glared back at her. *To address seventh-grade girls as "young ladies" is not simply condescending, but in truth patronizing, and although it might suggest apparent kindness, it actually betrays the sense of superiority of the speaker.*

"There is so much truth to what you say. As Harper Lee says in *To Kill A Mockingbird*, 'You never really understand a person until you consider things from his point of view . . . until you climb into his skin and walk around in it.'" He gave a little chuckle, and this was followed by a gigantic sneeze. "Sorry about that. I'm allergic to a lot of stuff, especially this season—holly, certain kinds of Christmas trees . . ."

"Cats?"

"Yes, some cats. But the point is, Rose, that I never considered how the term might sound condescending, and patronizing. . . . I failed to climb into a seventh grader's skin and walk around in it."

"It's okay," Rose muttered, and then paused.

"It's not okay," he said. Rose wanted to try to tell him that it would be impossible for him to climb into her skin and walk around . . . walk between two centuries. "Well, I'm sorry." He picked up a red pencil and marked the paper A++.